Alone

A MOTHER'S INTUITION...

A KAREN BLACKSTONE THRILLER
BOOK FOUR

NINO S. THEVENY

SÉBASTIEN THEVENY

TRANSLATED BY
JACQUIE BRIDONNEAU

SELF-PUBLISHED

Praise for Nino S. Theveny

Just as good as his other books, full of suspense. I recommend all of Nino S. Theveny's books. Can't wait to read the next one!

∽

A great story. Hoping the fifth volume will come out soon. Right from the beginning of the saga, I really got to like Karen.

∽

Here we are again in a cold case that hasn't been solved for years, with our journalist, Karen Blackstone, heading the investigation. Nino S. Theveny has an easy-to-read and fluid writing style, one that mixes suspense, betrayal and a crazy and surprising idea. A great summer read in my opinion.

∽

This psychological thriller is a true labyrinth, one that will try your nerves and make you break out into a cold sweat! Once again, with this magistral book, Nino S. Theveny is proving his talent to us by offering us high-

performing thrillers and terribly addictive ones! You can read this book without having read the three other ones.

∿

The 4th opus of a series where suspense and twists are omnipresent and where we're happy to find a character we love again!
   When Karen Blackstone investigates, and despite loads of wrenches being thrown into her work, she never gives up!
   A perilous adventure for that pugnacious detective who must find out what's true and what isn't, with a very surprising ending!

∿

When the author decided to create the character of Karen Blackstone, it was a stroke of genius. I really appreciate Karen, a brave and determined women who does whatever it takes to reach her goal, meaning find the truth. This is an excellent thriller, a captivating and addictive one, a great read and a book you won't want to put down. I personally think this is his best book yet, a successful cold case.

∿

"For me, the best of the four volumes of the Karen Blackstone series! You won't be Alone when you read it!

For Nini & Ben, with fond memories of the fun we had together wearing thongs on the beach. A unique and unforgettable moment!
Long live the happy newlyweds!

∼

En memoria de mi abuelo Juan.

∼

In memory of Grandpa Regis.

∼

For Spirou.

CHAPTER 1
Nothing bad can happen

Louisiana, *August 6, 2004*

It was slated to be one of the best days of their lives, illuminated by stars twinkling in their eyes, a day overflowing with fun and laughter.

There wasn't a cloud in the sky that day, at the beginning of August, above Six Flags New Orleans amusement park. Not a single cloud on the horizon, nor in Suzanne's heart, surrounded by those she loved the most: Ricardo, the love of her life and sweet Lisa, their beautiful little daughter who was nearly three, with her dark eyes like two tourmaline marbles and black onyx hair. Just like a gemstone, that child was the jewel he'd given her out of love.

They were amongst the first in line to enter the park. In the summer, people were waiting as of eight in the morning to get in: families, friends, colleagues, foreign tourists who'd taken a bus, mostly Asias. Nearly everyone was sporting a large grin. Though some people nonetheless looked serious, as if they were frightened of the wild and sensational rollercoasters.

You could see fear in their eyes.

But a contained and desired fear.

That kind of fear you like to have, one that stemmed from the near certainty that nothing could happen to you, that the rides were all safe, controlled and checked, not dangerous, even though of course, you'd be screaming, closing your eyes, your heart would be pounding, but all that would be "make believe," as little kids always innocently say. A fear with goosebumps that would only last a few seconds, a minute or two at the most. And once it was finished…

… *Frankly, nothing bad could happen in an amusement park, could it?*

THAT WAS the question that Suzanne was asking herself that morning, when going through the turnstile right behind little Lisa, who was following Ricardo's massive silhouette, her little hand tightly holding his big one.

Studying the site map, Suzanne asked Lisa where she wanted to begin.

"I want some cotton candy," the little girl said.

"It's a little bit early for that," her father replied. "But I promise you that after we have lunch, I'll buy you the biggest cotton candy cone in the whole park, so big that no one will even be able to see you behind it!"

"You promise?"

"Cross my heart, hun. How about starting in the Looney Tunes zone? We could begin with Yosemite Sam's Ferris wheel, that way when we're up on top you'll be able to see the whole park and it'll be easier to choose where you want to go next."

"The Ferris wheel, great!" the little girl exulted, while jumping up and down and making her blue skirt with its yellow polka dots swirl.

They walked down the central path with its souvenir shops on each side, the one that the customers had to take when their day at the park was over, and then right at the end of it, Ricardo noticed a hut with a sign on it: *Lost Parents*. He kneeled next to his daughter, speaking slowly and carefully to her.

"Sweetie," he said, pointing to the place behind the counter where young women with wide smiles on their faces inspired trust to lost kids. "That's never going to happen, because we'll always be holding your hand, but you never know. You have to remember where this is, okay? This is where you have to go, if ever, but it's not gonna happen, you can't find either of us. You won't cry or remain silent. If that should happen, you'll tell the ladies what your name is. And we'll find each other right here again, all three of us. Got it?"

"Yes, daddy."

"Great! Now let's all hit the Ferris wheel!"

The view they had on top was totally bewitching.

There was Lake Pontchartrain on one side, and on the other, the park's pond surrounded by a myriad of rides, with in the background the banks of Lake Borgne and the Gulf of Mexico sprinkled with its islands and peninsulas. Food both for the eyes and the heart.

From that artificial promontory they could see the impressive roller coasters with their carts rolling up and down at mind-boggling speeds, though a slight breeze masked the passengers' screams.

"I wanna do that," said Lisa.

"Sweetie, you're not tall enough," Suzanne replied. "You have to be over four feet tall. You'll just have to wait a couple more years, my little half-pint," she explained, running her fingers through her hair.

"Not fair," the little girl sighed.

"You're right," her father confirmed. "It's not fair, but rules are rules and they're there for a reason. Let's take advantage of the view. Then we can go to the 4D movies and watch SpongeBob SquarePants. Good idea?"

"Yeah!"

Hours thus went by without them noticing at all, going from one attraction to another, from a souvenir shop to a mini shooting range, where Ricardo, a skilled sniper, was able to burst ten balloons in only ten shots, allowing Lisa to win a stuffed animal as a prize. She chose a cute little monkey that she hugged against her heart. She named it Mookie Monkey.

After that they stopped at a food truck where they

purchased the cotton candy Lisa had been drooling over and she gobbled it down in a snap.

Above them, in the park, seagulls were squawking and swooping down on any leftover edibles.

Clusters of tourists passed each other by on the paths, followed each other in lines for rides, or waited in front of shops. Every once in a while, in the middle of a square or next to popular rides, the park's mascots, those poor employees who must have been suffocating in their heavy costumes, would wave at children or try to startle their parents by tapping them on the back.

Yet, in this friendly atmosphere, holding her daughter's hand, Suzanne suddenly had a strange impression.

A confused and vague feeling that someone was watching her.

Following her.

Scrutinizing her.

She tried to convince herself that it was stupid (frankly, what could happen in a theme park?), and quickly brushed aside that feeling, touched by Lisa's incessant laughter, a little girl who always seemed to be in a good mood.

A child though who they had to clean up, using disposable moist towelettes, to get rid of all that pink sugar around her mouth, on the tip of her nose, and on her pudgy little fingers. When they'd finished, they all agreed to take Lisa to the Mardi Gras zone. They'd spent a good hour there before Suzanne felt a sudden urge to go to the bathroom.

"Do you want to come with mommy?" she asked her daughter.

"No, I already went before."

"We'll wait for you here," said Ricardo, pointing at the hall leading to the restrooms. "Take your time, honey. Lisa and I will be studying all the different flavors of ice-cream in the shop over there."

And they walked away.

Never to return.

CHAPTER 2
The "Lost Parents" hut

WHEN SUZANNE CAME BACK from the restroom about five minutes later, her hubby and daughter weren't there waiting for her. She waited for them for a couple of minutes, but then as they hadn't come, she looked at the map of the park to find the closest ice-cream stand. The crowd was agitated. People were running around in all directions. And the funniest part of it — if you could actually call it funny — was that some of those individuals were mascots all dressed up in their hot and heavy costumes. *How can people want to run dressed up like that with this heat?* she thought absurdly to herself. Then she thought that it must be a part of some show, and that the park managers would do everything and anything possible to entertain tourists.

She still couldn't find Ricardo and Lisa though. She stopped in front of the sign with all the various ice-cream flavors and spoke to one of the employees, a jovial looking heavyset man with curly sideburns.

"You wouldn't happened to have seen a forty-year-old man and a little girl who's two and a half just a couple of minutes ago?"

"Lady, I see hundreds of people like that all day. All I pay attention to is the flavor of ice-cream they order from me! I'm sorry but I can't help you there."

"Thanks anyway," sighed Suzanne, turning around.

She walked back to the restroom block. After all, that was where they'd planned to meet. When she arrived though, neither Ricardo nor Lisa was there. She put the map into her purse and grabbed her phone.

She curiously was directed to voicemail, without any ringtones.

"This is Ricardo Gutierrez's voicemail. If I'm not answering, either I don't know who's calling or I'm busy. Just leave me a message and maybe I'll call you back! Your turn!"

"Rick, I hate your voicemail intro. So where the heck are you? I'm waiting next to the restrooms. I went to the closest ice-cream stand, but you weren't there. What are you doing? Call me back right away."

Suzanne paced back and forth, more and more irritated by the absence of Lisa and her dad.

Where can they be? she railed internally to herself. *What the heck is he doing?*

She walked up to the men's restrooms, thinking that maybe Lisa suddenly had to go to the bathroom and that Ricardo had taken her with him. She hesitated before entering the men's room where men of all ages began to stare at her when she stuck her head through the entrance door. Now she was really irritated. She was ready to pound on the doors of each stall, shouting out their names. Which was what she decided to do, but at the entrance.

"Ricardo! Lisa! You in there?"

She interrupted each man when they were leaving.

"You wouldn't happened to have seen a forty-year-old man with wavy black hair with a little two-and-a-half-year-old little girl, also with dark hair?"

"Nope."

"Not at all."

"I would have noticed them."

"No, sorry."

Frustrated, Suzanne leaned against the tiled wall of the hall leading to the restrooms, staring at her phone as if simply looking at it persistently would make it ring. But it remained silent, inert. Ricardo wasn't calling back.

She tried calling him again four times but was directed each time to his annoying voicemail message.

She quickly walked back to the ice-cream vendor, with a slim glimmer of hope that they'd be there, but as there was no one, she decided to return to the park's entrance, to the "Lost Parents" hut.

When she arrived, out of breath, she gave the employee Ricardo's and Lisa's names as well as a description of them. The lady shook her head.

"I'm so sorry, ma'am, but if I'd seen them, I would have broadcast an announcement for you. But if you want, I can do that now."

Full of hope, Suzanne listened to the announcement the young lady made with her sweet and reassuring voice.

"Will little Lisa and her daddy, Ricardo, please come to the entrance of the park, to the "Lost Parents" hut where Suzanne is waiting for them. I'll repeat myself…"

Suzanne didn't hear her repeat, because her phone rang.

"Miss Diggs? My name is Jason, from Trevor & Jones Marketing, and I'll just need a couple of minutes of your time for an investigation we're carrying out in Louisiana about leisure activities…"

She immediately hung up on him. At least though the call reassured her that her phone was working, and that it must be Ricardo's phone that wasn't. Dead battery? Was it turned off? In airplane mode? Forgotten in the car?

She tried to contact him once again. To no avail. She furiously put the phone back in her purse.

Shit! A good-for-nothing guy. And the day had started off so well.

Suzanne had been looking forward to that day, all three of them together in a venue catering to children and making them happy. All three of them, alone in the crowd. In their own little cocoon.

Instead of that, a type of undefinable apprehension

and anxiety was growing in her, taking root in her chest and not leaving her for many long minutes, then hours, days, months, years…

She was so choked up she could barely breathe. Then tears, tears she was unable to hold back, began.

While the seagulls were laughing above her head, while people around her were having a ball, while joyful music was being played, and happy songs were being sung, Suzanne Diggs collapsed into poignant despair.

She remained prostate for several minutes, tears streaming down her cheeks, her lips trembling, her fists clenched, and her heart broken.

Then, after having tried to call Ricardo for the umpteenth time on her phone, she left Six Flags theme park, walking to the parking lot to find the car they came into that morning.

Except that, victim of her own trust and blindness, she had no idea where they were parked and couldn't find Ricardo's Ford Kuga. She walked down the paths, examining each car. Several times she had a glimpse of hope because of the color or model of one of them, but each time it was in vain.

She thought she was going crazy, perhaps she was. Holding her head between her hands, she fell to the ground in the middle of one of the alleyways in the parking lot and burst into tears, her body shaking with nervous spasms.

Frankly, nothing bad could happen in a theme park, could it?

That was the question bouncing about in her brain.

Behind her, she could hear people screaming with fright on the roller coasters.

She also began to scream, like a wounded, lost and abandoned she-wolf.

The huge Ferris wheel spun slowly.

Slowly and inexorably, just like the wheel of fate.

That evening, after the park had been closed to the public, the cleaning staff picked up a forgotten stuffed animal, a sad little monkey, an orphan of a child who had, just a few hours before, hugged it so tightly…

CHAPTER 3
Blackstone Investigations

New York City, July 2024

I DIDN'T YET KNOW it at that moment, but my entire life was to be overwhelmed and overturned forever by a simple phone call.

FIRSTLY MY PROFESSIONAL LIFE.
    As for my personal life, it was up to me to choose the path I'd like to be taking. I had made up my mind after I'd returned from California, after the double Shondra Wallace and Jabaree Smith case. In Hollywood, that factitious district of Los Angeles, then in the Lone Pine desert and in Las Vegas, I felt too alone, too far from Paul.
    Paul Nollington, the guy who had been waiting for

six months to see what I'd be choosing for my love life. He obviously wanted me to get closer to the Big Apple, but I was dithering and dallying.

After I returned from the West, I plucked up my courage. I'd decided not to let my life go by, not to ignore the men who counted for me. Luke Virgil, my son I'd finally found, first of all. And then Paul.

In that French restaurant, where we had enjoyed our very first meal together when I was working on that Long Island case, and where I took him again, I announced to him between the main course and dessert, profoundly moved and visibly trembling, that I'd agreed to move in with him in his New York apartment.

THAT WAS WHERE, on the thirty-sixth floor of the building facing Park Avenue, while looking out over the lights in Manhattan, my phone rang, displaying an unknown number.

Today with hindsight, I understand that that phone call happened at just the right time, at a moment in my professional life where once again, I felt that I needed something new and some changes. I was searching for a meaning in my life. I'd been a journalist for several years for *True Crime Mysteries* magazine, reporting to my delicious yet oh so original boss, Myrtille Fairbanks, and had covered an incalculable number of cold cases concerning unexplainable disappearances, or unsolved crimes, things our readers gobbled up. Sometimes because of my research, cases were reopened, investigations were started up once again, thanks to new facts or clues that I brought to the cops in charge of them.

But much too often — and if I have to tell the truth, most of the time outside of those cases I'd already told you about —, all I could do was to emit hypotheses, generate new approaches, and nothing really changed for the victims. They were merely articles in a crime magazine. Something that did frustrate me, that feeling I had of working with no results, for nothing.

I was saturated, I wanted to be useful to someone. Solve cases. Find guilty parties. Tell families the truth, finally, something they'd been trying to find for months, years or sometimes even decades.

I no longer wanted to be a simple spectator or storyteller. I needed to become a player, not like Shondra Wallace was, but more like Philip Marlowe, a character in *The Big Sleep*, a movie directed by Raymond Chandler and admiratively played by Humphrey Bogart and Robert Mitchum, though I'd be passing on the cigarettes. Yes, I wanted to fly with my own wings at that time in my life, become a bit more mundanely a private detective!

Of course, I needed to do a bit more than putting a sign up outside my door, which I did do upon returning from California when I founded Blackstone

Investigations. I had to start by finding myself some paying clients! There is no shortage of people who unexpectedly go missing in the United States, as everyone knows that the police are often forced to close those types of cases much too quickly, when they don't have enough new elements to try to solve them.

Then, *those left behind*, spouses, husbands, children, parents, friends, everyone impacted by an unexplained absence and such a painful oblivion, *those are the ones* who never lose hope, though it's sometimes minute, of seeing the person again, or at the very least, finding what could have happened to them.

Those people would be my potential clients, I'd do my utmost to try to find what happened to their dearly departed, try to find an explanation that would heal the open and sometimes purulent wounds in their hearts.

But I knew that you didn't find clients like that merely by snapping your fingers. I'd need to be patient, accept less interesting jobs, like tailing husbands who had wandering eyes, wives who had become addicted to gambling or teens who were going out with people that their parents disapproved of. Jobs that just put food on the table, far from what I was expecting as a private detective. As for making a living from Blackstone Investigations, that was something that wouldn't happen immediately either.

. . .

But I could thank the Lord or whoever else had some influence on human fate for allowing me to count on my dear Myrtille, who didn't discourage me.

"Hey! My little chickadee, that's great news, this idea ! Go for its girl! That's a part of your ADN, I knew it the first time I set eyes on you."

"I'm aware that I'm abandoning you and *True Crime Mysteries* after all these years… But I'm afraid that maybe I'm cutting the umbilical cord too quickly. Would you take me back if this doesn't work out?"

My boss's totally original laugh instantly warmed my heart, as did what she added.

"Wait a second, you think I'm gonna forget you that quickly? You're dreaming sweetie! You know what? While we're waiting for your agency to take off and provide you with a decent salary, I'll hire you to write some articles for me as a freelance employee, so you can make ends meet. And when you get tired of working for me, just say, ciao, bye-bye. And we'll part as good friends. That okay with you hun?"

"You are so sweet, Myrtille."

"Bah! Don't try to bust my balls with sentimental crap like that, Karen. And shake a leg, you'll do great, Detective Blackstone!"

And I'm sure that you know that I didn't add any other sentimental crap like that to her conclusion.

I luckily didn't have to wait too long before an incredible case fell right into my lap: that phone call I was talking about earlier, the one that would kickstart my career as a private detective.

An enormous, frightening, unimaginable and yet such a real case!

A case that I'd fully embrace, fighting against my most primitive fears.

A CASE where I'd be risking my own life.

CHAPTER 4
Too perfect, too improbable

Hervey Bay, Queensland, Australia, July 2024

Austral winters Down Under* were usually dry with pleasant temperatures. On the eastern side of Australia, facing the coral reef, the tiny town of Hervey Bay was proud to call itself the humpback whales watching spot. It was in that bay, sharing the same name as the town, that each year the whales would migrate to and stay for a while, between the coast and Fraser Island, now renamed K'gari, its original aboriginal name.

Here, life-sized statues of whales were scattered

---

* The term **Down Under** is an expression designating Australia, New Zealand, as well as other islands in the South Pacific such as Fiji and Samoa. Its origins stem from the fact that these countries are in the Southern hemisphere, "down under" most other countries in the world.

about in town, in the middle of roundabouts, in courtyards, in front of the marina. It was near one of these that a fifty- or so-year old lady, taking advantage of the nice weather, was walking on one of the sidewalks down the main street that ran along the Pacific.

Suzanne Diggs had gifted herself with that trip, one that she'd been dreaming of for ages.

What could have made her want to buy tickets for *those* dates, in *that* town which was on the eastern coast and far from being one of Australia's main tourist towns?

What had brought here precisely at *that* time, on *that* sidewalk, in front of *that* ice-cream shop, the one touting over seventy-two different flavors?

Was it fate? Pure luck? Chance? Instinct?

Or perhaps of a mixture of all of that, like those multicolored scoops of ice-cream?

Whatever it was, Suzanne suddenly had an urge to treat herself to something cool and sweet. She walked into the shop where the A/C was on high, though the sliding door was constantly open.

The glass panel full of refrigerated containers of all sorts of ice-cream was nearly thirty feet long. Mountains of colored ice-cream into which employees put scoopers to serve their many customers throughout the day.

"In a dish or a cone? A sugar-cone or a chocolate one? One, two, or three scoops? An extra topping?"

It wasn't an easy task to choose with that profusion of flavors. Some were astonishing, like tomato-basil. Suzanne looked at each and every container, finally deciding to play it safe, try one of the flavors she knew she'd like: caramel and vanilla, with chocolate sauce for an extra dollar. The young man taking care of her, a guy named Kenny if his badge was correct, carefully put the two scoops into the sugar cone, and then, noticing that the melted chocolate container was empty, turned to one of his colleagues, who was restocking the cones she'd just taken out of the storage area.

"Hey, Ash! Can you get me another one of these, please?"

"Yep, mate!"

When the young lady turned around with the container, Suzanne was suddenly petrified.

Those eyes...

That hair...

How can this be possible? she asked herself. It was as if a ghost had materialized itself in front of her. The ghost of a little girl who had evaporated in ether nearly twenty years ago.

Twenty years ago, thousands of miles from there.

Twenty years without leaving the tiniest clue to help her understand something inexplicable.

Without a single proof of life.

Twenty years of her existence chasing that ghost.

No, I'm going crazy, Suzanne tried to convince herself. *That can't be true, it would be too perfect, too improbable.* Billions of human beings on earth, who live, who die, whose lives and fates entangle. Billions of billions of minutes that had gone by, and there, at that precise minute, in that precise place, that young lady whose badge said her name was Ashley would be the adult version of her little Lisa who had gone missing?

Too much of a hazard to be true, even more improbable than winning all the numbers in the lottery. Yet the fifty-year-old woman remained there, in front of the ice-cream containers, her hand out, her eyes staring at the astonished young lady. A mother's heart, soul and instinct could not be wrong. Things like that could not be explained, they were felt. They came from the soul or spirit, were transmitted from one being to another by pheromones or other chemical or esoteric substances, Suzanne wasn't sure of herself here, but she nonetheless believed it.

"Ma'am?"

Kenny's voice suddenly brought her back to the here and now. She shook her head, took the ice-cream cone the young man was handing to her while asking for four fifty.

Suzanne opened her purse, gave him a five-dollar bill, refused the change, and was tempted to call...

... *my daughter*...

... *Ashley*...

... the shop assistant, but she changed her mind. That was neither the moment nor the place. Plus what should she do? She couldn't just blurt something out like: "Miss, I think you're my daughter who went missing twenty years ago. Your name isn't Ashley, it's Lisa, I know, really though, I'm not crazy. Come with me then, we're going to get back to our old lives, like before, you'll see, it'll be great!"

No, all that was impossible. Unrealistic and unfeasible. The best way to end up in the loony bin, something that Suzanne certainly didn't want.

She left the shop, crossed the road, and sat down at a picnic table, to have her ice cream cone while keeping an eye peeled on the door of the shop. About a hundred and fifty feet behind her, after that strip of tropical trees followed by a sand dune, she could hear the tiny waves of the Pacific constantly kissing the long Hervey Bay beach, a sound which soothed her with sweet torpidity mixed with illusions. Suzanne was incapable of saying how long she'd been sitting there, her eyes glued to the ice cream shop, waiting for it to close or at least for *Ashley (Lisa)* to finish her day at work.

It was finally five o'clock and the young dark-haired lady left her workplace, with her purse slung over her shoulder, walking down one of the roads that were perpendicular to the town square.

Suzanne tailed her, sufficiently far though to keep an eye on her without being seen.

CHAPTER 5
A moving target

ASHLEY BOLT WASN'T PAYING any attention to the fact that she was being observed. As usual, upon arriving back home, she tossed her bag on the sofa in her little living room, then went to her bedroom while ripping off her clothes. She took off her work clothing and underwear to put on others which would be more practical for what she was about to do nearly every evening. Seamless cotton panties, a sports bra, a large sleeveless t-shirt and tight leggings. That regular and avid jogger then put on short socks.

In the front hall, she put her running shoes on, opened the apartment door, locked it, threaded the lock into one of her shoelaces, and tied a double knot around it. She rented out the top floor of a house from a couple of retired people. She rushed down to the town square, still being surveyed by a pair of binoculars as a moving target.

Her goal was to run to Urangan Marina taking

Maryborough Port Road. That was her usual jogging itinerary, mostly a flat one, but it had the huge advantage of following the coast over its twelve-mile round trip. Just what she needed to empty out her brain and purify her body.

When she reached the square, she didn't pay any attention to the bike following her, at quite a distance, on the lane that pedestrians, roller-skaters and strollers all shared. Her Airpods were tightly screwed into her ears and her stride now matched the rhythm of Tame Impala, a group she'd discovered a couple of years ago with their album *The Slow Rush*, a perfect playlist for jogging on the Pacific coast.

When she accelerated, the man pushed harder on his pedals, when she slowed down, he braked, when she stopped a moment to catch her breath or admire the ocean, he also put a foot on the ground, pretending to lace his shoe.

The cyclist was just another person in the crowd, another person, as was the case for many Australians, who liked to jog, walk, or bike after work when the temperature was more temperate.

When she returned home two hours later, the man stayed at the intersection. He watched her walk inside and went right up to the facade of the building. He remained immobile a few instants, as if making sure she wasn't coming back out again, then disappeared in the night, zigzagging so as not to be seen in the streetlights.

· · ·

The young lady, steaming with perspiration, whipped off her moist clothes, leaving them on the tile floor in the front hall and went directly to the shower, without even closing the bathroom door. She'd never even bothered to find out if anyone in the houses across the road could see her, or in the office building a bit farther down the road, in that peaceful Hervey Bay neighborhood, in Queensland, such a nice place to live.

But where, at any time, as was the case anywhere, you could also die.

CHAPTER 6
An impression, an intuition, a certitude

NEW YORK CITY, *July 2024*

I FOUND myself in an extremely uncomfortable situation, one I'd dreaded, in a nutshell, I now was regretting my decisions. Blackstone Investigations wasn't taking off as I'd hoped it would, and I was scraping by authoring a few articles for Myrtille and a couple of investigation gigs that were neither interesting nor lucrative.

Up until that phone call that would overturn my professional life.

At that time, I hadn't yet acquired my own office, and I was working from the apartment in Manhattan that I shared with Paul. He was actually there when I picked up, and though he pretended not to hear the conversation, I could see him pacing in the loft and looking at me with inquisitive eyes.

"Is this Karen Blackstone, from Blackstone Investigations?"

"Speaking. What can I do for you, ma'am?"

"Miss! Diggs. Suzanne Diggs. I must tell you that it's a bit special and I don't want you to think I'm nuts."

"Don't worry, in my job I never judge people, all I do is try to understand and above all, help them. So, why did you call me then?"

"My daughter disappeared."

A bell I only knew much too well immediately rang in my head when she used that word. Finally! I'd finally be working on a case that didn't involve a lady whose husband was catting around or someone trying to screw their insurance agency. I grabbed my pen and began asking her some questions.

"When was she reported missing?"

"August, 2004."

I gulped.

"2004? Like twenty years ago?"

"Correct. Precisely twenty years ago."

"But please allow me to ask you why you're calling me now? Are there any new elements in the case?"

"I don't know if you could call it a new element, it's more of an impression, an intuition. Or even better than that, a certitude for me."

"Meaning?"

"I've been on vacation in Australia for the past two weeks, in Hervey Bay, a little town in Queensland. And I think I found my daughter there!"

I was getting mixed up now.

"Miss Diggs, I don't think I understand the object of your call. You told me you found your daughter who went missing in 2004. In that case, there's nothing for me to do."

I could hear her sigh on the other side of the line.

"You're right, it's not that easy. Like I told you, for me, deep down inside, it's a certitude, but in real life, I'm afraid that I'll provoke incomprehension, or even hostility for that young lady, who, and I'm sure of this, is no one else than my dear daughter, Lisa."

She broke down and began to cry.

"Were you able to talk to the young lady?"

"Briefly. Very briefly."

Then she told me about how she happened upon her missing daughter at the ice cream shop while she was buying a cone with two scoops.

"On the badge she was wearing, her name was marked as Ashley, but I'm sure that's not her real name. She's my dear daughter Lisa, there must be a mistake someplace. Like maybe her top was in the wash and she used one that belonged to one of her colleagues who wasn't working that day. That must be it," continued Suzanne Diggs, almost as a soliloquy, "there must have been an exchange of uniforms. Miss Blackstone, do you have any children?"

My throat tightened up at that question.

"Yes, I do. I've got a son who must be about as old as Lisa, your daughter," I admitted, my eyes sparkling at that thought.

"So you can understand me then! You must realize that us mothers can feel things like that, when we're near someone who's from our own flesh and blood."

"Yes, I do," I admitted, as the very same thing had happened to me just a few weeks ago. "But tell me, were you able to speak to her? Ask her a question or two? It would seem to me that it would be the most direct way to confirm your suspicions."

It took a while before she answered me.

"I tried to approach her discreetly. Tried to learn more about her, without putting her under any pressure. You have to understand, I couldn't just pounce on her when she left work and shouted out 'Lisa, I'm your mother. You're my daughter.' She would have thought I was crazy!"

That was about what I was thinking too, without admitting it. I mentally tried to visualize the scene.

"So did you speak to her? Even a word or two?"

"I was afraid to. To be frank with you, Miss Blackstone, I followed her, you could even say spied on her to find out more about her. Who she was, what she did every day, who she was friends with, what she did when she wasn't working, basic stuff like that."

"Basic? Because you think you can follow people like that? That's something called voyeurism, or harassment, and it's an offense that's punishable by law. Or else it's a profession, mine you could say."

"That's exactly why I'm calling," she rebounded immediately. "I thought that you, a professional used to investigations like this, maybe you could help me shed some light on this affair that's eating away at me."

When she said that, it was like flashing lights went on in my head. An ancestral fear twisted my gut. I knew myself well enough to dread what would be coming next. I cut her off before she could continue.

"There is no way I'll be going to the other side of the world based on such tiny and intangible elements you've told me, Miss Diggs."

"I'll pay you whatever you want, don't worry," she replied. "I've got money, it's not a problem for me."

"That's not the sticking point," I stammered.

"What's the problem then?"

"I hate flying," I shamefully admitted, well knowing that it was something that closed doors for me.

And it was true that flying to Australia, being cooped up in a metal container that was subject to whims of the wind for twenty-four hours, and that was just a one-way trip, same thing to return, that was something I could never do.

Paul, who was listening to our conversation idly, raised an inquiring eyebrow. Irritated, I made a movement telling him to get lost.

"You know there is medication to quell a fear of flying," Suzanne Diggs added. "Or hypnosis."

"That's nice of you to be concerned about my health, but no, I could never do that. What I can do however, is to refer you to one of my colleagues who would be able to assist you."

"I want you though," she insisted.

"Why me?" I asked, astonished.

"Because I know what methods you use, and your results too. Your reputation too, because I'm a *True Crime Mysteries* reader. I know how you excel in cases linked to missing children."

She was a tough cookie. As for me, I was dithering. On one hand, I was sure that it would be a fascinating investigation, one that I'd love, but on the other, I was afraid that the case boiled down to mere elucubrations of a disturbed woman. I decided to split the difference.

"Okay then, if I'm really the person that you want to work with, here's what I could propose to you to start. You told me that you're still in Australia?"

"That's right, I'm still in Hervey Bay. I rented a little apartment and I'm staying there."

"Here's what we can do then. You try to get a bit closer to that Ashley. But without making her suspicious. Don't go barging in with your story of her being your daughter who went missing twenty years ago, that would be counterproductive. Try to make friends with her, or at least make her a person that you could talk to about this or that. And then, little by little, try to learn more about her. Ask her a few questions about her life, her past. As for me, I agree to use all the resources I have to investigate the disappearance of Lisa back in 2004. Past cases always help us understand what is going on in the present. What do you think about that?"

She thought that over for a few moments.

"We got a deal."

"Perfect. Let's begin to work like that with you in Australia, me in the States, you in the present and me in the past. Then we'll swap our discoveries and try to see if the two ends of the string join each other logically. Let's start with the beginning of this. What was the precise date when your daughter disappeared? And where?"

"I'll never be able to forget that horrible date. It was August 6, 2004. That was when Ricardo and I took Lisa to the Six Flags amusement park, in New Orleans."

CHAPTER 7
With a red-hot iron

IN THE FOLLOWING MINUTES, I asked Suzanne to tell me everything she remembered about that event that had branded her with a red-hot iron in her memory and scarred her soul as a mother, without interrupting her even once.

She told me how Ricardo and she had taken Lisa to that amusement park, a day that was supposed to be a fantastic one for them as a family.

And how it had turned into a nightmare.

As she was telling me this, I jotted down details in the notebook that never left me side, because I liked writing things down with my own little fingers, rather than using a computer when my clients tell me things. You could say that I'm old-school, but I'm not ashamed of that at all.

When she finished, her voice cracking with emotion, as if those events had just taken place, though they'd happened twenty years ago, I had a couple of questions for her.

"So you told me that the last time you saw Lisa and Ricardo and spoke to them was right before you were going into the restrooms."

"That's right. We agreed to meet up there, at the end of the hall."

"And they were going to an ice cream stand."

"That's right."

"Did you see them head in that direction? I mean, did you see them leave the hall?"

She hesitated for a few seconds, trying to recall those twenty-year-old souvenirs.

"All that dates back so far. I don't know, I don't know anymore, I don't think so. I think I ran my fingers through Lisa's hair, telling her something like not to exaggerate on the number of scoops of ice cream, or something like that and then I went into the ladies' restrooms without turning around again. That's the last image of her I have, so joyful... so alive."

And then I heard her sobbing. I tried to soothe her with a few comforting words, but I know how hard it is to stem painful memories like that, and how they seem to come back like a wave in your tear ducts.

"What did you do then after leaving the park?"

"I went to the parking lot to try to find the car. I called Ricardo dozens of times, but he never answered. And I finally contacted the police in New Orleans. What else could I have done?"

"Go back home to see if for some or another reason, they'd gone back there without you."

"That doesn't make any sense. Why would they have done that? Of course, I took a taxi and went back home after. And no one was there, of course."

"So then you contacted the police."

"A whole 'nother story there," she said bitterly, cutting me off. "You know how it goes. They told me to come, they nodded while listening to me, asked me the typical questions — more or less the ones that you're asking me now — and then politely took note of what I said. And never a kind word."

"You mean they didn't take you seriously?"

"Exactly. I'm not teaching you anything new when I tell you that loads of people go missing in our country, Miss Blackstone, and generally speaking they're not considered as something that is a priority for our police force unless they're children."

"But there was a child. Except that Lisa disappeared at the same time as her own father. So, in the first hours or even days, it's not a crime. As long as the disappearance isn't considered as a worrying one, there's no need to be alarmed. That's the philosophy of those investigators, and you can't blame them, they don't want to be drowning in files to process. But they must have continued with your case."

Suzanne laughed dryly.

"They didn't have the choice. I harassed them each and every day. I still didn't have any news of my two loved ones."

"You probably thought it was a simple case of kidnapping? That wouldn't be the first time that a father kidnapped his child from their home, took them far from their grieving mother. In that case, is it really a disappearance? The first suspect when kids go missing is often the father."

"That what the New Orleans cops kept telling me."

I suddenly thought of something.

"One more question, Miss Diggs. Since then, has your husband ever come back?"

"No, never," sighed my client. "Neither him nor our little Lisa."

"That means we've got an unexplained double disappearance and above all... an unsolved one."

Deep down inside I thought back on all the many cases I'd investigated and where, more precisely, I had to solve multiple disappearances that were either fresh ones, or on the other hand, ones that had taken place many years later. I could feel my interest in this case concerning Lisa and her father growing inside me.

"I suppose, if we're talking about them being missing, that their remains were never found around the park nor in New Orleans?"

"No where in Louisiana. Had that been the case I wouldn't be here asking you to lead an investigation on them and telling you that I'm sure I found my Lisa."

"It was a purely rhetorical question to allow me to rule out one line of investigation. Of course, had their remains been discovered, the case would have been closed."

"It is," Suzanne said. "It's been closed for over ten years. No new elements."

"Do you remember the name of the inspector in charge of the investigation?"

"Of course! I called him so many times with the hope deep down inside that some tiny clue would make them do something. His name is Stanford, William Stanford."

I jotted the name down in my notebook. I'd already taken three pages of notes and had decided to take on Suzanne Diggs's case.

"Do you still live in New Orleans?"

"Good Lord, no! And as time has gone by, I've tried to put as much distance as possible between myself and my Louisiana years. You understand…"

"Of course, it's always hard to live in places so full of painful memories."

As for myself, I no longer could approach a certain cursed cul-de-sac in Boston without my entire body trembling. It was thus easy for me to have empathy for Suzanne.

"So, Miss Blackstone, will you work for me?"

"I will and I'll try to understand what happened on August 6, 2004 in New Orleans."

CHAPTER 8
In the time it takes to snap your fingers

AFTER HAVING AGREED on the monetary conditions with my new client, which included an advance payment for expenses, I asked her to email me some photos of Lisa, Ricardo, and herself at the time when those tragic events took place. It was often useful, when questioning any eventual witnesses, to possess the photos of the players — both guilty parties and victims — of the case.

When I hung up, Paul quickly sat his cute little butt down next to me on the sofa.

"So? You got something new?"

"Um... I don't know yet. But finally something that should be an interesting case. I can't wait to begin."

"Not that I was eavesdropping or anything, but I thought I understood that you might be leaving for a while? I heard you say, 'the other side of the world.' Where are you off to?"

I rolled my eyes and sighed.

"Don't even mention that. My client is sure that she found her daughter, who went missing twenty years ago, in Australia. You see me taking a plane to the Southern hemisphere, on the other side of the planet?"

Paul's wry smile confirmed the fact that he now knew me only too well.

"What's sure is that your old Ford Ranchero won't be able to drive you there. Unless you put it on a cargo boat. But that trip would take quite a while."

"Quit being sarcastic, you horrible person," I teased. "I'm going to start by going to New Orleans, where the little two-and-a-half-year-old girl and her father disappeared. They apparently vanished in the time it takes to snap your fingers. Twenty years without any news, any clues, any suspects. So it'll be up to me to unearth witnesses, investigators, and find out what happened."

"Have a nice flight honey," said Paul ironically, kissing me on my neck, "that'll warm you up for your departure to Australia."

I lowered my head with a resigned sigh.

* * *

New Orleans, July 2024

I OF COURSE decided not to cross the United States from north to south with my dear Ranchero. The Big Apple was about 1,300 miles from the Big Easy, and I was afraid that my old clunker would give up the ghost and I'd never even make it there. Without even including fatigue, something to be avoided when kicking off an investigation.

So when I disembarked at the well-named Louis Armstrong Airport, and despite my slight air sickness, I had to admit that the approach to the runway next to Lake Pontchartrain and the north of the Mississippi was stunning. The day was drawing to an end and by the time the cab had taken me to my hotel in downtown New Orleans, night had fallen over the city. I went up to my room, unpacked, took a well needed shower and then as I was starving by that time, went downstairs where I ordered a seafood gumbo, trying to get used to the local cuisine. Though I had chosen not to eat meat and was forced to only consume gluten-free products, I still enjoy eating and know how to appreciate the specialties of the cities I work in. I thus devoured this dish made from seafood, rice, celery, peppers, onions, and spices, a thick and hearty soup-like dish, not even leaving a spoonful. I went back to my room to begin working.

Sitting cross-legged on my bed, with my laptop on my thighs, I opened my emails and clicked on Suzanne Diggs's mail. It contained a series of photos of herself, the guy named Ricardo, and of course little Lisa.

Suzanne seemed quite different from the image of the lady I mentally had from her phone call, as if her voice didn't match her body. Then I thought how idiotic it was to think like that, I knew weaklings who had strong tenor voices and musclemen with voices of castrates! Her round and pale face with almond shaped eyes extended by crow's feet wrinkles made me think that this was a recent photo of her. She had short slightly curly hair that was so blond that I was sure it came from a bottle.

On the contrary, that Ricardo — and what was his last name? I'd forgotten to ask Suzanne about it, — had dark skin like South Americans did, and chiseled features including an angular jaw, topped with ink black hair. On that photo he must have been thirty at the most. Taken before his disappearance.

THEN I OPENED the last file where I was astonished by how beautiful the little girl was. She had delicate features, a long face, surrounded by black hair that was braided with long braids falling on her shoulders. On that photo where Lisa was looking right at the camera, she seemed a bit melancholic to me with her large dark brown pupils, a nostalgia that didn't fit her very young age.

That photo must have been taken on the day she went missing, because in the background I could see a huge Ferris wheel, a must for all theme parks.

The young child was holding a stuffed animal tightly against her chest. A brown little monkey with a huge smile.

On Lisa's face, an identical smile twisted my gut.

. . .

I closed my computer with a sigh, took the glass of water on my bedside table, swallowed my daily dose of pills and pulled the sheets over me.

Before falling asleep, I couldn't get the image of Lisa's enchanting smile out of my head.

Was it her last one?

CHAPTER 9
A feeling of desolation

When I begin most of my investigations, I like to go to where they took place so I can experience the conditions, atmospheres, areas, volumes and generally get a feel for the place. Does someone go missing in the same way in the middle of a desert or in Chinatown in Manhattan? Do people disappear similarly in the Rocky Mountains and the Norwegian fjords? My experience has taught me that they don't.

So the first place I went to in New Orleans was logically the Six Flags amusement park.

I had the hotel lobby reserve a taxi for me and a couple of minutes later I hopped into black and white Chevrolet, one that was different than the eternal and regulatory New York Yellow Cabs.

"Morning Miss," said the driver with a southern accent that I supposed was type of Cajun, that dialect that came from Acadian immigrants, who were themselves descendants of French settlers. A delicious asset though it was not easily understandable with French words right in the middle of an English sentence. "Where you going today?"

"To Six Flags."

He burst out in a thundering laugh.

"My little lady, if you're hoping to have a good time there, you'd better make a U-turn!"

I wasn't really going there to have a good time.

"Is there a problem? Is the park closed today?"

It was true that I'd presumed that the park, at this time of year, was logically open every day of the week.

"Not just today," the driver said, "but until further notice... You still want to go?"

Even more now, I thought, while nodding. All mysterious things interested me. The driver set off towards the park.

"Why is the park closed? Was there an accident there?"

I could see that he seemed to be astonished by my question, looking into the rear-view mirror.

"What? You just get in from Mars or Jupiter, Lady?"

"Excuse me?"

"No, I just want to say, without offending you, where have you been for the past twenty years? You're not from here! Because us, people from here, from the South I mean, there's no way we could forget the tragedy."

The tragedy? That word was like a bad omen for me. I instinctively associated it with the disappearance

I was working on but couldn't see why the park would be closed for a thing like that.

"What are you talking about?"

"Katrina."

For a split second I wondered who the heck Katrina was, before suddenly realizing the breadth of my loss of memory. How could anyone forget that destructive and devastating hurricane that happened in August of 2005, causing so much damage in New Orleans. Those born in Louisiana must have been traumatized forever by that natural disaster, a disaster both for the town and for humanity.

"I'm so sorry," I sincerely answered, "I didn't realize that..."

"*Cest la vie*," he answered in French. "You have to keep going, repair, but... you can never forget. For Six Flags, there were never any reparations. The park has been closed for nearly twenty years and each rehabilitation project has been rejected. Isn't that awful! All the kids in New Orleans loved that theme park. It made them happy. But if you still want to go there, no problem."

"Yes, please."

I was boiling over though inside, fearing that my investigation would fail as of the first day. The doors of the park that were now closed wouldn't allow me to access the zone where the events took place, and that irritated me. But I still wanted to get as close as possible. A quarter of an hour later, the man dropped me off in front of the former main entrance gate. What a shock.

That abandoned theme park looked terrible. I had trouble imagining that people had laughed there, children had shouted with joy, cotton candy and toffee apples had tempted everyone, with the background noise that the roller coaster cars and their passengers screaming out loud made when they looped around.

"Miss, you want me to wait for you here?"

There were weeds overgrowing the main plaza leading to the entrance, behind which I could make out the ticket huts, a Ferris wheel, and a bit farther, an infernal roller coaster that no one would ever ride on again on its rusty tracks. I turned to the cab driver.

"No, that will be fine. I'm going to spend some time here. But if you give me your number, maybe I could call you to pick me up?"

The driver handed me a dog-eared business card.

His name was Mason Lacassagne.

"*Pour sûr*," he replied in French. "At your disposal and watch out for yourself, this isn't a place for someone like you."

I thanked him and assured him I'd be careful. He politely waved at me before driving off. I turned around and walked to the gates.

To get there I had to step over the reinforced concrete blocks that had been laid there to avoid any vehicles entering, sort of like those things that you see when there are riots or there's a risk of intrusion by a ram raider.

All this plus all that put together gave the premises a feeling of desolation.

Beyond its neglected and abandoned state, the silence here was heavy. Gusts of wind blew between the branches of the trees, making the weeds lie on the ground like hay. Behind me, as I was walking to the main gate, I could hear the buzzing of the few cars on Michoud Boulevard.

Quite unsurprisingly, the gates were locked, with a huge padlock that only a specialized pair of plyers could have cut open. Over six feet tall, with rusty pikes at the top, the gates were impenetrable, unless you were a Yamasaki, something I certainly was not.

On the other side of the fence, the park looked like a ghost town years after the Gold Rush out West, a town that Lucky Luke in the cartoon albums could have gone through. I was chomping at the bit to get in but stopped by those few inches of metal. Not giving up, I began to walk next to the fence around the site, between empty lots and weeds. The park didn't seem to be that huge, but going around it would take me a while. I was hoping to stumble upon a part of the fence that had been vandalized, with a hidden entrance, but couldn't find any. After having been abandoned for twenty years, I was surprised that no one seemed to be squatting it, as people were always attracted by deserted venues like that to throw parties, down a couple of cold ones, or for a couple, find a discreet and original shelter for their own session of intimate attractions.

My hopes though were finally rewarded when,

after having circumvented nearly the entire park, I found a dirt path, parallel to I510, a busy Interstate, which led to the employee entrance. Here there was another gate, one with a sign on it. *No entrance. Danger*.

Except for my defense, Mr. Attorney General, the gate wasn't really closed! Its two crooked gates had a gap that was just big enough, after a few contortions, to let a slim lady who was five feet six inches tall slip through.

And that lady kneeled, wiggled and squirmed, making sure she didn't rip her clothing.

Before penetrating that forbidden zone.

CHAPTER 10
An eerie silence

THE STRAIGHT PATH went on roughly thirty feet after the rusted-out gate, next to an impressively high roller coaster, then up to a square that angled off into a parking lot, then to some sort of building that must have been a warehouse, garage, or workshop for Six Flags' employees.

I walked next to that building made from metal sheeting and ended up in the middle of the deserted theme park. Quite a mind-boggling view of such peace and quiet in a place that ordinarily would be so crowded and noisy. The only sound was the wind whistling grimly through the metallic rides, breaking that eerie silence. Here, twenty years ago, thousands of people were there, walking down the paths, waiting impatiently in lines to go on rides or have an ice cream cone, just like Ricardo and Lisa did, on August 6, 2004.

Was that the one, falling apart, that I was standing

in front of today? It was easy for me to imagine the little dark-haired girl, with her brown, twinkling eyes looking at the ice cream containers, trying to decide between chocolate and vanilla, that scrumptious looking red raspberry or that sugary and delicious caramel.

Did she have time to choose before disappearing? Was she able to taste her favorite flavors before she was taken away, kidnapped, hidden?

By whom?

Her own father? Someone else? An unknown person, some psychopath who happened to be there? Was she the one who was targeted or was it her father? Or both?

A scenario began to write itself in my thoughts. I visualized the little girl, brutally separated from her father, while someone was forcing him to go in the opposite direction. The little girl was holding her ice cream cone in one hand and in the other, that stuffed animal she'd won earlier in the day. Then the unsettling image of the ice cream cone on the ground, the scoop of raspberry sherbet melting in the sun, spreading like a pond of coagulated blood...

I shook my head to rid myself of those thoughts. I was being ridiculous! How could I believe in a kidnapping in the middle of the day in a joyful crowded park and that no one had even noticed? Often, during my investigations, I have flashes like that, some that turn out to be true, whereas others are totally a product of my over productive imagination. And I do have a powerful imagination!

I strode down the paths from one ride to another. I spent quite a while in front of an unarticulated ride with a twisted metallic structure, the sides of which had fallen into inert rubble, then a collapsed stand or ticket hut. Most of the structures had been tagged, proving that despite the 'no entrance' signs, I certainly wasn't the first person to have gone inside. Many of the windows had been broken and shards of glass were omnipresent on the ground. I walked, paying attention to where I put my feet down, on the ground strewn with miscellaneous rubble, rusted out iron bars and broken planks of wood, from that violent hurricane back in 2005. Paradoxically though, some of the structures had remained standing despite the wear and tear to be expected and Katrina's terrible winds that I remembered reading that gusts had reached 175 mph. Nearly two decades had gone by in that deserted theme park and the unexplained disappearance of Lisa and her father.

I took my phone out, I needed some info. I didn't even think about the time difference between New Orleans and the eastern coast of Australia.

Nothing ventured, nothing gained, my favorite leitmotiv. Suzanne picked up after the phone had rung only three times.

"Miss Diggs? This is Karen Blackstone. I hope I'm not waking you up in the middle of the Australian night?"

"I've always got my phone next to me and I'm sure you understand that for the past couple of days I've hardly slept at all, haunted by my disheveled thoughts."

"I understand. Right now I'm at Six Flags. I know all this dates back, but do you remember where the restrooms that you were supposed to meet Ricardo and Lisa in front of were? Because of course there are several of them."

Suzanne astonished me by answering without a moment of hesitation.

"Like I told you, I haven't forgotten a thing about that terrible day. I remember perfectly well that those restrooms were at the back of the park, close to where the Interstate is, right at the foot of that roller coaster named Mega Zeph, that's the wooden one, you can't miss it. Why are you asking me that?"

"Just to situate myself in the park. So the ice cream stand was near those restrooms then?"

"There were several of them, but we'd walked right in front of one, and you're right, it was near those bathrooms. Lisa had spotted it a bit earlier. So I'd imagine that Ricardo and she both went there."

"You'd imagine? You can't be sure of it?"

"That's right. When I walked in, they were still standing in the hall."

"Okay. I'll call you back if I need anything else. And thanks for the photos. Lisa was such a beautiful little girl."

"And now she's a striking adult, you can believe me."

I didn't know what to say after that, so I just hung up after having said goodnight to her.

Then I walked to those restrooms. They were in a two-story building, on the ground floor. What a terrible sight! Those public restrooms, naturally quite an unesthetic venue in the best of times, were now completely abandoned and terribly destroyed. The hurricane had caused flooding, and the uncontrollable water had rushed in with mud, vegetal waste and divers detritus, all of that forming a foul and unequal crust on which I was walking, albeit with disgust. I remained in the hallway, too afraid to go into the toilet area itself. And what would that have brought me anyway? I saw a door at the end of the hall with a metallic bar on it, that you pressed down to exit. I pressed it and found myself outside now, where there was a path winding through the tall weeds to the warehouse that I'd gone past a bit earlier.

I suddenly jumped, and screamed when, out of breath, I heard a throaty voice yelling at me.

"Hey! You there! Whatcha doing here? This is private property!"

I turned my head to the upper part of the building across from me, something that must have been their offices where the voice was coming from and discovered an old man with an unkempt beard covering the whole bottom of his face, staring at me from one of the windows with its broken panes.

I couldn't have been more frightened had I seen a ghost.

CHAPTER 11
That Katrina bitch

"You almost scared the living daylights out of me," I admitted.

"Who are you, lady? You didn't see them *No Entrance* signs?"

"I could ask you the same question," I blurted out, my heart pounding and on the brink of hightailing it out of there.

"Ha! Ha!" the old man with his blackened skin and gray dirty beard said. His dreadlocks were just as unkempt as the park itself. "You got some guts my little lady. Whatcha doin' here anyway? Nothing left to steal here you know."

"And you?"

"Is this game of verbal ping pong going to last forever? Don't move, I'll be down."

I naively hadn't even thought that I'd be coming face to face with someone in that abandoned and prohibited theme park. Nonetheless, the graffiti proved to me that squatters or unoccupied young people must sometimes hang around there. I suddenly realized that I could have been disturbed by a junkie or other more or less dangerous disenfranchised individuals. The old man seemed to me to be more quirky than dangerous, yet I was thinking of running off before he came down to meet me. But my legendary curiosity made me wait. A minute or so later, there he was. Wearing rags of clothing of a very doubtful cleanliness, totally matching his neglected aspect, he looked me straight in the eyes before speaking.

"You a cop?"

My eyes popped wide open. Because I looked like a cop?

"Not at all! And you, you're the guardian of the temple?" I asked ironically.

"You're not too far from the truth," he replied with a smile that showed many missing teeth as well as those yellowish and nearly brown ones. "What's yer name?"

"Karen. What about you?"

"Moses. Call me Mo. At least you don't look like no junkie. Plus, it's always nice to have a visit here. So whatcha doin' here? You looking for the water slides or the bumper cars? You're a little late for that!"

"Almost, I'm looking for souvenirs. Without meaning to offend you, you must be old enough to have gone to this amusement park when it was still up and running."

"For sure! And let me tell you, it was a success! It was only open for five years, but wow, they were great ones. Fucking hurricane! She destroyed so many things and lives that Katrina bitch... Wanna beer? Sorry, my coffee machine is on the fritz, I've been waiting for the repair man to stop over since 2005," the old man chuckled.

"No thanks," I replied, disgusted. "On the other hand, as long as you're here, could I ask you a couple of questions?"

"Come on in," he said, with a movement of his chin towards the building.

I hesitated to go inside. I had no idea who that man could be, his dark eyes sunken below his bushy eyebrows seemed to dissimilate his dark intensions, and I had no idea what could have happened inside.

"It's nice out, let's stay outside," I illuded the question. "We could talk here on this bench, if that's okay with you."

"Whatever you want. But I'm still gonna get myself a beer. I'll be right back. Sit right down, my dear little lady, this bench is for you" he said with a wide gesture of his arm.

I sat down, my mind boiling over with thousands of questions, and Mo reappeared a couple of minutes later, limping. He handed me a light soft drink that I accepted and pulled the cap off his can of beer, taking a long pull on it. He exhaled with a sigh of pleasure, looking up towards the sky and its clouds on that nice summer day.

"Ah! It was really nice here back in the day."

Then he shook his head, as if thinking 'what can you do?' and I jumped right in.

"If I'm here, it's because I want to go back in time. Till August 6, 2004 exactly."

Mo nodded his head.

"That is a while. How come that precise day? You came here for a fun-filled family day?"

Family day... I thought bitterly. I realized that Luke Virgil must have been four that year, just a bit older than Lisa.

"That day," I began to explain, "a family, just like loads of other families, went here to have fun, a day they were looking forward to. Up to the moment when that family was broken apart, shattered, dismantled. A two-and-a-half-year-old girl, named Lisa, disappeared with her father, named Ricardo. Their mother, Suzanne, never knew what could have happened. The investigators didn't find anything. Twenty years! Twenty years without any news! For Suzanne, twenty years without living, twenty years of being alone. Up until a couple of days ago, when she thought she'd found her daughter working at an ice cream shop in Australia! And she asked me to investigate that double disappearance."

"Wow! Crazy scenario! A lot better than the movies shot here ever since that bitch went through..."

"Movies were shot here?"

"For sure! *Jurassic World*, for example. Or a recent episode in *Planet of the Ape*s, I wouldn't be able to tell you which one, as I haven't seen any of them. Ah! I also heard of a thing like *Percy Jackson*, something like that, I don't know if the guy's related to Michael, or if he's one of the Jackson Five... Anyway except for Michael and Jermaine, I've never been able to remember their names. Did you know that Jermaine is a guy? Crazy name... Anyway! That's not what's important here, right! Maybe I witnessed your story..."

"Really?"

"Believe it or not, I worked here in 2004. That's right!"

"What did you do?"

"I was one of those guys no one notices. Lots of people like that... One of those dudes wearing overalls who's on his feet all day — and even after closing hours — with a long gripper in his hand to pick up the waste that indelicate tourists *forget* to throw into the bins. See what I mean?"

And I did. I've always pitied those anonymous cleaning staff. How many times had I run across them, pitying them internally because maybe they'd not studied hard enough at school, or they didn't have enough money or smarts to hope for a better job.

"Not an easy job," I said understandingly.

"Bah! For me it was fine. Not really hard work, you could say. You didn't hafta think. And I wasn't bothered by all those little middle managers on my back, plus the park was nice. And all those kids with huge smiles on their faces, that was what I really liked, I never had any. I mean kids, not smiles."

"A discreet and transparent employee... an anonymous one," I bounced right back. "And one who maybe saw something... Who knows, maybe without realizing it, you did see or hear something that could relate to my investigation."

The man burst out laughing.

"And you think that my memory, me an old fart, twenty years later, still remembers that tiny little thing? You're dreaming, lady. I don't got powers like that, and I'm sorry but I can't help you. All I can tell you today is that if something like that had happened then, I imagine that it would have really created a commotion, and if so, I would have known. But frankly, nuttin at all, at least I don't remember nuttin."

I sighed after having taken a sip of my warm soda. I had to be realistic: the first person I talked to in my investigation wasn't going to unravel it for me and serve it to me on a silver platter. That would have been too good to be true. I remained silent.

"Me, I didn't see nuttin, but that over there, maybe it did!"

I followed the direction that he was pointing to with his gnarled index finger.

Above us, hanging on lopsided by an electric wire that had somehow resisted Katrina's fury, I saw a surveillance camera whose eye was shut tight.

CHAPTER 12
Reduced to eternal silence

I shook my head, incredulous.

"Those electronic devices are over twenty years old and were hit by a hurricane. They're good for nothing."

"You're right there, sweetie," confirmed Moses. "Those antiques are totally useless! And squatters broke the few that resisted Katrina. Except that I think they're like us humans, they got eyes to see, but they also got a brain that records stuff, right?"

"Of course, they've got digital or back up disks. But still, in the same way, would they have survived? I'm sure the investigators put their hands on them."

I could see a smile in the middle of Moses's bushy beard.

"Don't be so sure of that. Nothing ventured, nothing gained. I got my little idea where they might be."

"Come on!"

"Sure do! You know, here it's like my home. I know every nook and cranny. Did I tell you about that?"

"About what?"

"About my life!" said old Mo with a guffaw. "Y'all interested in my life? Yer not? Tough luck, I'm still gonna tell you about it. I'll make it short, don't worry. So like I told you, I worked at Six Flags back in the day, before Katrina. That bitch destroyed everything: the theme park, businesses, jobs and especially lives. Holy shit, you shouda seen that! Imagine this place where we're sitting buried below nearly twenty feet of muddy water, all that water that escaped from Lake Pontchartrain, right next to us. 'Bout twenty feet! It took weeks before the zone started to look normal, like you see it today, which isn't great, you gotta admit. And in the meanwhile, the big bosses did estimations on how much it would cost to clean everything up and rebuild. It was close to a hundred million bucks! They gave up, laid their employees off, at least those they couldn't send to other Six Flags theme parks in the country. I got laid off, I was already over fifty, and let's just say that the hurricane and society both did me in. You gotta remember how much damage there was. Over half of Crescent City was devastated, nearly two thousand people died or disappeared... More than a million people living in Louisiana had to move.

As for me, I decided to stay, though my house got blown away, it's probably floating some place in the Gulf of Mexico! But rather than walking up and down New Orleans' devastated streets with other vagabonds, homeless people or even hoodlums who were taking advantage of the chaos to scare people and rob them of the little they had left, I decided to go back here. I knew that I'd be better off. I moved in up there, where you first saw me. It was dry, the windows were still intact on that side, and it wasn't too cold. Ever since then, each day I wander around in the streets of this artificial district where people used to have fun, all alone, but nice and peaceful. Every now and then, the cops, 'coz they gotta earn their keep or maybe the mayor asks them to do something, come here to chase out local thugs, but I know where they won't be looking. Know where to hide. And my little lady, it's been like that since 2005. But I no longer pick up the junk and litter in the paths, I'm sure you understand."

The man ended his tirade with a guffaw that turned into a coughing spell.

"The hand of fate," I simply said.

"Okay then, so you wanted to see them recordings? Just follow me into my office," said Mo, getting up from the bench, a hand on his back. "This time you can't say no."

I COULD FEEL that I didn't have anything to fear from that man, a poor guy that society had left behind and followed him towards the administration building. We walked upstairs, went down a dark hall, and passed in front of a door that was slightly ajar.

"My apartment! I won't show you around, I didn't do any cleaning today."

That was quite the euphemism: I saw an old yellowish stained mattress in the middle of the room on the floor, surrounded by boxes, cans, clothing and a huge quantity of eclectic and undefinable objects.

"It's here, at the end of the hall," continued Moses. "If you'll just follow me," he added with an exaggerated stilted tone.

A few more feet and even though there was no electricity of course, I could make out what was written on the door: *Central control station*.

Moses opened the door.

Inside, I discovered what looked like all the control stations in public places that were equipped with video surveillance systems. There was an office chair with wheels, a desk with several computer screens side by side, keyboards, a microphone, metal cabinets, archive boxes, a walkie-talkie, as well as scattered papers and magazines.

"I'll leave you to rummage around," said Mo. "You need something, just holler!"

What could I learn from that abandoned office? All those electronic machines that hadn't worked for nearly twenty years, reduced to a virtual eternal silence. I couldn't turn them on and make them speak to me! The only hope I had was to scavenge around in the drawers and archive boxes, hoping that I'd find some disks.

But my hopes were quickly dashed. In the drawers

I found loads of things — including magazines for men only — but no cassettes, CD-ROMs or other support devices.

But on the archive boxes, the years covered were written on the sides. It didn't take me too long as the Six Flags amusement park had only been open from 2000 to 2005, and in the 2004 box that I ripped open, there were differently colored envelopes with CD-ROMs month by month.

I picked up the box, tipped it over and everything in it fell out onto the desk.

There were eleven envelopes.

ALL THAT WAS MISSING WAS the one from August 2004...

CHAPTER 13
Supermax

California, 2004

PELICAN BAY STATE PRISON, located on the edge of Crescent City, a little town with a population of six thousand, on the north-eastern corner of California just south of the Oregon border, was a cold, gray inert mass, sitting in the middle of a dense forest with all the trees cut down immediately around it, when seen from above.

If you were flying over the prison, you might think that its architecture looked like a recreation facility located near a marina, but that was completely misleading. Inside its walls, daily life was light years away from any touristic activities for the three thousand or so inmates in that high-security prison. And even less fun in the part that included the white buildings in the form of a cross, a whole block, surrounded by electric fences and desolate planes. That part of the prison was known as a super-maximum-security prison or super-max, one that housed the most dangerous convicted criminals. Dangerous for society, dangerous for themselves, dangerous for the wardens and other inmates.

Those inmates enjoyed special treatment you could say, spending twenty-two and a half hours out of twenty-four in solitary confinement in their cells, with one hour of physical exercise in a tiny courtyard of the facility, handcuffed and bound with fetters with the remaining half hour reserved for a brief visit, though rare, in the visitation area. And those visits were strictly controlled, monitored, secured, and were reserved for the "lucky ones," who had accumulated a certain number of "bonus points." The others had to settle for a monthly phone call.

The detainee, that day, was expecting a visit.

Lying in his 80 square foot cell, on a concrete bed, he was staring up at the florescent light on the ceiling. The light was turned on and off by the prison guards outside the cell and did little to alleviate the lack of sunlight in the cell. Outside of that neon light, there was a four-inch-wide arrow slit or loophole, equipped with an opaque glass people called a window, just because it was easier that way, giving just enough light to see your way around during the day.

The harsh neon light fell on the man lying on his concrete bed. His long wavy hair framed his face with its thick beard. Looking at him, you might have said he was almost Christlike.

He could hear the subdued steps of the prison guards approaching his "apartment." Steps that stopped in front of the heavy armored door with its electronic key.

After an acoustic click, the door opened and the three prison guards walked into the security portal where a locked grid separated them from the inmate. That portal ate away another nine square feet of the total area of the cell and all it did was to protect the wardens from some attempted escape or aggression from prisoners.

One of the three prison guards stood in the portal, one hand on his nightstick and the other on his service weapon, whereas the two others opened the grid bars.

"Inmate 45-287, to the visitation area!" barked one of them, probably the highest ranking one, without further ado.

In his orange jumpsuit that was two sizes too big for him, the prisoner slowly rose, rubbing his sore back and winced. A wince of pain or of irony? He was the only one who knew. Now docile because he knew the drill, he turned his back to the prison guards, holding out his joined hands through the hole in the grid so they'd be able to handcuff him. After that, in the security buffer zone, he kneeled so they'd be able to fetter his ankles and put a chain around his waist.

Escorted by the three prison wardens – one man on each side of him holding him by the arms and the third one pointing his M16 rifle at him –, he slowly walked down the labyrinthic halls. Door after door, buffer zone after buffer zone, the group was followed by the inquisitive eye of a multitude of surveillance cameras linked to the central security office. Each door opened and closed itself electronically as the four men advanced up to the room where on rare occasions prisoners could speak to a friend or family member, *de visu*, or simply by phone. Both of course, strictly monitored by the penitentiary administration.

It took them a good five minutes to walk through all the infrastructure leading to the visitation area in the complex. That area was a mere soundproof three-by-three-foot cabin with a concrete shelf and stool in front of an armored glass window. A phone hanging on the wall allowed inmates to converse with their visitors.

Today, he had a female visitor.

Sitting across from him, a young lady with long brown hair and a light complexion was looking at him sadly. She understood, when reading the message on the gate of the prison, — *Abandon all hope, ye who enter here* — that this was a one-way trip, and there'd be no going back home. The judge had sentenced him to two hundred and sixty years of imprisonment. All he could do would be to mark the days on the walls of his cell.

The young lady sat down on the seat on the other side of the window and picked up her phone. Then the prisoner, as he'd now had his handcuffs taken off, picked up his. The line had no dial tone, it was merely a disguised interphone, just a bit more sophisticated than the phones little kids make with two yogurt cups linked by a nylon string. Just a simple link between the inside and the outside, between freedom and detention, between life without hope and hopeless death.

At first he could only hear the lady breathing, nearly panting, and she wasn't able to utter a single word. They both looked at each other in the white of their eyes, with that armored glass window separating them, with those sentences without words, without the least bit of punctuation. A comma, suspension points, that was all they needed to ease their respective souls, but even that was impossible for them.

She soon began to sniffle. He was pained to see tears dripping slowly on her face. She finally was able to speak.

"Oh…"

Before bursting into tears.

"Ten minutes," shouted the prison guard through a loudspeaker.

"Asshole," mumbled the inmate.

That interlude was enough to allow separated couple's seawall of words to open.

"How are you?" the lady asked.

The man snorted.

"Just have a look: it's a palace here! They treat me like a prince. Prive room, all amenities, three meals a day. Water and heat on each floor, my clothing is washed and dried, a bit monotonous for the colors, but I'd say that orange goes well with my complexion. Plus, a view of the sea... of desolation. Like I said, a real palace here!"

"Good Lord, how could that have happened?"

"You know how it happened... But let's not talk about that anymore! Now you have to look towards the future."

"What future?"

"I'm talking about your future sweetheart, because mine... You saw what it looks like outside, all those concrete walls with barbed wire on top, glass shards and miradors all over, you can't even go outside for a walk..."

The metallic voice of the prison guard interrupted him.

"No details on our facility or I'm immediately stopping this visit. Those are the rules."

The prisoner raised both hands.

"Okay, okay. Got it. I was saying, your future sweetie, you gotta think of yourself. Enjoy your life, take advantage of your freedom, you're not like me, locked up in this hole. Have fun. Have fun, you and our little girl. Our treasure. You'll tell her how much I love her, won't you? I'm crazy about her. Go out, get around, take vacations, go to movies to laugh, take her on rides in amusement parks..."

The lady smiled timidly.

"Amusement parks. Remember?"

"How could I forget? Those moments will be engraved in my heart till the end of my life, I mean for the next two hundred and sixty years at least," said the inmate bitterly.

"Five minutes," the prison guard announced coldly. "Start to say your goodbyes. Or adieus."

"Shut your filthy sewer mouth you son of a bitch," hissed the inmate between his teeth. "So my dear, you see, we already have to say goodbye, time flies so fast when I see you and goes so slowly when I'm waiting for you."

"I love you, my angel."

"I love you too babe, but like I said, you gotta live your life, don't wait for me, I'll probably be a bit late for our next date... Come on, you have to be strong now. Promise?"

The lady swallowed a sob that shook her chest.

"I'll be strong, I promise."

"You say hi to our friends," asked the inmate, tilting his head sideways.

He slowly rubbed the tattoo on his neck with his fingertips, two artistically tattooed figures.

"Of course," replied the lady with a hint of a smile.

"Tell them not to forget me and to take good care of my business. From here it's gonna be hard to take care of it myself... They know which contract is the high priority one."

CHAPTER 14
Those who remain

New Orleans, July 2024

As Lady Luck didn't seem to be on my side for the surveillance cameras at Six Flags, I had to turn my investigations towards the authorities. I opened my notebook and found the name of Inspector William Stanford, the one that Suzanne Diggs had given to me. She said he was the policeman in charge of the investigation about the disappearance that she reported back in August of 2004.

I thanked my unexpected host for his welcome and promised to get back to him if needed in my investigation, and then walked towards the exit. I took Mason Lacassagne's business card out of my pocket, and the taxi driver showed up a few minutes later, at the Six Flags entrance, on Michoud Boulevard.

"Hey! *Comment ça va M'zelle?*" he asked in

French, opening the car door for me. You weren't too scared on the roller coasters? Ha! Ha! Back to the hotel?"

"Not right now. Could you take me to the NOPD* headquarters please?"

"Okay. South Broad Street, I know it by heart. Consider it done! Ready Freddy?"

Sitting in the back seat, I let myself be lulled by the Cajun music coming from the radio. I had the impression of hearing country chords mixed in with sentences that I had no idea what they were saying, as they were sung in some sort of French dialect I didn't understand at all. Mason tried to teach me a few lines that I did my best to repeat, like: "Oh yeah! *Donnez-moi des haricots! Les haricots sont pas salés,*" telling me that it meant something like 'Gimme some beans. Them beans ain't salted,' whatever signification that could have had.

Outside, the suburbs of Nola[†] went past us as we drove next to the peaceful Mississippi towards the center of New Orleans. Half an hour later, the chauffeur stopped his cab in front of an ordinary looking five or six story building, made from unesthetic concrete: the New Orleans Police Headquarters.

"There you go *M'zelle*. Call me back whenever you need a ride, Mason's always ready! Your hotel is only a ten-minute walk from here, towards the river, but I can pick you up if you want."

---

[*] New Orleans Police Department
[†] NOLA: **N**ew **O**rleans, Louisiana (**LA** is Louisiana's State code)

"That won't be necessary Mason, thanks."

I PAID him and turned around, going into the police station. I introduced myself as a private detective to the agent at the reception desk and asked to see Inspector William Stanford.

The young lady raised an inquiring eyebrow.

"Stanford, you said? Doesn't ring a bell. Wait a sec, I'll check it out."

She clicked away on her computer, then looked back at me.

"It's Stanford? S.T.A.N.F.O.R.D?" she spelled out. "There's no one here with that name, ma'am. I do have an inspector Stanton and an officer Sanford, but no Stanford. Maybe you made a mistake."

"It's possible," I humbly recognized, thinking that perhaps Suzanne Diggs did give me a wrong last name of the inspector in charge of the case twenty years ago. Plus I said to myself that the title of officer Sanford probably referred to a younger police officer, and that it was unlikely that he would have been in charge of the case back in 2004. My logic anyway.

"Okay, maybe Stanton then. Could I see that inspector?"

"Please wait."

She speed-dialed him. That time Lady Luck was smiling down on me. He accepted to see me and a couple of minutes later I saw a forty or so year old man, quite tall, holding his head up aristocratically, and with the regulatory short salt and pepper haircut. After we greeted each other, we went to his office on the third floor.

"Do we know each other?" he asked when we sat down. "Your name rings a bell…"

It was hard for me to believe, but I briefly gave him my resume, in particular the articles I'd written for *True Crime Mysteries* as well as the Jabaree Smith case that had made headlines all throughout the country, at least enough of them that a cop in Louisiana would remember.

"Yeah! That's it! That Hollywood kid-star! So that was you?"

"It was," I replied, blushing. "But I wasn't alone, of course. I worked hand-in-hand with the LAPD police. Without them…"

"Of course," he replied proudly, "it's always a good idea to ask for assistance from our efficient police force. What would the world be without cops?"

"Totally!" I flattered him while thinking of the crazy number of cold cases in America. Which, between us, represented the majority of my activity.

After that little newspeak contest, Inspector Stanton got down to business.

"So, how can I help you?"

"Two people who went missing back in 2004 at Six Flags amusement park, remember that?"

The policeman squinted, as if calling upon his long-term memory.

"Wow! That's not recent. Twenty years! I was still in the police school then. Not working here. Frankly I don't know what to say to you. But you're looking for some specific inspector, William Stanford, right?"

"That's the thin little clue that my client gave me."

"Because you're working on that disappearance for a client? Someone involved in that case?"

I briefly outlined what led me to see him today.

Stanton thought that over.

"As for the name of that policeman who Suzanne Diggs had spoken to at that time, it is someone I know. There was a William Stanford here. But now he's retired."

Once again, I seemed to run into a brick wall at the beginning of my investigation. I suggested a workaround.

"You must have archives of cases that the NOPD was in charge of. Especially evidence, here I'm thinking about elements such as surveillance cameras tapes," I insinuated, thinking that those shot in August of 2004 were missing in the Six Flags control station.

"If I understand correctly, it's a cold case. There's been nothing new since the events took place, so I don't have much hope."

"*Nothing ventured, nothing gained*," I tried.

"Why do you want to reopen this case? Just on the basis of an old lady's elucubrations who thinks she saw her daughter who disappeared in New Orleans twenty years ago. You think that's all we got to do, Miss Blackstone? I'm not going to teach you anything when I tell you about the mind-boggling number of unsolved cases each year. And they'll remain unsolved *ad vitam aeternam*..."

I sighed.

"I'm quite aware of that, Inspector. Believe me when I tell you that I know it's like looking for a needle in a haystack or isolating stardust in the universe. Just one case amongst hundreds of thousands of others in this world. But it's my job! And even though I maybe only solve a couple of cases each year, for me it's the joy to know that I've been able to explain what happened, or I've saved memories, or repaired lives, at least for those left, people who had been crying and suffering until I helped unearth the truth."

While my heart was speaking, the policeman was nodding, more and more visibly, my arguments seemed to have made a dent.

"Okay, after all. It's not going to cost us much. As long as this story won't make my guys lose time, it's alright for me. I'll give you what I find, and to be polite, then it's in your hands. Deal?"

"Deal!"

I remained silent while he was typing — with his two index fingers, believe it or not! — on his keyboard and tried to figure out what those various expressions on his face meant. I thought I could make out, in order, concentration, questions, frustration, stubbornness, doubt, anger, incomprehension, and at the end, resignation.

He looked up. "Well, Miss Blackstone, I regret to inform you that we have no records at all of any cases of disappearances at Six Flags in August of 2004."

CHAPTER 15
Empathy

Hervey Bay, July 2024

THOUGH SHE WAS FAR from dying for an ice cream cone, Suzanne Diggs didn't see any other way to get a bit closer to Ashley. Following Karen Blackstone's advice, she went once again to the ice cream shop that touted seventy-two different flavors, just a few minutes before closing time. She made sure that Ashley was there, spotting her behind the counter putting the refrigerated containers in order, and walked in.

At that time of the day, she was the only customer, so she walked straight up to Ashley, forcing herself to smile to try to mask the uneasiness she felt when approaching the person she thought was her daughter.

When the employee raised her eyes, she had a puzzled expression. Though every day at this time of the year she had dozens or even hundreds of clients, she was pretty good with faces, and some people, because of their features or attitudes printed themselves more easily on her memory. She unconsciously thought she'd seen that lady once or twice and smiled at her, as if they knew each other.

"Hi. What can I get you? We've got an end-of-the-day special, one free scoop for two that you buy or the chocolate cone for the price of the regular one."

What she could *get* Suzanne was something she wasn't able to admit openly in the middle of the ice cream shop, even with no witnesses. So she just asked for two scoops of ice cream, caramel and stracciatella, in a chocolate cone.

Ashley carefully prepared her order and gave it to her with a wide smile.

"Enjoy!"

"Oh! I'm sure I will, you have excellent ice cream here, that's why I stop in so often."

"I thought I'd already seen you. Do you live in Hervey Bay?" asked the young lady pleasantly.

As they were alone in the shop, she had time to exchange a few friendly words with her customer. And being friendly was undeniably one of Ashley's qualities, as was empathy.

"Let's just say I'm on an unlimited vacation here. Are you from here? If you've got any good addresses or tips to give me, I'm all ears."

"I'm from Darwin, in the Northern Territory, but I've been living her almost a year. For addresses and tips, it all depends on what you're looking for. Shops? Tourism? Sports? Bars? Culture?"

Right then the door opened, and a noisy group of teens rushed in.

"Oops! Gotta go," she said. "If you come back, I'll give you some good tips."

Suzanne paid for her cone and walked out.

She stayed close though, eating her ice cream cone on a bench across from it. About twenty minutes later, she saw Ashley walking out and heading towards the marina. Suzanne threw the rest of her cone into the nearest bin and discreetly followed her. She tried to stay about thirty feet behind her, and when Ashley stopped to do some window shopping, she'd go to the other side of the street, ahead of the young lady, before crossing the road again in the opposite direction of Ashley.

As Ashley was looking at the dresses in the shop window, she couldn't avoid the collision. Someone had just run into her.

"Excuse me, I'm sorry, I was thinking of something else and..." Suzanne said, apologizing.

"You have to watch out! Oh! It's you?"

"What a small world... Really, I'm so sorry, Miss. It's Ashley, isn't it? You're the young lady who sells ice cream? Without your uniform, I wasn't sure. Are you okay?" Suzanne asked. "I'd blame myself if..."

"No, I'm fine, don't worry," replied Ashley with a smile. "Nothing's broken. What about you?"

"I'm pretty tough. But I don't know how you can forgive my clumsiness. Could I buy you a drink, if you have time?"

Ashley thought it over for a few seconds, looked at her phone to see what time it was and accepted.

"There's a cute little bar not too far from here. That's already one good tip," she added with a smile.

The two women walked towards the bar, side by side, just like two friends would do. Or a mother and a daughter.

When they walked into the bar, a cyclist stopped his motorbike on the sidewalk on the other side of the street, attached it to a metal railing, then walked in after them.

CHAPTER 16
The black sheep

New Orleans, July 2024

Just as intrigued as Inspector Stanton, I asked him to repeat. He confirmed what he had just said, in other words.

"Something just ain't adding up here. I don't understand. Even if the hard copy of the file can't be found after so many years, at the very least, I should find something about the case in the database. But there's nothing."

"But how is that possible? Even in 2004, most of the work must have been done on computers."

"Of course, it wasn't like we were back in the Stone Age."

The image of him awkwardly typing with his two index fingers on the keyboard curiously popped up in my brain and I had to force myself not to laugh. I let him continue.

"I'll tell you what I think, Miss Blackstone, because I can only see one explanation. In my opinion, your client is totally off her rocker. Or she's lost her memory, or she's a pathological liar, who knows! I think that before you lose your time, which is undoubtedly worth just as much as mine," he said bitterly, "in fastidious research, you should clarify things with her. Have you actually met her?"

"For now, I've only spoken to her on the phone."

"And for you that was enough to kick off your investigation of the past? Just because what she said?"

I suddenly felt like a little kid being scolded by my grade schoolteacher . But Inspector Stanton wasn't totally wrong there. Was that simple idea of an interesting and lucrative job enough for me to have rushed into the first real case that I had been contacted for? Was I so anxious to kick-start my budding activity as a private investigator that I'd forgotten all the basics? Circumspection, prudence, objectivity.

"That lady seemed so sincere to me, so afflicted. I think that I can feel things like that in people who, each day after an unexplained disappearance of a loved one — and here it was two loves ones — are no longer living, they're just existing, surviving."

The inspector smiled at me mockingly.

"Well I've been around the block a couple of times myself and I saw people like that too. Sincerely destroyed ones. Alive, though dead inside. Human waste, devastated by the loss of a husband, a child, a mother… Except that experience has shown me that in a herd, sometimes you stumble upon a black sheep. You might say that you should be able to recognize them right away. But you're there, a shepherd in the middle of your livestock, with your dog who knows what it's doing too, and you don't see it coming. As soon as you turn your back on them, that black sheep, or sometimes a ram, rushes up to you and kicks you in the butt! And you end up on the ground rubbing your behind asking yourself how you could have been so dumb that you didn't see it coming."

"But… um… no," I stammered, troubled by the policeman's vivid line of thought.

It's true that I often have been quite surprised in my investigations. Theoretically improbable reversals of situations that nonetheless turned out to be true. Inspector Stanton seemed to be reading my thoughts.

"Meet her in person before you continue."

"Um, she's in Australia."

"So? There are things called planes!"

"True, but that's exactly the problem, I'm afraid of flying."

"Have her come here then. Seeing her face to face should allow you to understand her a bit better. How many people who looked like the salt of the Earth then turned out to be real demons? And how do you know that she didn't invent that disappearance act to mask her double crime? Infanticide and a black widow… But then again, these are just a few thoughts of an old cop used to tackling the horrors our fellow citizens are capable of. Or who knows, maybe it's just a computer bug in our data base!"

Once again his fingers began walking on the keyboard.

Resigned, I thanked the inspector for his time, asked him to keep me in the loop, if he ever was able to find out a bit more about this case, then gave him my card and left.

"If ever..." I repeated, pitifully.

NIGHT WAS SLOWLY FALLING over the Mississippi, a river as peaceful as the inhabitants of Louisiana. I walked along the bank to reach my hotel, which, as the taxi driver had told me, was a mere ten-minute walk.

As soon as I got back to my room, I sat on the bed, opened my laptop, and using all ten fingers and not just my two index fingers, started an internet search about what happened on August 6, 2004 in Six Flags. If Inspector Stanton wasn't really gifted enough to access the database of cold cases in his department, I was hoping to find something on the web. And I said to myself that it must have been at least mentioned in the local papers.

Suddenly, in the search bar, I realized I had committed professional negligence, not having asked Suzanne to give me Ricardo and Lisa's last name. I'd assumed she had her husband's last name. I thus entered *disappearance + Lisa + Diggs +Ricardo + Six Flags + 2004*.

The results though were disappointing.

Google gave me articles about Six Flags, mainly dating to post-Katrina, about the destruction of the park, and the rebuilding projects, which had all failed.

Other results hit the keyword *disappearance*, sometimes associated with the first names of Ricardo or Lisa, but never both of them together. But there was no mention of anyone named Diggs. And even less Ricardo or Lisa Diggs.

The farther I scrolled, the more missing terms I had from the search engine.

As if it was true that no one had disappeared on August 6, 2004 in the New Orleans theme park.

NOW A BIT PISSED OFF, I immediately called Suzanne Diggs.

CHAPTER 17
Conspiracy

Hervey Bay, July 2024

SITTING across from one another at a table in the corner of the bar, Suzanne and Ashley looked at each other, smiling. Suzanne was proud of herself for her little trick, while Ashley was thinking how strange fate could be. How could she be drinking a glass of fresh fruit juice so quickly with a lady she didn't even know a few minutes ago? But that lady had a look on her saying she could be trusted, though she had no idea why she thought that. For Ashley, with some people and without knowing why, it was sometimes easy to get to know them and you immediately felt at ease with them. Close to them, if you could put it like that. Something you couldn't explain, you simply experienced it. Ashley was like that, open-minded, empathic and friendly.

So she replied to Suzanne Diggs's insidious questions without a second thought.

"What made a young lady like you come and live in Hervey Bay? It's not the town in Australia with the most to do, I'd imagine. Why not Sydney, Brisbane, Canberra or Perth?"

"And what made a woman like you decide to come to Hervey Bay on vacation?" replied Ashley with a smile. "I was joking. I understand why, it's so beautiful here, and for tourists, they can either explore the coral reef, or go whale watching when they're migrating twice a year. So that creates jobs for Australian people and foreigners too. That's how I ended up here, a job! And I'm sure you agree there are worse places to work!"

"You're right. You told me you were from Darwin I think. Were you born there?"

Of course that was not an innocuous question.

"Yup! Totally from the Northern Territory," joked the young lady proudly. "The most northern city in Australia, Ma'am."

"Please, just call me Suzie," replied Suzanne, trying to win her over. "Ma'am gives me the impression of being an old lady. Even though I could be your mother..."

"I doubt that," Ashley said, "I don't know how old you are, but you certainly don't look that old!"

Suzanne nearly choked on her fruit juice.

"Ashley, you were well brought up. From a well-educated family. If I showed you my ID card, you'll see that my wrinkles at the corners of my eyes and around my mouth totally match my age. But you... I have trouble believing that your... parents... allowed you to leave home to work on the other side of the country. With your angel face, you look underage."

The young lady burst out with a crystal-clear laugh.

"You know how to flatter people, Suzie. I guarantee you that I'm a responsible adult. Totally emancipated. I've got my driver's license, but I don't have a car yet because my legs are enough for me to move around wherever I want in a five-mile radius."

Suzanne shook her head, meaning she didn't believe her allegations. On purpose, she disagreed with her.

"No, I don't believe you. I've got a daughter who's... who's twenty-three. And you look younger than her."

"That's normal!"

"Why?"

"Because I'm a lot younger than your daughter, it's true! I'm almost nineteen."

The two women looked each other in the eyes like two duelists right before then final skirmish. The American's winced smile against the Australian's angelic one. Suzanne insisted, falsely naïve.

"Seriously, I don't believe you. I need proof."

"Okay," replied Ashley, opening her purse hanging on the back of her chair. "I'll give you some proof. Here's my ID card, you can read it yourself."

Suzanne grabbed the official Australian document that did stipulate that Ashley Marta Bolt was born on December 26, 2005 in Darwin, Northern Territory.

Though she was proud of herself for having obtained the proof of her identity, she now had to do her best to hide her frustration. For her, that just wasn't logical. Ashley couldn't have been born in 2005 in Australia as she was already two and a half in 2004 when she disappeared in a theme park in Louisiana. Those documents must have been false. In the tortured mind of that mother separated from her child, for her it was evident that somehow the young lady was hiding her true identity. Otherwise that would have meant that Suzanne was crazy! But why would she have wanted to look younger than she was in reality? Why pretend she was born in Australia and why have the alias 'Bolt.' No, frankly all of that was just some huge hoax. A large-scale conspiracy to trick Suzanne. She had to understand the reasons for it, its logic. But just like that, right off the bat, she couldn't reveal the truth about her origins to that young lady. She never would have believed her. That was why she had to, with the help of the private investigator she'd hired, reveal what really happened in 2004 in New Orleans.

Suzanne handed the ID card back to its owner.

"I have no other choice than to agree with this proof of the infallible Administration: you're still a teenager, and me, I've got crow's feet at the corner of each eye. That's life! Whatever, you still could be my daughter…"

Her voice crackled a bit when she uttered that, and the young lady noticed.

"Are you okay, Suzie? You're really pale all of a sudden. You want me to get you a glass of water?"

Suzanne raised her head, leaned back against the chair rest, and took a deep breath.

"Thanks Ashley, I'll be fine. I'm just a little tired. I'll rest at home. Anyway, I already feel better. I was delighted to have spent a few moments with you, Ashley. And I do hope we'll stumble upon each other another time."

"Me too, Suzie. And if you ever feel like you need an ice cream, you know where to go. You want me to walk you home?"

"No, I'll be fine. Thank you, Ashley. Have a nice evening."

The two ladies left, one going to the right and the other to the left.

When she got back home, Suzanne Diggs took out her phone and saw that she'd had a voicemail in her absence.

Karen Blackstone's slightly irritated tone added an additional layer to her uneasiness.

"Miss Diggs, Karen Blackstone here. Can you call me back as soon as possible, whatever time it is for you? I think we need to have a frank conversation now. Thank you."

CHAPTER 18
The meanders of the Mississippi

NEW ORLEANS, July 2024

I DOZED OFF, irritated and a bit discouraged by the beginning of my new investigation with its bewildering roots.

My morale was, if not in the basement, maybe on the ground floor, and before going to bed I needed to hear my boyfriend's voice, my chum's voice, as they say up in Quebec. I wondered if the Cajuns, their distant cousins, also used that term. Paul, always quite the night owl, picked up on the third ringtone.

"My beautiful Cajun, so glad you called. Did you learn any French words?"

I sighed.

"Sweetie, it's nice of you to try to make me smile but tonight my heart's not in it. I'm sort of demotivated you could say."

"What's going on, my beauty? You're already missing me? Because you can believe me, I miss you terribly. What about me hopping into my jet and flying down to Louisiana?"

"You're so sweet, but if you were here, I wouldn't be able to concentrate at all. Even though your warm skin... Anyway."

I briefly outlined what I'd done and what I'd discovered. The abandoned theme park, meeting old Moses, the missing August 2004 footage in the archives of the park, the police file that had also gone missing, and then — adding insult to injury! — the absence of anything in the papers about that case.

"To sum it up then," said Paul with his ineffable synthetic spirit, "you're investigating an event that never happened, is that right?"

"I'm afraid that you're not too far from the truth there. This is the first time I've been stuck in a swamp like this."

"That's normal, you're in the bayou of the meanders of the Mississippi," joked my dear man, who outside of this synthetic spirit also had the gift of a sense of humor, Dad joke style. "If you think she is trying to pull the wool over your eyes, just walk away. Call your client, thank her, pay her back what you owe her and go on to the next case."

"She already paid me quite a comfortable advance... I was sort of counting on it."

"Bah! You'll get other juicy cases too, don't worry. Your reputation precedes you. Come on back home!"

"No, not yet. I don't want to be made fun of! I have to understand what happened."

"If there was something!"

"When there's smoke, there's a fire someplace. I'm going to wait till my client calls me back. Put the dots on the I's, separate the wheat from the chaff in her incredible story, you get what I'm saying? You know I hate admitting that I'm not going to win every case when I hit the first speedbump."

"Ah! There's my real Karen back again! A fighter, a winner, a Rottweiler who doesn't drop its prey after biting it in the calf. Get going honey, have a good night. Love you."

"Love you too."

I FELL ASLEEP a bit more reassured after our conversation, but less than three hours later my phone rang, waking me up.

"Miss Blackstone? This is Suzanne Diggs. I got your message. You wanted to speak to me, I hope with the time difference…"

"Don't worry about that," I replied, after having shook my head to get the cobwebs out.

I looked at the alarm clock. Three in the morning. What time was it on the Australian coast? Probably about fifteen or more hours later.

"Did you make any progress?" Suzanne wanted to know.

I felt destabilized by her question. How could she dare ask me something like that?

"Listen, Suzanne, I must admit I'm having problems. Like I'm lost in the middle of a forest, surrounded by misleading paths and cul-de-sacs. Can I be frank with you?"

"Of course."

"But, how can I say this without offending you? Let's just say I've got the impression you didn't tell me everything."

"What? Of course I did! Why would I hide something from you, you the person I hired to help me shed some light on the past that is driving me crazy?"

"That's the question I was also asking myself. What would you stand to gain by sending me on a wild goose chase?"

"I'm sorry, but I don't get what you're insinuating."

I sighed, hesitating to spit out the words that were burning my tongue.

"Okay, I'm not going to beat around the bush. The New Orleans police don't have your file of a missing person's case. They even wonder if it actually did exist. The officer you told me about has retired. I'll still try to find him though, he might be able to tell me something. And there weren't any articles in the paper about a double disappearance that occurred in August of 2004 at Six Flags. I don't think something like that could have missed being in the local papers and that the police authorities didn't keep any archives of the case. In conclusion, Suzanne, I'm wondering about the veracity of what you told me."

An uneasy silence followed. On the other end of the line, I perceived a sort of lamentation, soon interrupted by a few words.

"How... can you... affirm things... like that, Karen? That's horrible! I've been... suffering for twenty years. I don't have... a life anymore. I'm dying inside. Me, lie to you? Why would I do something like that? I'm not crazy you know!"

"Suzanne, that's not what I'm insinuating. But you must tell me everything. If not, this story will remain a complex web, something I'll never be able to untangle."

"I swear to you I told you everything. On August 6, 2004, Ricardo, Lisa and I were at the New Orleans theme park. And that was the last day that I saw them alive."

I jumped.

"Alive? A wise investigator could deduce that you saw them later... dead!"

"That's horrible what you're saying!" burst out my client. "I lost my man and my daughter and you... you... that's despicable!"

Once again all I could hear was painful crying.

"Calm down, Suzanne. I'm sorry. It's not my role to interrogate you. It's the opposite, I want to help you. Understand. Find them, maybe... Let's work together. Speaking of which, how are things going in Hervey Bay?"

I gave her time to get her wits back.

"I started to get closer to Lisa… I mean Ashley. I think she now trusts me and little by little, I'll learn about her past. And I'm sure that you and I, we'll be able to pool our respective investigations. You'll see, Karen, you'll end up understanding that I'm telling you the truth."

CHAPTER 19
Twenty years of fantasies

Hervey Bay, July 2024

Suzanne was afraid to tell Karen Blackstone that she had certainly made a mistake about Ashley Bolt, who, according to her ID, could not have been her twenty-three-year-old Lisa. Unless those documents were false...

That was what was running through her mind, over and over again, while she was preparing a frugal dinner in her vacation home.

But still, that young lady was the spitting image of Lisa. However, was it really possible to compare the features of a child who wasn't yet three with those of a person who was going on nineteen? Was Suzanne imagining things? Sparked by a bit of vain hope, was she losing herself in her fantasies? How many times, in twenty years, had she thought she'd recognized her lost daughter in the features of a child at an intersection, a teen in front of her school, a young lady coming out of the movies with her boyfriend? Too many! But it had never been as strong as the day when she found herself face to face with the girl in the ice cream shop in Hervey Bay. *This time*, she was persuaded, *it was her*!

Or, if it wasn't her, like in the Laurel and Hardy movie, maybe it was her sister?[*]

Or a true look-alike.

Or, who knows, Ricardo's *secret daughter*? She looked so much like him: the shape and color of her eyes, her hair, the same nose. And Ricardo, back in the day, travelled so much. Including to Australia, for business.

No, that couldn't have been true, it was impossible. Suzanne mistook her dreams for reality, hung on to the smallest hypothesis, was sure of the most minute coincidence that matched her desires.

Could twenty years of unfulfilled hopes lead to insanity?

Or could insanity generate twenty years of fantasies?

Suzanne swallowed the Chinese noodles she'd cooked in the microwave while going over her obsessional thoughts. Sitting cross-legged on the sofa, in

---

[*] Reference to *Our Relations*, a burlesque American film produced in 1936 by Harry Lachman, starring the comic duo Laurel and Hardy.

front of the TV, she mentally was preparing the next step of her plan to approach Ashley... her Lisa!

As of the following day, she went to the ice cream shop once again where she could nearly recite the whole list of flavors now.

There was a chubby girl, with an ungrateful face but a nice smile, behind the counter. Suzanne asked her if she could speak to Ashley, if possible.

"I'll go see if she's in the back," the obliging employee replied.

And just a couple of minutes later the brunette appeared, with a big smile on her face when she recognized Suzanne.

"Hi, Suzie, you want another ice cream?"

"No, I don't want to gain weight, every day would be too much. I just came to get a tip or two and ask for a favor. Would you have five minutes for me, Ashley?"

"My break is in twenty minutes, if you want to wait."

"Great! I'll be on the bench outside."

True to her word, Ashley came out and surprised Suzanne who was admiring the little waves licking the dunes a few yards below.

"Here I am," said the young lady enthusiastically.

"Oh! You scared me, I was lost in contemplation.

It's so beautiful here. So peaceful. So moving that it makes me nostalgic."

Ashley sat down on the bench next to her and also looked out over the ocean.

"What are you nostalgic about?"

"Oh! A long, sad story... I'll tell you about it one day, if you're able to endure my tremolos."

"No problem," replied the young lady. "So, you want some tips?"

"That's right. I've seen so many statues of whales all over the city that I thought it would be fun to go out on a boat ride and observe them. That must be an extraordinary experience. Except there's quite a few companies that provide this service and I don't know which one I should book with. That's why I was hoping you could help me. I'm sure you must know lots of people."

"Ah! You're right! It's THE thing to do here in Hervey Bay! During this season the whales swim between the coast and K'gari Island. You don't want to miss that, you're right. I went last year when I first arrived. And I found a little company that offers all sorts of outings in a catamaran, it's fantastic, there's only twenty-five people max on their boat, and you almost feel like it's your own! A family type atmosphere, a great skipper and welcoming crew. What was their name again? Wait a sec."

She took her phone out of the back pocket of her jeans and quickly scrolled down her list of phone numbers.

"Got it! It's *Blue Dolphin Marine Tours*, with Jodie and Peter Lynch. I remember their names now, the owners are a couple, and Peter is the skipper I told you about. Remember, I said it was a family business. Sound good to you? You want me to check their availabilities?"

Now Suzanne was smiling again. She hesitated though, before answering.

"That would be nice, but… There's something I'd like to ask you again. Would you go with me Ashley? Of course, my treat!"

The young lady thought that over for a couple of seconds, wondering why the lady was so persistent and friendly, though they'd just met a couple of days ago. What was she trying to do? Just meet the locals?

"Why me?" she asked.

"Because you… you're… I mean, you could be my daughter, or almost. You remind me so much of her. Plus I feel alone here. And I like talking to you, so if you agree, I'd be overjoyed. But I would understand of course if you don't want to."

Finally Ashley's empathy with the lonely lady clinched the deal.

"Let's go! Tomorrow's my day off, let's see if they've got any availabilities."

She checked, and they reserved their ocean cruise for the following day.

A beautiful outing in the sea, full of unforgettable and varied emotions!

CHAPTER 20
A wolf hidden in the shadows

New Orleans, July 2024

Right before I hung up, I remembered in a flash to ask Suzanne what Ricardo and Lisa's last name was.

"Gutierrez," she replied.

"Ricardo and Lisa Gutierrez."

"You weren't married then?"

"No, he never wanted to tie the knot," regretted Suzanne with a long sigh.

That nocturnal conversation with my client disturbed my sleep, which was filled with stressful dreams all night.

I woke up at about six, out for the count, swallowed an aspirin and went back to bed, collapsing on the still warm mattress. I woke up again about half past nine, my headache was gone, and I had the firm intention of continuing my investigation and not giving up. Someplace there was a wolf hidden in the shadows of this case, and I had to track it down and force it out of its den so I could slaughter it.

My hunger to know more about that case sparked my physical hunger and I went down to the hotel restaurant right before it closed to have some breakfast. I quickly gobbled down a good-sized serving scrambled eggs served with smoked salmon and had a strong and hearty cup of coffee that really perked me up.

While I was dozing that morning, nearly in a deep comatose sleep after, I remembered a method of investigation that could be useful in this case. A method that a famous journalist had imagined and developed, also a cold case specialist like me, someone I'd run across in a conference he'd held in Los Angeles a couple of years ago. Billy Jensen had more or less patented a research technique to find witnesses that was based on the power of social networks and Facebook in particular, omnipresent in the lives of our fellow citizens, from age thirteen to seventy or eighty. That astute guy had first tested that principle, then, as time went by, had succeeded in solving cases that even the police had abandoned for lack of new elements. One day, after a host of developments, trips, and interviews, he was the one who'd succeeded in putting his finger on a serial killer who had never been caught for over a decade in California. His conference was fascinating, as was his book* that I'd read. I decided to give it a try for the disappearances in Six Flags.

His job, like mine, was to tackle cold cases and try to introduce new elements, such as statements from witnesses. To accomplish that, Billy, using his Facebook profile, would create a page about the case in question, post photos — of the victim or potential suspects — and then write a few lines about the crime, where it had taken place, the dates, as well as any verified facts or assumptions. Then with those posts, he would invest a couple of hundred bucks in a publicity campaign on the social networking service with a target audience, who he thought would be the best to give him any valid information. For example, he could target people around a town, a district or even people living on a given road. Just men, just women, or both. Young people or not so young ones depending on how old the case was. Sometimes his advertising campaign would last for a couple of days, other times for a couple of weeks, according to what he needed, and of course he was counting on this being shared by those reading it.

That was what I wanted to try.

I rushed back up to my room, opened my laptop and went straight to Facebook.

I, using Jensen's method, also created a page enti-

---

* Billy Jensen, *Chase Darkness with Me: How One True-Crime Writer Started Solving Murders* Sourcebooks, 2020

tled: Disappearance of two people in Six Flags, New Orleans, on August 6, 2004.

For my cover photo I used the photos of Ricardo and Lisa that Suzanne had given me and uploaded the file.

Then I wrote the following post, which would be my targeted ad.

On August 6, 2004, Ricardo Gutierrez and his daughter, Lisa, two and a half years old, went missing while they were at the now-closed Six Flags theme park in New Orleans. Neither the father nor his daughter were ever seen after that day and the two victims vanished during the afternoon. Today, Lisa's mother and Ricardo's partner is still grieving and suffering from their unexplained absence and the pain she has of not knowing what could have happened that day nor what has become of them.

So, if you happened to be at Six Flags on that day of August 6, 2004, and using the power of social networks, and you think you'll be able to give me some information, however minute it may be, however insignificant it may seem to you, please, I'm begging you: do it! Contact me!

Please don't hesitate to respond to this post or contact me by direct message (especially if you've got some names to communicate).

Your testimonial could be a game-changer, please be assured of that. Little streams make powerful rivers and details are what solve cases.

Think of that grieving mother, someone who hasn't had any news of her partner and daughter for twenty years now. Think of that little girl, just over the age of two, someone we have no idea of what could have happened to. And her father, what role did he play in this case?

Any information you can give me will be taken seriously, processed with discretion, and you can remain anonymous, should you wish to.

Thanks in advance for your contributions.

THEN I ADDED Lisa's photo, so the call for assistance would have a larger impact, as posts with images on social media are seen by ten times more people, opened, clicked upon, than posts with only a text.

Moreover, that little girl's angel face could only attract attention and move people.

Last but not least, I sponsored the publication, with money from Blackstone Investigations, targeting a twenty-mile radius around New Orleans and men and women from thirty to seventy years old, hoping that this could spark the interest of those who were between the ages of ten — and potentially able to have some memories of that day — and fifty.

I clicked on "launch the sponsored ad," which sent it into the secret Facebook system, awaiting validation. And hoped it wouldn't take too much time.

Now I was going to start knocking on doors, something that had often yielded a host of first-hand information for me in the past.

CHAPTER 21
A scar on my heart

Hervey Bay, July 2024

You had to be an early bird to embark on the Blue Dolphin at seven in the morning, the Lynch's catamaran that was docked at one of the pontoons in the marina, surrounded by a slew of private boats and yachts. The boat, about thirty-six feet long, only had one mast and was nearly invisible amongst the other luxurious behemoths. Suzanne liked that intimate feeling she had as soon as she set eyes on the boat.

She'd joined Ashley a few minutes earlier in front of the marina's gate. She had been waiting for her at the foot of a gigantic statue of a humpback whale that was on the sidewalk. Impressive. Announcing what was to come perhaps?

"It's already so nice of you to accompany me, Ashley," Suzanne said to her warmly.

"No problem. Plus last time I went, we only saw the whales from quite a distance, you never know where they'll be. Maybe we'll be luckier today, who knows? Here, have a look at these photos," she said, pointing at signs along the wharf, "some passengers were even able to touch the whales' rostrums with their hands!"

"Wow! Do you think that's possible? I mean, like they weren't photoshopped to attract tourists? That's crazy!"

"It's all completely true," the young lady confirmed. "Let's go! Hop right in."

Peter Lynch was on the dock, helping them board his boat.

"Welcome ladies."

They greeted the other passengers already sitting on the cushioned benches. An athletic looking man with a square jaw and sunglasses was the last one to board. He just had enough time to attach his bike to the railing before hopping in himself.

A FEW MINUTES LATER, the skipper gave them a reassuring briefing that was not without a touch of humor. Then it was anchors aweigh and the catamaran began to slowly make its way through the port before picking up speed in the channel. The calm sea promised them smooth sailing, and the blue sky, a pleasant day.

All that was missing were the whales, the stars of the trip.

Lulled by the slight roll and tiny pitch the sailboat had, Ashley and Suzanne were sitting on the net in the bow. The waves were flying by below them in a magical shimmer. They could hear the little waves lapping against the double hull and drops of water shot up intermittently, splashing their summer clothing. They both laughed and Suzanne had the impression she was sharing an unforgettable moment with a loved one. And in return, Ashley was delighted to see Suzanne with a big smile like that.

"We'll keep on sailing towards K'gari, which is east, and then after we pass it we'll go straight north," announced the skipper. "Yesterday we were able to admire a beautiful adult whale who came up to greet us. We'll keep our fingers crossed for today."

The morning went by peacefully with passengers talking to one another according to their affinities in a warm atmosphere. The sun above them was pounding down on them and crew members reminded their clients to slather sun cream on whatever was exposed, as UV waves didn't spare this part of Australia which was known for its record amount of skin cancers. Here everyone used 50 index sunscreen, especially because of the shimmer the sun gave off over the sea.

That perfect moment led Suzanne and Ashley to tell each other more. Side by side, their arms touched each other as the boat tilted. Suzanne let out her feelings first.

"Ashley, I'm so happy you came with me. It's doing me a world of good. I felt so alone…"

In an affectionate gesture, the young lady put her hand on Suzanne's.

"My pleasure," she replied. "I was actually wondering why you came here, in Hervey Bay, alone on your vacation."

Suzanne closed her eyes, letting her soul drift just like the catamaran cutting through the waves. She finally began.

"My past is what brought me here. My past, and especially… fate! Painful things happened to me back in the past, a long time ago, but I still have the stigmas of them in the deepest part of my heart and soul. Something that will never be able to heal."

Ashley nodded, comprehensively.

"Do you want to talk about it?"

"I don't know if I'll be able to without breaking down in tears," Suzanne sighed. "I don't want to spoil the atmosphere onboard. Though I must say that sometimes I really need to vent, to talk to someone, someone who knows how to listen to me. I feel so alone, so abandoned. Lost."

"Suzanne, I'm here for you. Look at the scenery, that's something that'll help you trust me. You can talk to me."

"Thank you, Ashley. I consider myself truly blessed to have stumbled upon someone like you. A good listener, so empathic. So here's what happened to me. Twenty years ago, Ricardo, my partner, Lisa, our daughter, and I went to an amusement park in New Orleans. That day started off great, we were all having fun. All three of us were together, happy. Laughing. Up until I went to the ladies' room for a few minutes, alone. Ricardo and Lisa, my little darling, went to buy an ice cream cone while they were outside waiting for me. We had agreed to meet at the entrance of the restrooms, but... I never saw them again in my life!"

"Your husband kidnapped your daughter?" That's awful."

"I'm afraid I'll never know what happened. No one saw anything, no one heard anything. I went to the police, they carried out an investigation with a lot of reticence but didn't have any results at all. The case was quickly closed. As if nothing had happened that August 6, 2004. But I'm not losing my marbles! The last twenty years have been a nightmare, without any respite. Up until..."

"Until?"

"Until I came here. I honestly don't know what to think about that... A sign of fate? A huge mistake in my judgement? A fantasy blinding my eyes? Up until I saw you, Ashley."

The young lady squinted, taken aback.

"What do you mean?"

"No, it's too idiotic."

"You can tell me."

Suzanne hesitated, first looking out over the ocean, then down at her feet, finally looking the ice cream vendor straight in the eyes.

"When I first saw you at that ice cream shop, it was as if I'd seen a ghost! Ashley, you're the spitting image of my daughter, Lisa! Your eyes, their shape, their color. The same smooth black hair, the same nose. It's so unsettling."

And this time she did burst into tears, attracting the attention of crew members and other passengers, including the man wearing sunglasses seated behind them.

"Is everything alright?" one of the crew members asked.

Suzanne nodded reassuringly, drying her eyes while Ashley put her arm around her shoulders.

"I can understand how hard this must be for you. Sometimes we run across people who remind us of others. And I understand that it must have been quite a shock. Now I understand better why we're here, both of us, and why we're so close. I remind you of your daughter who disappeared. But Suzanne, I don't want to hurt you, you know, but you have to understand that I'm not your daughter! You told me yourself the other day at the bar, Lisa would be twenty-two now. And I'm not even nineteen!"

"I know… I know that it's completely idiotic, crazy, insane, stupid, all that. And I also know that I thought I saw my Lisa in the street dozens of times, the teen she'd become, the young lady she now would be. But Ashley, the first time I set eyes on you it was so powerful. Never like that before! I've got the feeling that there's some intangible link between us, something that's invisible, yet present. I don't know how to explain it to you."

"Perhaps alchemy between two people, sometimes that happens, even though they don't come from the same family."

"I know. Maybe so much suffering has led me to imagine things. I'm sorry, Ashley, I warned you, I wrecked the atmosphere here."

"It's no big problem and talking things over is always a good idea. Your Lisa must be very beautiful, if I look like her," joked the young lady to relax Suzanne.

"An angel," Suzanne smiled. "But tell me, Ashely, are you an only child?"

"No, I've got a sister! A little older than me."

"Really? What's her name?"

"Johanna."

"How old is she?"

"Twenty-two."

Suddenly someone began to shout.

"Whale on port side!"

CHAPTER 22
To dust you shall return

New Orleans, July 2024

I'D ASKED Suzanne Diggs to give me her address in New Orleans before Ricardo and Lisa had disappeared. I'd told her that I had to go there, to better comprehend the decor and the way they'd lived when the events took place. Of course, I was sure that in twenty years a lot of things had changed, including of course the residents themselves. In any given neighborhood, when the profile of its inhabitants' changes, the whole neighborhood changes. Places shape people and people change places, just like in any ecosystem where living things interact with the environment. And vice-versa. A neighborhood is born, lives, declines, falls apart, dies, is born again, thrives, disappears... just like human beings.

Chestnut Street was in the Garden District, on the

northern banks of the Mississippi. I learned that it was one of the wealthiest places in New Orleans. A peaceful place with colonial-style houses, most of them two-story ones, surrounded by white picket fences. The road with trees on both sides of it afforded a pleasant haven of greenery for the residents as well as much appreciated shade for those walking down the street.

To feel freer in my movements and avoid depending on Mason Lacassagne, that taxi driver who I'd used the first days I was here, I decided to rent a car. I parked in front of Suzanne's former home and admired the place they'd lived in until that disappearance ripped their lives apart. I remembered what the client had told me when I asked her what she'd done with her home. "I never could step inside our home anymore. Much too painful, do you understand? I didn't feel at ease after that." And I did understand her. What a pity though, I thought looking at that beautiful property. It wasn't the most luxurious house on the block, which was full of classy places, but it certainly didn't feel out of place there. Wealth was exuding from each intersection, and I remember Suzanne telling me that money wasn't a problem for her. Now I understood.

I got out of my car, immediately hit by a gust of hot wind over Nola that day. The coolness of the river, though not far, didn't seem to make any difference up here.

Where should I begin? The current residents of the

former Gutierrez house? Their neighbors? Twenty years later, would I even find anything useful? I nonetheless had learned that all approaches could be profitable. Even though they seemed to be absurd after such a long time.

I rang the bell at the former Gutierrez house. It was in the middle of the morning, there were some passersby on the shaded sidewalks, one walking a dog, another one pushing a stroller, and another one dragging a shopping bag towards an outdoor market I'd passed when driving here. Some people were working in their gardens, but behind that fence, no one was outside. I rang the doorbell once again and was getting ready to leave when the door finally opened.

"Can I help you?" asked a fifty- or so-year old lady, wearing a cleaning lady's clothing, an apron, latex gloves on her hands and a dust rag thrown over her shoulder.

"Are you Mrs. Clarks? I read the name on the mailbox."

"Not at all. My name is Julia, and I work for the Clarks. What do you want?" she asked with a slight Hispanic accent. "They're not home."

I quickly introduced myself and asked her if I could have a few minutes of her time. She accepted grudgingly and walked down the front steps to me. She didn't invite me in, but that was no big deal as the tragedy didn't occur there so I wouldn't learn anything from going inside their former home.

"Have you worked for the Clarks for a long time?"

"For them, no, because they've only been here two years. Before that I worked for the Donahue family, the previous owners. And for the Rappaport's before that. I've worked in this neighborhood for various families for fifteen years."

"So you never know the Gutierrez family who were here until 2004?"

"No, not at all. Why?"

"You never heard that Ricardo, and this daughter Lisa went missing that year?"

"That doesn't ring a bell, sorry. I should have?"

"Something like that should have left traces in the neighborhood. But it was before you started working here. Do you know anyone who lived in the neighborhood twenty years ago and is still here?"

The cleaning lady called upon her memory.

"You know, I've been here for fifteen years and there's been loads of new owners, left and right. But I think that Mrs. Kellermann, she's a widow who lives in that house over there," she said, pointing at a house about fifty feet away on the other side of the road, "was already there at that time. As far as I know, she's certainly the last survivor of that era. The last one who could have known that Gutierrez family you were talking about."

"Do you work for her too?"

"I do. Poor lady, she's in a wheelchair. There's a nurse who comes in every day and someone who helps her take a shower and get dressed. You know, all that stuff. And I do the cleaning twice a week for her, even though it's not really dirty. But you know, dust always comes back!"

Remember that you are dust and to dust you shall return, I thought by a biblical analogy.

"You think she's home now?"

"Like I said, she's impotent. In her wheelchair all day long. Of course she's home. "But..."

"But what?"

"I sort of think she's like losing her marbles a little bit."

Just my luck! When I told you that this investigation didn't look very promising...

CHAPTER 23
That unforgettable moment

Hervey Bay, July 2024

It was a unique, fascinating, unforgettable show that the couple of whales slowly swimming up to the catamaran gave us. A show that interrupted Suzanne and Ashley's conversation.

"They're teens," said Captain Lynch joyfully, turning off the motors. "They're already over twenty feet long, perfect. At that age they love to play, you'll see. You can call them, whistle, clap your hands, they love interaction, it's something that stimulates them."

Suzanne, as were all the other passengers, was delighted by their show. The cetaceans revolved around the boat with grace and agility that contrasted with their imposing mass.

Everyone followed the comings and goings of the animals, rushing from port to starboard, from the bow to the stern, jumping on the nets, so as not to miss a single moment of the whales.

"Don't run and hang on to the rails," the skipper, who was on the roof of the boat, his hand shielding his eyes, recommended.

The cetaceans suddenly dove under the hull. Suzanne, as did all the others, held her breath, worried. What if those behemoths weighing several tons decided to capsize their little skiff? She'd read articles about orcas who'd attacked boats.

"Don't panic," Peter Lynch reassured them, "whales are very pacific animals and they're very careful."

And it was true as a few seconds later the two whales emerged on the other side of the catamaran, with their white stomachs facing the surface. The passengers whistled, called, and held their hands out towards the water with unexpected hopes of touching their rostrum, which would have been once-in-a-life-time experience for them.

They shouted out with joy and incredulity at each of the graceful figures those gigantic ballerinas did. For a whole hour the cetaceans stayed and played with the humans, without even touching the boat once.

"This is a first time for me too," the captain, who went out each and every day during their migratory season, admitted to them. "It's already pretty rare to have a couple so close to the boat. But for them to stay so long, what a unique experience. My dear passengers, you are lucky dogs! Let's thank our friends the whales for this unforgettable moment!"

As the cetaceans dove back into the depths of the ocean, all the passengers thanked them, clapping their hands with joy. They saw them one last time a bit farther on as they were heading towards K'gari.

This unforgettable moment, Suzanne Diggs mentally repeated to herself looking at Ashley from the corner of her eye. She then went back to the conversation they were having before the whales came to distract and brighten up the tourists.

"That was magnificent," she said to the young lady while they went back to their seats on the nets in the bow.

"Splendid! I'm so happy to have, you could say, allowed you to experience that magical moment, one that must warm your heart."

"Being close up and personal with nature was comforting. But Ashley, you told me that you've got a twenty-two-year-old sister? Johanna, isn't it?"

"Yup, my big sister Jo. I love her."

Suzanne thought about the best way to place her pawns without arousing suspicion while innocently leading her to give her some useful information."

"Do you see each other often?"

She could tell that the question saddened Ashley.

"Unfortunately not very much since I left Darwin."

"Ah! She's still there then?"

"Yeah."

"And you don't get to go back very often."

"You know, when your family's far…"

Suzanne shivered, something Ashley immediately noticed.

"Oh! I'm sorry Suzanne, I wasn't paying attention to what I said."

"Don't worry. And is Johanna as pretty as you?"

Then Ashley laughed.

"You're joking! She's a thousand times prettier than I am!"

"That's not possible. I can't believe that!"

"Swear to God."

"Prove it."

The young lady got up and ran to the cabin where the skipper had stored everyone's stuff and came back with her wallet in her hand. She opened it and took a photo out.

"What do you think?"

What a shock! Even bigger than when she'd found Ashley in that ice cream shop. Johanna was not only to die for — what a horrible association of words — but she looked even more like the mental image Suzanne had of her Lisa as an adult. *Her* Lisa, who couldn't be Ashley, but who could, on the other hand, be Johanna. Suzanne's vision suddenly blurred, things began to spin, and that wasn't just due to the boat's rocking. She went ashen gray, dropped the photo that nearly slipped between the cracks in the net and would have fallen into Hervey Bay. Ashley luckily grabbed it just in time.

"Oh! Excuse me, I nearly lost your picture."

"Good thing I've got good reflexes!"

The skipper had just changed tack and told them they were now heading towards the marina after an exceptional day at sea. The two hours it took to return to Hervey Bay went by quickly, though they didn't see any other cetaceans, except for a shoal of dolphins jumping afar. The atmosphere on the deck was excellent and about four o'clock the crew served snacks, much appreciated by everyone except for that man with his dark glasses on who remained alone at the stern of the boat, but who seemed to be staring at Suzanne and Ashley.

When they reached the port, the two ladies went their separate ways with Suzanne thanking Ashley once again and promising to see her again soon.

"You know where I work," said Ashley as she walked away.

Suzanne decided to walk back to her flat, strolling through the plaza while taking advantage of the last rays of the setting sun.

She walked slowly, her head stuffed with images of the cetaceans and her mind full of that unsettling portrait of Johanna Bolt, when she suddenly heard the noise of tires rushing towards her.

She didn't have time to turn around. A cyclist passed her on the right and grabbed her purse that she just casually had slung over her shoulder.

"Hey!" she screamed, panicked.

But the man had already pedaled away, though she did try to run after him.

A few passersby witnessed what had happened, but no one had the presence of mine to try to stop the thief.

He disappeared at the first intersection.

CHAPTER 24

Like an open book on the past

New Orleans, *July 2024*

I rang the interphone at the Kellermann residence, one of the neighbors of the Gutierrez family when they lived there on Chestnut Street.

The morning was drawing to an end, and I thought that the old lady must have been up by now and not yet napping. A young voice answered.

"Hello. Who's there?"

"Hello, ma'am, I'd like to speak to Mrs. Kellermann for a few minutes. Julia, your cleaning lady, sent me."

"About what?"

I had to be diplomatic for a few minutes before that highly protective lady finally opened the door, saying that a visit would only do her employer good.

I heard a beep when the gate unlocked and went

into their property, much more luxurious than Gutierrez's house. The nurse's aide was waiting on the porch for me, and I followed her to the back of the house, to a veranda where the Kellermann widow was looking out over her back yard through the picture window.

"Mrs. Kellermann? There's a Mrs. Blackstone who'd like to speak with you."

"Ah."

That was all the old lady said and she didn't even bother to turn her head towards us.

"Mrs. Kellermann has mobility issues," the nurse's aide explained as we went back to the wheelchair where she was sitting.

She rotated it so I could see her. She must have been eighty-five, ninety. Her light blue yet lively eyes seemed to be lost below her curly white hair that framed a deeply wrinkled face. That face that was like an open book written about the past.

"Hello," I said to her gently. "My name is Karen Blackstone."

"You're here for my shower?" Lucy Kellermann asked, astonished. "You're not the same gal as usual."

"No, Mrs. Kellermann," her nurse's aide said, "I'm the one who helps you with that. This lady would like to ask you some questions about the past."

"Hmm! The past! We'll see. What would you like to know, young lady?"

Thought I did appreciate the "young," I figured that visibly that lady no longer possessed all her cognitive capacities.

"Thanks for accepting to answer my questions. I'll be brief, don't worry," I added both for the old widow as well as her aide who was staring at me with a disapproving eye.

"Bah! I got all the time in the world. My husband is on a business trip, he won't be back till Friday, he told me."

My fears were confirmed, a widow with a husband, something hard to do!

"Ma'am, does the last name Gutierrez ring a bell with you?"

"Gutierrez? Let me see... It's not my cleaning lady, the one who comes twice a week?"

"No, that's Julia Menendez.

"Menendez, Gutierrez, they sound alike."

To cut off any racial insinuations, I quickly continued.

"They lived right across the street, there where the Clarks now live. They lived there twenty years ago, up until the middle of 2004. Ricardo and Suzanne Gutierrez, and they had a little girl named Lisa. Do you remember them?"

The old lady squinted, her eyelids looked like two rolls of papyrus, and she seemed be calling upon her ancient souvenirs. Then she opened them suddenly.

"Oh! Right! A cute little blondie?"

Not really, I mused.

"Let me show you a photo."

I rummaged around in my purse and took out the pictures that Suzanne had given me and showed the old lady Lisa's photo. She leaned over so she could see it better and then nodded several times. She made me think of those plastic dogs you put in your car with their heads bobbing up and down as you drive. Her eyelids suddenly popped up, sort of like blinds that you opened.

"Yes! Now I recognize her, it's little Lisa Gutierrez!"

"Right, that is her," I said, happy that she'd had a bit of lucidity.

"She's so cute. A little doll. But it's strange, I haven't seen her in a while. I hope she's not ill. Or something happened to her."

"Actually Mrs. Kellermann, about that subject, do you remember some dramatic event that took place in the summer of 2004? That was the year before Katrina."

"Katrina who? I don't think I know anyone named Katrina."

"Not a person. The hurricane."

"Good Lord, of course! What was I thinking of? What a tragedy! Did you come to tell me that the little Gutierrez girl was swept away in the flood? That's awful! Such a beautiful child."

"Not at all. Like I said, something that took place *before* the hurricane. I'm talking about when Lisa and her dad, Ricardo, disappeared."

I slipped the photo of the Gutierrez family under Mrs. Kellermann's eyes then.

"Good-looking guy," the old lady approved. "They

went missing? That's so sad. Now I understand why I don't see them so often."

I tried to imagine what notion of time Mrs. Kellermann still had. She seemed to be confusing eras, mixing them into one same period of time. For her, past and present were the same thing: her husband on a trip, the Gutierrez family she saw less and less. I insisted though.

"That's normal. The Gutierrez family moved out in 2004."

"I know," she replied, surprising both of us. "They moved in the summer! I saw them move."

Now I was interested.

"You saw them leave? Would you be able to give me a rough date? And when you say they left, do you mean they moved house?"

"Well I saw one of those big trucks you use to transport furniture and boxes, you know one of those with a platform behind it that you can raise or lower."

"A tailgate lift?"

"I guess so. I remember now because it was unusual."

I had no idea why people moving would be unusual.

"What do you mean by that?"

"Well, when you move in the middle of the night..."

"In the middle of the night? You're sure about that?"

"Without a shadow of doubt. Are you insinuating I'm losing my memory?"

"Not at all."

Though I did believe quite the opposite. She continued.

"I remember that well because that night, like other nights that summer, it was really hot out and I stayed in my veranda for hours on end, with the windows wide open to try to get some cool air in. I spent my time doing crossword puzzles — that was my hobby — while gazing at the stars and listening to the sounds of nature. And I remember very well that noise that disturbed my nocturnal harmony. The moving van parking, the tailgate opening, going up and down with a creaking sound, men who entered the property, came back out pushing furniture on trolleys, or even carrying them, from the house to the van, and that went on for the whole darn night. I thought to myself it sure wasn't logical to move at night. Nor could it have been practical."

"And the date? Do you have any idea? I mean was it before or after August 6th?"

"After that, I'm sure. Because I remember I'd nearly finished all the crossword puzzles in the double summer edition. I hardly had any left and I thought I'd have to buy another one to finish the season, but I preferred the one I had because it wasn't too hard. Yes, that must have been in mid-August."

"That's interesting," I said out loud. "Do you

remember having seen Ricardo Gutierrez with the mover crew?"

"No, I don't think so," replied Mrs. Kellermann after a moment of reflection that seemed interminable to me. "No, I really don't think so. I'd never seen any of those men. Total strangers!"

I thought over that new information that confirmed the disappearance of the Gutierrez family, but still, do people disappear and take their furniture with them? Unless Suzanne herself set that up after her partner and daughter went missing. I'd have to quickly get to the bottom of that. In the meanwhile, I realized I hadn't yet shown the photo of my client to Mrs. Kellermann. I fished it out of my purse.

"I'd also like to show you the last photo of the Gutierrez family. Though they weren't married. Do you recognize this lady?"

The old lady with her parchment skin leaned her neck out, reminding me of a turtle, towards the photo, squinted, concentrated and shook her head.

"Not at all," she replied categorically. "You're sure it's that adorable little brunette girl's mother?"

CHAPTER 25
Your former identity

Hervey Bay, July 2024

Panicked, Suzanne, in tears, plopped down on one of the benches in the square. After that perfect and emotion-filled day, now she found herself without any ID papers, without any money, without any identity.

Seeing her like that, a young obliging man stopped and asked if he could help her. In a few words she told him what had just happened and asked him if he knew where the nearest police station was. He not only explained where it was, he offered to accompany her there.

Fifteen or so minutes later, the American was standing in front of a police officer who pleasantly took her statement while telling her that luckily, that type of offense, a snatch and grab, was actually quite rare in Hervey Bay, a nice little down in the peaceful

Sunshine State. That it was probably committed by some foreigner, because Australian citizens had the reputation of being more hospitable and respectful to tourists. Or maybe it was a teen who'd had too much *XXXX Bitter*, Brisbane's local beer. And could Suzanne describe her aggressor so they could find him more quickly?

She unfortunately wasn't able to describe the cyclist, though it was a man for sure, one with wide shoulders. That was all her brain had been able to assimilate during the few brief seconds in which the probably well-planned robbery had taken place.

"What did you have in your purse?" the policeman asked.

"Everything," Suzanne said tearfully. "I mean everything that's important. My ID papers, my wallet, a bit of Australian and American money, photos, my passport, my phone, my agenda, the keys to the apartment I'm renting. Everything you need in your life!"

She burst into tears again.

"Don't worry too much, ma'am, most of the time losers like that guy are only after money. Sometimes they keep credit cards and use them for contactless payment until they've reached the threshold. You can contact your bank to stop payment on any transactions that took place after the theft of your papers, as I've written this all up in your statement. After that, they generally toss everything into a bin, or at the worst, into the sea. And you'll find your papers and your former identity…"

"My former identity?" Suzanne cut him off.
"Before the theft, I mean."
"Ah! Of course!"
The lady dried her tears and signed the policeman's statement.

AFTER THAT, she wondered what she'd do now, with no ID papers, no money, no keys, not knowing anyone in Hervey Bay, except Ashley Bolt. Except that they'd also stolen her phone, and anyway she didn't have Ashley's number. At this time of the evening, the ice cream shop where she worked was already closed and she'd have to wait until tomorrow to phone her. What could she do until then? Where was she going to sleep? What was she going to eat? Would the legendary hospitality of the Australians include feeding and putting up a foreigner?

Finally, she headed to the sea and walked along the dunes where the waves in the Pacific crashed on the shore, where the rumbling backwash filled the night. Her feet sunk into the sand as if it were powdered sugar and she thought about sleeping there that night, right on the beach, lulled by the waves. Up until — and why not anyway — she'd be swept out by the tide, putting an end to twenty years of torture.

Suzanne dwelled on those dark thoughts until the cool night began to shift into a cold one and she started to shiver, sitting there on the sand, her arms crossed holding her legs against her bust.

She got up and walked towards her lodging. The owner lived only two roads from there. She should go there and ring the bell, she'd certainly have a spare set of keys. Why hadn't she thought of that earlier?

To reach the owner's house, she had to go in front of the apartment she was renting. She ran across a few passersby, but the roads were mostly empty at that time of the night. Not that she was feeling vulnerable, but still, she remembered how terribly frightened she was when that guy had snatched her purse. At each corner of the road she was afraid she'd see that cyclist that she imagined might be following her.

Suddenly, just a few steps from her apartment, she froze.

A bizarre vision attracted her attention.

She didn't believe her eyes, the darkness must be playing tricks on her subconscious.

Yet, no doubt was possible, that object on the ground in front of the doorstep, she knew exactly what it was.

Her half-opened purse had been tossed there.

She sped up, kneeled down, and tears in her eyes picked it up. And went through its inventory.

Then there was a second stupefaction.

Absolutely nothing was missing...

She took her keys out, went into her apartment and locked the door behind her, her mind fraught with mixed questions and fears.

Her aggressor, a weird person, now knew where she lived...

CHAPTER 26
The authenticity of her fantasy

New Orleans, July 2024

My mouth was still hanging open after Mrs. Kellermann's last sentence. The old lady — a tad senile, I'd noticed that several times during my interview with her — hadn't recognized Lisa's mother on the photo Suzanne had given me.

"You don't recognize this lady?"

"Is it a recent photo or an old one?" the eighty-year-old lady asked.

I hesitated, not too certain myself.

"I think it's pretty recent. Why?"

Lucy Kellermann nodded several times.

"Like I told you, I like to do my crossword puzzles in my veranda overlooking Chestnut Street. I can see everything that's going on in the street, but it's not like

I'm spying on people. Day or night. And if I can tell you something — Janet, is that right?"

"No, it's Karen."

"Well, Karen, I don't know where you got that picture, but what I can tell you without the shadow of a doubt about that photo, is that I do know that lady in it."

"Who is she?"

"Oh, I don't know her name... Or maybe I just don't know it anymore. I'm not too good with names, but I'm sure I saw her several times."

That certainly aroused my curiosity.

"Here?"

"Yes, here in the street. She often walked up and down on the sidewalk, in the shade, across from Gutierrez's. Sometimes she sat down on the bench at the angle of the block and stayed there, staring at their house. She nearly almost wore sunglasses, but every once in a while she'd take them off to read the paper, but then she'd raise it in front of her face, as if she was hiding behind it."

"She never went into their property?"

"No, I never saw her go in. At least not when the Gutierrez's were there."

'What are you insinuating, Mrs. Kellermann?"

"I think I'm right, but I could be mistaken, huh! I think I saw her go inside, surreptitiously, through the gate that closes really slowly when the Gutierrez's leave by car, for example. She'd be waiting at the corner, behind some foliage where she couldn't be seen, she'd walk along the wall and then at the last second, she'd slip in between the wings of the automatic gate."

"When was this and how did she get out?"

"My little lady, I have no idea! Like I said, I wasn't spying on her, just looking out. Something I saw and remembered. After that, I continued doing my crossword puzzles as usual."

"You never thought of telling the police that someone was in your neighbor's property?"

"No, and I regret that today. Especially what with you told me about the disappearance."

"And you didn't tell Mr. Gutierrez either?"

The widow lowered her head, ashamed.

"We weren't really friends, them and my late husband and me. You know, around this neighborhood it's sort of everyone for himself and God for us all."

I thought back on the information Lucy Kellermann had just given me and then had an idea.

"After Ricardo and Lisa's double disappearance, I would imagine the police must have started knocking on doors. Did you think of telling them about that person who snuck into the Gutierrez's property?"

The old lady seemed to think this over, her eyes disturbed.

"No police ever came to question us about this. Who are you talking about?"

Once again I took Suzanne's portrait out of my purse.

"This person."

"She's beautiful," said Lucy stupidly. "That's Lisa's mom, right?"

That question bothered me. The old lady's memory was visibly off track once again. Unless the opposite was true: it had been misfunctioning and now there was suddenly a type of lucidity. A roller coaster memory!

The nurse's aide made a gesture, so I'd understand her boss was starting to get tired. And as for the moment, I didn't have any other questions, I thanked her and left. As I was walking out, Mrs. Kellermann shouted out to me.

"If you see my husband, could you tell him to shake a leg? With all this wind outside, I'm afraid we'll soon have a hurricane."

"I will," I reassured her, though saddened.

Then I left, looking at the house where the Gutierrez family used to live, and where the Clarks now resided.

THERE WAS something in what Mrs. Kellermann had told me that had left me puzzled. She'd said that the police hadn't questioned the inhabitants living in the neighborhood, or at least she didn't remember that. Yet, when someone unexpectedly goes missing, isn't that one of the first things that's done, just like I was doing right now?

But for that, there had to be a disappearance. And

after that, people who start worrying about them, then trying to find them.

But ever since I'd landed in New Orleans, I'd run into the same roadblock: no one could confirm that the Gutierrez father and daughter had disappeared.

They no longer lived on Chestnut Street, but that certainly didn't prove that they'd gone missing. Just, if we could believe what the old neighbor lady said, that they'd moved. At night, okay, that was strange, but did it prove anything?

At the end of the day, only one person had told me there was a disappearance: my client, Suzanne Diggs.

Could I believe her?

And why would Suzanne hire me to investigate a disappearance that she was the only one who believed in? Why pay me to check the authenticity of a fantasy?

Once again, I was faced with an inexplicable and grotesque enigma.

I mentally thought over everything that could implicate, and internally chastised myself, saying that I'd allowed myself to be guided by a *presumption*: what proved that it was Ricardo and Lisa Gutierrez on the photos that Suzanne had sent me? All I knew about them was what my client had told me. I had no reason to doubt what she'd told me by cross-checking the pictures on the internet, for example. But still, I'd drawn a blank looking for articles about their disappearance.

So? Did they really exist? Or had Suzanne invented that whole story?

I even wondered if the photo of Suzanne actually was Suzanne. After all, I'd never set eyes on her!

Was she really the person she'd told me she was?

Was I going to have to investigate my own client? That would have been a first! And to do that, would I have to hire one of my private detective colleagues, or could I do it myself?

I needed to set up a video call with her.

When I finally arrived in the shady Garden District, I took out my phone to get to the bottom of this.

That was when I discovered that I'd had several Facebook notifications, and I immediately clicked on them.

CHAPTER 27
Advice... from a friend

Hervey Bay, July 2024

IT HAD BEEN an exhausting and grueling day for Suzanne, who laid down on her bed without even getting undressed. Up before the break of dawn to be on the catamaran before seven, she'd finished her day at night on the sandy beach after someone had relieved her of her purse... that she'd then found intact on her doorstep.

"What a day!" she sighed.

When she picked up her phone, she found that Karen Blackstone had called her several times, including some video calls.

She listened to the messages that the detective had left her, asking her to call her back as soon as possible about something very important. But Suzanne had other fish to fry at that time, and felt so terribly tired, both physical and psychological fatigue. She'd call her back tomorrow.

She needed a good night's sleep.

When she woke up, still dressed, she hadn't even pulled her covers back, she was still troubled. Her head was spinning, making her nauseous. She leaned on her elbow, looking around the room that at first she didn't recognize. It took her a couple of seconds to adjust her vision and understand where she was, both geographically and the circumstances that had led her there.

She was in Australia, she was sure of that. She believed she'd found her daughter, intimately persuaded that was also true. And she needed a strong cup of black coffee. She had to make an effort to sit up and saw her purse at the foot of her bed, where she'd tossed it before falling into a deep sleep.

Part of it had spilled out on the floor, a brush, makeup, a notebook, wallet, pen, some gum, crinkled receipts, a paperclip, her keys... And in the middle of that hodgepodge, a piece of paper that had been ripped off her notebook, with several words jotted down on it, words that Suzanne was sure she hadn't written.

She leaned down cursing her headache and picked up the piece of paper.

She squinted and read:

Quit trying to stir up the past.

. . .

Suzanne dropped that piece of paper as quickly as if it were on fire and might burn her fingers.

No flames, but an unequivocal threat.

Or was it? A threat or just advice from a... friend?

Who could have slipped that piece of paper in her bag? The most logical hypothesis was that cyclist who had snatched it.

That guy, who hadn't taken a thing, not even her cash, was perhaps trying to warn her of some danger? But why that snatch and grab scenario? What not simply tell her?

Anyway, the subject of the message seemed clear.

Stirring up the past...

Someone knew what she'd discovered in Hervey Bay. Someone was following her, watching her.

Someone knew she'd met Ashley Bolt and even more troubling, knew that she thought that she'd recognized her as being Lisa, her daughter who went missing twenty years ago on the other side of the globe.

Someone had been spying on her, that was clear. Or maybe her phone was bugged! But Karen Blackstone had been the only person she'd talked to about that.

Plus, Ashley, a little bit too. Before concluding that the young lady couldn't have been her daughter, but on the other hand, her sister, whose photo she'd seen yesterday on the boat, could be.

Her mind still fuzzy, Suzanne began to panic. She

was now sweating. She looked all around the room, trying to spot hidden cameras or mics. Thinking of which, she dumped the rest of her bag out on the bed, wondering if the robber hadn't slipped in some sort of micro-spying device as a bonus to his not so sweet words. But she didn't find anything.

Her paranoia and nearly inexistant knowledge of spyware today however didn't allow her to think that nowadays you could insert a mic into a pen, the cap of a mascara tube or an earring.

HER HEART POUNDING, she dragged herself to the kitchen to make some strong coffee. Hoping that the beverage would give her enough lucidity to understand the situation in which she was wading through.

Blowing on her hot cup of coffee, Suzanne thought of something.

Who could that possibly hurt if she ever found her partner and daughter?

The kidnappers?

Ricardo and Lisa?

Why did they want her to abandon her research?

And what was the big deal about stirring up the past?

Helped by the steam spiraling off the hot coffee, just like a crossfading in the cinema, Suzanne Diggs toppled into her memories that she kept hidden in the deepest part of her subconscious thoughts...

In hell

"Sit down, please. Wherever you want. Whatever is the best for you, on this armchair or chair or on the sofa. You can lie down if you want. From now on, this space is yours. Your space of trust and confidence, for the whole time our session will last."

The young lady hesitated, looking all over the room with its subdued decoration, then chose the white sofa with black cushions on it that seemed soft and welcoming. Like a protective cocoon. She remained seated though, her hands clasped between her knees, her fingers so tight that her articulations were white.

That was her second appointment since the event took place and the first where she was expecting to enter the heart of the subject. The heart, the word was correct to designate her feelings.

Yet she hesitated to respond to Dr. Petrossian when he began his session.

"How are you feeling right now, at this precise moment, in this room?"

She took a deep breath and raised her eyes to the ceiling.

"Okay I guess."

"Okay I guess," repeated the practitioner, mirroring his patient's tone. *"What does that mean for you?"*

"That I'm okay! As okay as possible considering the circumstances."

"Well then. On a scale of one to ten, where would you situate your current mood? One would be a complete depression and ten total well-being."

After thirty or so seconds of reflection and sighs, the lady said that two seemed right to her.

"In that case, Miss, the object of our work, or rather your work in this venue and these moments with me, will consist first of all of determining the causes of those feelings, then trying to affront and accept them, to try to climb the ladder to reach higher rungs on it. Is that alright with you?"

"Going up to rung number ten? I know that's impossible."

"And you're right! Very few people actually reach that level. Or only for fleeting moments, during events that are heavy with senses and emotions, like during the birth of a child. Others reach higher levels with meditation. Here we're talking about nirvana, supreme peace. What would you say about rungs seven or eight?"

"That would be wonderful," the patient replied. *"But I don't believe it. I dropped down too far... I think*

pretty soon I'll have to dig... go down even farther... down to hell! But... if I think about it, I'm already in hell!"

The practitioner nodded, with no facial expressions, taking notes in a moleskin notebook with an expensive pen. He came back to his session.

"*As this is your space, you're the one who will lead this session. What do you want to talk about?*"

The young lady didn't hesitate this time.

"*Them!*"

"*Who do you mean by 'them?'*"

"*Those two. My husband. My daughter.*"

CHAPTER 28
An unusual commotion

New Orleans, 2024

My fishing trip for statements had worked. I'd cast my line into the vast ocean of social media, and some fish had taken the bait. Billy Jensen's method had borne fruit, and I had the proof with direct messages that had been posted in response to my call for witnesses that I'd posted on Facebook: `Disappearance of two people in Six Flags, New Orleans, on August 6, 2004.`

Besides messages of compassion under the photo of Ricardo and Lisa, as well as a few troll comments of course, two people with good intentions had sent me messages.

The first one came from a lady named Josefina Kalinka, or at least that was her pseudonym on Meta

— I guess that's what you're supposed to call it now, even though I find it hard, just like X for Twitter — who'd contacted me.

I don't remember any event such as a double disappearance in the park at that time. I had a summer job at Six Flags then. I was a student. I only worked there in July and August. My job consisted of doing what no one else wanted to do, such as cleaning the restrooms, fun stuff like that. I remember a mini-event which probably is not important and that I'd totally forgotten, up until I read your call for witnesses, which is heartbreaking. I don't know if it's important, probably not, but why not share it with you. If that could help you with your investigation and allow the family to understand what happened... So let's just say that my statement concerns other employees who are somewhat different. If I remember correctly — but that goes back a long time!— there was an unusual commotion that day.

. . .

That Josefina made me want to know more. I answered her in the same thread.

Thank you so much for having contacted me. Could we speak? Here's my phone number...

Then I clicked on the other direct message, from a guy named Felix McBride:

Hey. Damn, I remember that summer, but nothing that related to your disappearance case. On August 6, I was working at Six Flags: one of those idiots walking around in the park dressed up as a mascot, see what I mean? *Hi kids, how are you today? Having fun! Let the good times roll!* So anyway, bet you get how fun a job it was. Anyway, if it actually was that day, there was some weird thing that happened with our costumes. It's a little hard to explain in writing and I gotta admit writing's not something I like, so if you wanna know more, call me.

. . .

THIS TIME FELIX gave me his number and I clicked on it directly in the app.

He picked up on the second ring and I introduced myself and thanked him for having contacted me.

"No problem, if that can help. So like I said on Facebook, I don't know if it's worth anything what I have to say. I hope you won't make fun of me."

"Why would I do something like that? It's already so nice of you to try to help. Any little detail could have its importance. And I'll gladly listen to whatever you have to tell me," I reassured him.

Felix told me, with his cute Cajun accent, that I was slowly getting used to, what he remembered and what he thought had taken place on August 6, 2004.

"Anyway, like I said, I was a student then and I needed money. I was ready to accept any job at all, as long as it was paid work. So I took anything and everything and when I saw the ad in the paper for Six Flags, I thought, why not! And I didn't care about being ridiculous. The job consisted of walking around in the park after having donned one of the costumes of the park's mascots. There was Catfish Rod-N'Reel, a brown cat with brown slacks and suspenders. Then all the well-known ones like Daffy Duck, Bugs Bunny, Pac-Man, Scooby-Doo, and even Superman and Batman. And yeah, the Mr. Six costume too, you know that old bald fart with a black suit, a red bow tie and suspenders, who you saw in the ads and who went all over the country in a bus sporting the franchise's colors. A great dancer."

"I don't know who he is," I confessed humbly.

"That's not important anyway. No big deal. So, that day, I won first prize: I had to wear the Daffy Duck costume made from some sort of hide. You can't even imagine how hot that shit is, especially in the summer! Like you are roasting in a pizza oven! That summer I thought I'd finish the season transformed into a margarita or four cheese pizza! So, I was supposed to be the Looney Tune's duck. A shitty job, and the worst part of it was that you were supposed to talk to the kids by imitating his voice. See what I mean? With a twangy voice and sputtering drops of saliva?"

"That I do," I replied with a smile.

"So you understand me! Anyway, all us 'hosts' were always there before opening hours and we'd meet up in the changing rooms. Some people keep their clothes on under their costumes. I personally just wore my boxers, it was a bit less hot that way. You gotta know that there were always several of us walking around in the park as the same characters, so there were several Daffy Ducks, Scooby-Doos, etc. except that on that day, we were missing a costume. I looked all over, but the duck costume was missing. I didn't complain though because I finally got the Batman costume which is a tad more virile than Daffy Duck. And not as hot, not as thick. Mady from cotton, not wool! So, that's all."

What did he mean, that was all? How could the fact that a Daffy Duck costume was missing help my investigation? Misfortune had been raining down on me ever since the beginning of that investigation, had I hit an umpteenth red herring? A poor and useless statement? From a guy who just wanted to talk and tell me about his little school year anecdotes? Yet, with experience and according to the old saying, the devil often hides in the details. I continued with the witness.

"Felix, I'm not sure I understand here. How could the missing costume be linked with my double disappearance case?"

He hesitated.

"Um, I don't know, but as you said the tiniest detail, even an insignificant one might help, I thought that... But that's not all."

"Yes?"

"Several other costumes were missing too, not just mine. Some colleagues even had to be transferred that day. And they ended up cleaning out the toilets instead of walking around saying, 'quack quack.'"

"Several? How many?"

"Six at least. Quite a few. Plus it was the very first time something like that had happened at Six Flags."

"What did they conclude?"

"First, everyone wondered if the costumes hadn't been sent off to be dry-cleaned. But in that case, they always delivered clean costumes. Management finally concluded that they had been stolen."

"Costumes that had disappeared," I meditated to myself.

So maybe, I thought after having thanked Felix and

hung up, that was the disappearance of August 6, 2004!

Except here I didn't understand a thing.

Up until the other witness, Josefina Kalinka, called.

CHAPTER 29
The enigmatic Samaritan

Hervey Bay, July 2024

Her coffee had gotten cold while she tried to travel back in time. Her cup was still half full, and after Suzanne had sipped it, she made a face and immediately dumped it into the sink. That now cold beverage was just as bitter as her distant memories. Bile from the past filled her throat, making her nauseous. And the burning present didn't sooth that unpleasant feeling.

She knew deep down inside that she'd have to progress, whatever it took. Whatever risks, threats, or wrenches thrown into the works to slow her down. She hadn't traveled thousands of miles and decades for nothing: fate had brought her to the eastern Australian coast, here and now, with a purpose or plan that only she could understand.

Whatever could happen to her now, even endangering her own life, she would never give up.

She preferred to die a thousand deaths rather than remaining in ignorance or uncertainty forever.

She took a shower to refresh her ideas, a nearly cold one, an energizing one. Dressed for another hot Australian day, she put her purse over her shoulder and went out.

Determined, she walked down the sidewalks of Hervey Bay towards the ice cream shop. Her phone vibrated. Karen Blackstone, again. Suzanne sighed, clicked on "refuse call," and continued. When she arrived, she saw Ashley behind the counter. The young lady smiled when she saw her, asking her if she wanted an ice cream cone so early in the morning. Suzanne replied that she'd pass for the moment but wanted to talk to her as soon as possible. Did she have a break coming up soon?

Ashley looked at her watch and frowned.

"All I've got is my lunch break."

"How about having lunch with me then, I saw that there's an Asian restaurant near, if you like Asian food."

"Fine with me! Plus it's one that I recommend! Will eleven thirty be okay for you?"

People eat early in Australia, which suited Suzanne fine, and at half past eleven she was seated in the veranda of the restaurant.

"Thanks for the invite," said Ashley upon arriving. "What did you want to talk to me about? We should exchange our phone numbers, that'll be more practical to talk to each other rather than you going to the shop all the time. My boss is going to end up thinking you're harassing me!"

"Good Lord! I'd never do anything like that!" protested Suzanne.

A waitress came and took their orders. Then Suzanne gave her her phone number and Ashely immediately entered it into her cell phone.

"I'll call you, that way you'll have my number," she said, putting her phone down on the table between the bottles of sweet and savory soy sauce. "So? Tell me more. You look annoyed, Suzie. Am I wrong? You got a problem?"

"Something completely crazy happened to me yesterday after we went our separate ways. Believe it or not, just a few minutes after we left the marina, I was mugged."

Ashley's eyes popped wide open, stupefied.

"What? So what happened? Were you injured?"

"No, nothing like that. Someone grabbed my purse. A guy on his bike. I didn't even have enough time to understand what had happened before he disappeared at the intersection."

"I hope you went to the cops."

"I did. But that's not all. The strangest thing in this affair was that when I got back to my apartment, my purse was waiting for me on the doorstep, intact, and nothing was missing!"

"That is completely crazy! He didn't steal anything?"

"I know! My phone was there, no money missing from my wallet, nothing! Either the guy had some remorse, either someone took it from my aggressor, or Lady Luck was smiling down at me!"

Ashley frowned, thinking of something.

"Something intrigues me here. How would that person, whoever it was, know where you live?"

That's true, Suzanne thought. She didn't think she had the address of her apartment in her bag. So? Who was that mysterious thief? Who was that enigmatic Samaritan who brought her bag back? Who, in Hervey Bay, knew where she lived?

"That's what's worrying me the most," she said, as the waitress brought them their piping hot and terribly appetizing meals.

But deep down inside, what was worrying her the most was that threat that had been placed in her purse. She decided not to tell Ashley about it. Worrying her too wouldn't help. For now, she was hoping to find something else out from her, a crucial bit of information. Except she really didn't know how to go about it. This time Lady Luck would smile on her a bit later.

When the waitress left, Ashley was scandalized.

"I never would have believed that something like that could happen in our peaceful little town. Like Hervey Bay isn't Sydney or Brisbane! Now I understand why you look annoyed. If I were you, I'd be freaking out! I get all emotional about things."

"Bah! All's well that ends well," said Suzanne philosophically. "Let's eat. What time do you start work this afternoon?"

"One. Fine. Enjoy!"

Digging into a vegetarian satay for one and a char kway teow for the other, both delicious, they remained silent for a moment.

"Ashley, I have to repeat how sorry I am to have almost lost the picture of your sister in the water yesterday. I realize how attached we are to little material things we carry around with us in our purses, especially when they've got a sentimental value, how much we'd hate to lose them!"

"You can replace a picture," said Ashley. "Not a sister! It's not like you almost dropped her in the channel!"

"A sister... a daughter..." Suzanne sighed. "You must like your sister a lot, I can feel that when you talk about her and your eyes brighten up too then. Johanna, isn't it?"

"Yup, my Jo! My role model, just like lots of little sisters for their big sisters, don't you agree?"

"It's true that often we try to imitate our older brothers or sisters, and on the contrary, rebel against our parents. Plus, even if the picture had fallen in, I still have tons left on my phone!"

To illustrate what she said, she unlocked her phone and opened the photo gallery. She was proud to show Suzanne photos of her sister and her, both smiling.

"Here this one was taken in Darwin, actually

Zuccoli to be more precise, at our parents' house. This is the Darwin Waterfront, you can see the pool in the background. And here is Jo's place, her cozy little apartment with the balcony overlooking Tipperary Marina. I love her place!"

"It is cute," agreed Suzanne, looking at the numerous photos that gave her all the time she needed to study Johanna Bolt's face and features.

Ashley suddenly put her phone down.

"Oops! An emergency pit stop," she said, rushing to the back of the restaurant where the restroom was.

Suzanne's eyes were glued to her phone, which was still open on a portrait of Johanna. That was too much of a temptation for her. She turned her head towards the back of the restaurant and reassured, picked up the phone. With hers, she took pictures of Ashley's photos, and then as quickly as possible, opened her contacts menu. She found Jo and took a picture of her number and then opened the digital business card. All that info in such a little device, isn't that crazy. Her professional address, personal address, email, geolocalization of photos, etc. A goldmine! Seconds were flying by, and Suzanne was afraid that Ashely would see her manipulating her phone without understanding why. She took one more photo and quickly closed the contacts menu and put the phone back down next to the soja sauce bottles.

"Sorry," said Ashley when she returned. "I didn't get a bathroom break for the whole morning."

. . .

THEY FINISHED EATING while talking about this and that, avoiding difficult subjects, and left the restaurant.

"By the way, I'll be out of town for a couple of days," Suzanne said to her new friend. "I hope when I get back we'll share some time together, you have no idea how much I enjoy this! Thank you, Ashley!"

"Same here, Suzanne! See you soon then. Where are you going?"

She hesitated.

"To Sydney, I really want to see the Opera there…"

But Suzanne wouldn't see anything in the capital of the State of New South Wales. That afternoon she went back to her apartment, packed a suitcase with clothes for a couple of days, rented a car, and drove the hundred and seventy-five miles separating her from Brisbane Airport.

THAT EVENING she boarded a domestic flight to Darwin, Northern Territory.

CHAPTER 30
A mad Daffy Duck

NEW ORLEANS, *July 2024*

PEOPLE OFTEN TELL you that God works in mysterious ways.

I was able to verify that with my second statement that came from Josefina, a Six Flags employee back in the summer of 2004.

"Thanks for helping me, even if it seems like a detail to you," I said, after having introduced myself.

Praying that her memories would be less — insignificant — than Felix's.

Taken separately, both were minute, but they strangely met in the middle. Here is what she told me.

"That day, like all the others that week, I was working in the cleaning service. That sure wasn't our favorite week, I can tell you. But like I told you on Messenger in response to your Facebook post, people with summer jobs like me have to work wherever needed. Whether the need comes from more clients or employees who are either on vacation or sick, etc. I'm sure Karen you won't be astonished if I tell you that all of us preferred a thousand times working in the cafeteria or at an ice cream or waffle stand rather than cleaning the restrooms. But that was my tough luck that week, I had a mop and toilet brush! What happened isn't really memorable, except for the characters that took part in it."

"Meaning?" I encouraged her.

"If I told you that it concerned Bugs Bunny, Pac-Man and Daffy Duck, you'll think I'm nuts."

After what the first person had told me, that was certainly the last thing I would have thought about Josefina. Now I was getting interested.

"I'm all ears."

"Okay. I think it was nearing the end of the day because I'd just signed the restroom quality sheet after having cleaned it. So that was the third time that day, the last time before the park closed to the public. The last one took place after the park was closed. Anyway, I'd just finished scouring the urinals and I was in the hall leading to the restrooms with my mop, pail, and latex gloves, and guess who comes running in - Daffy Duck!"

"The park mascot?"

"Exactly. And when I said running in, he was really running. As if his tail was on fire, running without paying attention to anything or anyone. And I was right in the middle of the hall with all my cleaning equipment. He literally ran right into me. And I fell over on my butt, with my pail and mop. And instead of saying he was sorry, know what he said?"

An outages silence followed Josefina's totally rhetorical question because of course I had no idea.

"He yelled 'get the fuck out of the way, bitch,' which hurt me more than my butt on the tile floor. Seriously, how vulgar can you get?"

"And I don't imagine he stopped to help you up."

"Spot on, and then right after Bugs Bunny and Batman rushed in too! That time I moved to the side of the hall to let them through. They ran up to the service door at the end of the hall, shouldered it open and disappeared behind the stages of the park. When I understood what had happened, I couldn't see where they were off to."

That scene was unusual enough to be remembered, which Josefina confirmed.

"It's not every day that you get run over by a mad Daffy Duck!"

"I believe you. Do you know why they were running like that? I would imagine that it was unusual."

"It was! All the employees had been briefed on that subject: running in the park was strictly prohibited. And even less so in the slippery halls of the restrooms. Plus it's really hard to run when you're wearing costumes like that."

"Would you say they were running after someone,

or they were fleeing something, or they were running after one another?"

Josefina sighed.

"I can't answer that question. All I know is that they were in a hurry... and impolite! Ah! I remember one more little thing. I also saw Bugs Bunny throw himself onto SpongeBob SquarePants! Something that made all the little kids who saw it crack up."

I had a hunch that the former employee's statement was priceless, though it left me puzzled. I asked her a question.

"Do you remember hearing about a theft — or maybe I should say a disappearance — of costumes at the same time?"

It took her a while to answer me.

"Not that I know of. But I was never a part of the mascots. And I didn't know anyone who was."

"It's no big deal. Thank you so much for your statement, Josefina."

"I'm not sure that this microevent could be useful to your investigation, but who knows!"

Yup, who knows, I repeated *in pett*o after having hung up.

Finally something a bit positive to get my teeth into!

Luckily, because what was about to follow, very quickly and in an unexplained manner, would undermine my investigation.

CHAPTER 31
In the lobby

Australia, July 2024

Karen Blackstone, worried, had left her yet another message. Sitting in the Brisbane Airport lobby, where like in all airports throughout the world you run across the same tired eyes, the same sighs standing in line, the same people dozing on the benches, Suzanne finally decided to call the detective back. After all, she'd hired her to get help, no use in playing Lone Ranger while putting blinkers on your horse. Maybe not Lone Ranger, but Suzanne was now galloping down another trail, one that Karen didn't know about.

"Miss Diggs!" said Karen not too warmly. "You're alive! I hope you're alright at least?"

"I'm fine. I've had a couple of minor setbacks, but everything's fine now. And I learned quite a few interesting things, what about you?"

"I thought we'd agreed that you'd keep me in the loop about your discoveries?"

Suzanne told her about how she got close to Ashley as well as her tenacious impression that Johanna Bolt, Ashely's older sister, was her real daughter — something she more and more was intimately persuaded of. Then she told her about the purse snatching and how it was returned with everything in it, as well as the message. She said she was going to go to Darwin to try to see Johanna.

"That's why I thought I saw my daughter in Ashley. Except that her age wasn't right. But Johanna, I'd bet my life on it! I have to get to the bottom of this. Have you made any progress on your side, Karen?"

Deep down inside Karen was sure that it was just wishful thinking, but after all, as she was paying her to help her find her long-lost daughter, the detective had no other choice than to continue her investigations. She then told her about her progress — or lack of it! — in Six Flags, at the police station, at Mrs. Kellermann's house and on Facebook. Then, still intrigued by the affirmations — or also delusions — of the old lady on Chestnut Street, she figuratively threw a rock into the pond.

"Suzanne, be frank with me. Who are you?"

In a mirror

"*Miss, who are you?*"

Dr. Petrossian's question left the patient unprepared. She'd learned that her therapy firstly consisted of knowing herself. Profoundly. Intimately. Before apprehending the world that surrounds us all.

What could she say?

It wasn't an easy question. Who would have been able to give a clear, honest and precise answer to that open question? As if you asked a passerby in the road: "Who is God?"

Even more difficult when, like the patient, you were suffering deep down inside, in the blackest part of your soul.

Of your mind.
She did, however, try.
"*I'm a woman. I'm a wife. I'm a mother.*"
"*And? Before that.*"

"I'm... me?" she sputtered.

The practitioner nodded as if saying "Miss, you're getting close."

"What do you think of that 'me?'"

"What I think?"

"Let's think of a concrete situation: you're looking at yourself in a mirror. Imagine that that person, the one in the mirror, is someone you don't know, someone walking down the street. What does she spontaneously make you think of?"

The patient dwelled on that question.

"Fear," she finally said. "I'm afraid of her."

"Why?"

"Because... I don't know her," said the young lady, hesitating.

"And like people say, you're afraid of things you don't know, is that what you mean? You see that 'me' as a stranger? A foreign body? Another person?"

"Yes! You're right. That's the feeling I have when I look at myself in the mirror. Being another person. Is it serious, Doctor?"

The doctor had a hint of a smile, surprised by the formula that out of the blue made him think of Bugs Bunny saying, "What's up, Doc?" He tried to reassure her.

"It's no longer serious when you're aware of it and you're ready to work on it. That's what we'll be doing, Miss. If you agree, of course. Like I already told you, we're not going to get anywhere without you buying into

this. So, I'm asking you: will you cooperate with me during our next sessions to try to define and differentiate that 'me' and that 'other' who both live together in you?"

"*I'd like them to become only one person,*" the young lady agreed.

CHAPTER 32
An undesirable visitor

NEW ORLEANS, July 2024

"KAREN, that's a strange question. I feel like I'm talking to a psychiatrist! Who can actually affirm who they really are? I sure can't."

"Suzanne let's not beat around the bush. I've got the feeling you're not telling me everything and for some unknown reason, you're trying to bamboozle me."

That seemed to have hit home, and she remained silent before continuing.

"Why would I lie to you or try to hide things from you, Karen? All I want is the truth. And I need your help."

A couple of days ago, she'd already given me that very same speech. I immediately jumped in.

"Do you know Mrs. Kellermann?"

"Of course! She was our neighbor. She's still alive? Did you meet her?"

"Yes, I spoke to her and showed her photos that *you* gave me of Ricardo, Lisa, and yourself. And speaking of which, her answer intrigued me."

"Why?"

"Believe it or not, when I showed *your* picture to her, at least the one that you said was you, Lucy Kellermann found it hard to be categorical. She wasn't sure it was Lisa's mother. Her neighbor at that time."

"And you believed that old lady's delusions? That shrew? Twenty years ago, she was already losing her marbles, I can't even try to imagine the state of her brain and memory today. Poor woman..."

"Suzanne, wait, I haven't finished. The woman on *your* photo, she recognized that one, on the contrary."

"Or maybe she thought she did," my client cut me off.

"Maybe. But Mrs. Kellermann affirmed that that person, in other words *you*, or *the lady in the photo*, often prowled around your house, or should I say Gutierrez's house, and sat on a bench, wearing dark sunglasses and hiding behind a newspaper. And that she even secretly entered the house when the owners weren't there. What have you got to say about that?"

Suzanne laughed bitterly.

"I'd just say it's an argument in favor of saying she's senile. How could she mistake me for that lady? Though I must say, part of what she said is true. I can see that everything's all mixed up in her head, but she's not wrong when she talked about some lady who was spying on us and who went in the house when we weren't home."

A red light went on in my detective mind.

"Ah… that's interesting. So you'd confirm that?"

"Yes, I would. We were sure there were intrusions back then. Footsteps on the lawn, a poorly closed window, a picked lock, an alarm that had been disabled… Plus stolen objects!"

"What kind of objects?"

"Strangely things that weren't valuable, or at least didn't have a commercial value, except for a bit of jewelry, earrings, rings and necklaces. But mostly objects with a huge sentimental value! Mostly framed pictures. Portraits of us as a family or only of one of us. Often pictures of my beautiful Lisa too. All throughout her life. Don't you think that's awful? Breaking into a house and stealing what's the most precious in the world, priceless in our hearts. Almost as bad as rape!"

I totally agreed with Suzanne on that point and was also horrified. You had to be crazy to do something as pitiful as that.

"I would imagine you filed a complaint?" I hoped.

"I did. But nothing ever came of it. We never got the pictures or anything else back!"

"Could you tell me about when all this took place?"

"I'd say about the whole year before their disappearance. Yes, that's right," Suzanne said. "It happened a couple of times during the same couple of months and up until the summer of 2004, I think. Up until I found the message..."

"What message?" I asked brusquely.

"A threat. That said, in a nutshell:

> *The next time, it won't be just Lisa's portrait that's missing...*

Meaning, it would be Lisa herself... That was just a couple of days before we went to Six Flags..."

CHAPTER 33
Game over!

CALIFORNIA, 2004

IT WAS visitor time again for one of Pelican Bay's most famous inmates. Rainbow day, they all called it. Sunlight in the middle of gloomy, cold and damp days that went by endlessly in that super-maximum-security prison. He'd already been there several weeks, probably months, – he'd lost track of time – vegetating in that rathole, in his concrete seventy-five square foot cell. And even rats would never have agreed to live in that lifeless and squalid cage. They'd just die off.

The same ritual. The neon light came on, the door opened with an electronic click, the arms you put behind you through the hole in the door so they'd be able to handcuff you, the three prison guards escorting you, their weapons visible, the echo of their boots in the deserted hallways, the multitude of doors that they unlocked and locked, cameras following the progression of your little group, then finally that narrow cubicle they called the visitation area. Behind that armored glass window, always the same visitor, the same loyal and opinionated lady, who never lost faith though everyone knew, on both sides of the window and fake yellow phone that you only left Pelican Bay feet first in a wooden box.

"Hey, beautiful," said the inmate who had been freed from his manacles. "What's new under the sun?"

"It's still shining, my love. How do you...? It's..." she articulated with a strained smile before bursting into tears.

Her eyes moist, she opened her purse and took out a miniature game of chess, putting it on the shelf. Through the armored glass window, the prisoner saw her install each piece on the black and white squares.

Through the cameras on the angles of the visitation area, one of the prison guards saw what was happening. He smiled when he saw the game. *A healthy way to pass the time*, he thought.

"Come on sweetie, don't cry", the inmate said softly. "Don't cry, I don't like to see tears on your cheeks. Life goes on, even without me. It has to go on for you too. You have to be strong, strong for me. From here I can't do anything, it's true. For me, I've finished playing. Game over! But others can play for me, there are still key pieces... Though the king is out, the queen is still alive. Plus the rook is still standing. The bishop, knight, and devoted pawns are still there."

The lady nodded while making sense of her man's metaphors. He continued.

"Now you'll be moving my own pieces on the big chessboard. Can you do that for me? Let's say we're starting a new game. A rematch!"

"I can try, honey," murmured the young lady. "What piece do you want to move?"

"The bishop."

She understood him without words.

"Where do you want to move it to? And how? What's his target?"

The inmate with his orange jumpsuit had an evil looking grin.

"His targets," he said. "The opposing king. And his princess..."

"His princess?" asked the lady, astonished. "There are no pieces with that name in chess."

"Of course there are. She's the king's daughter."

When she heard that, she shook her head, horrified.

"She's innocent! We can't..."

"Collateral damage," declared the inmate. "If we can't defeat that piece, ours — the black pieces — can encircle him at the minimum, imprison him, use him as an exchange currency."

"To exchange him against..."

"The white king! Not that white! He's the one I want to kill! He fucking tricked us, now he has to pay!"

On the other side of the window, the visitor put her index finger with its red nail on the cross on the head of the white king and slowly laid the most important piece down on the chessboard.

"Checkmate," sneered the prisoner.

CHAPTER 34
A real person

New Orleans, July 2024

"Why didn't you tell me about that anonymous message?" I scolded her, irritated.

"I forgot about it. I'm sorry. All those years... And the impression to have gone crazy trying to figure out this story in my head."

I mentally noted to check if there were any traces of her complaint but had no illusions. I had a question.

"Did you ever find out the name of your undesirable visitor?"

"Never."

One last thing was nibbling on my brain.

"I still can't understand why Mrs. Kellermann thought she recognized that woman in *your portrait*, the one you sent me.

"She must have gotten mixed up."

I insisted.

"Miss Diggs…"

"Suzanne!"

"Right, sorry. Suzanne. Can we continue this conversation as a video call? I'd like to *finally* see my client and employer! It'll be less impersonal."

There was a moment of silence before she responded.

"Right now that'll be complicated. I'm at the boarding gate for my flight to Darwin. I'm afraid it'll cut off."

"We can always try," I insisted, clicking on the "camera" icon of the app.

Immediately though, there was a message on my screen saying that my correspondent had rejected my request for a video call. At the same time I heard an announcement in the loudspeakers.

"I'm boarding," said Suzanne. "I have to hang up. I'll call you back soon."

She hung up, leaving me alone with my doubts.

Then I saw I had a Facebook notification, one that paralyzed me.

I CLICKED on it and the application directed me to access the page that I'd created for my ad.

While reading the content, I broke down, my investigation once again was a victim of an unfortunate incident. This case was being hampered and slowed down by a thousand details and disillusions.

I had the feeling that with each step forward, fate was forcing me to take two backwards.

Dear Administrator,

Your Meta account will be disactivated after 24 hours. This is because your advertising campaign or activity on your page does not comply with Meta's general conditions of use.

Should you believe your account has been banned by mistake, please contact us. To avoid your account being permanently restricted, your page will no longer be published, and all related advertising campaigns shall be disactivated.

We shall inform you of Meta's final decision by email.

After 24 hours, should the system not have received a request for review, we shall automatically close your Facebook account, and you will no longer be able to use our services.

Should I respond to this? I knew that fakes like that proliferated on social networks and in messaging systems. That all they aimed for was to trick people into giving them their personal data so that web pirates would be able to defraud them. I remembered the unfortunate experience that one of my friends who owned an online shop selling works of art had. Once, she had had the misfortune of clicking on a link like that and entering miscellaneous elements concerning her advertising account. She'd brutally lost access to her account, as well as potential visitors and clients. After forty-eight hours, she noticed an unusual explosion in her advertising budget: the hacker had used it to broadcast religious messages about Jesus Christ. In just two days her bill amounted to seven hundred dollars! She quickly had to move heaven and earth, cursing Jesus Christ, to block her account, curb that hemorrhage and recover her Meta access rights. So much work, so much stress!

As for me, deleting my sponsored ad to find witnesses on August 6, 2004 wasn't really dramatic. It was something I could do without, though it had allowed me to obtain some good results with Josefina and Felix. I had other leads to explore, but still, I was slightly pissed about that.

But how could my little ad have broken Meta's rules? Was it a crime to try to find information and, who knows, the truth about a tragedy? I wasn't praising terrorism, inciting hatred or blasphemy!

Why block me then?

Had someone flagged me? Some internet user saying my ad was inappropriate? If so, who and why?

A sole individual? An organization? An official one, unofficial, the Mafia?

Now I was the one who was making up stories in my head!

Though I envisaged several scenarios, none of them seemed sufficiently plausible to lead to my account being closed.

Someone who's never tried to contact a living and breathing human being at Meta can't understand what an uphill battle it is!

As I refused to think this was a fake message, I wanted to contact Meta. I wasted a whole hour going through the FAQs and assistance forums, "talking" with a Chatbot, etc. That conversation with an artificial intelligence quickly began to loop around and was driving me crazy. As I progressed a bit deeper into what I imagined as some concentric circles which, I hoped, would allow me to talk to a real person, I had to validate emails, receive codes by SMS, prove that *I* wasn't a robot (the ultimate paradox!) by clicking on images of bikes, stairs, bridges or cars, and move a piece of a virtual puzzle into its empty space. Then log off, log back in, during which I of course forgot my password, which then required a reinitialization with a new SMS, etc.

I was tearing my hair out!

Whatever I tried, whatever I asked, I ended up with the same response, though it was formulated differently: `Your advertising campaign or activity of your page does not comply with Meta's general conditions of use.`

Okay! Thank you, I think I understood that!
But... why?

Finally though, after two hours of cold sweat and irritated sighs, I got through — by miracle? — to a living and breathing person on the phone, to whom I had to explain everything I'd already explained on their site and who made me wait while listening to unbearable music while he examined my account, my access and my parameters.

Ten minutes later, which seemed like hours to me, the Meta help desk employee got back to me.

"Miss Blackstone? I can confirm that your advertising campaign was not hacked. I can't see any anomalies for access authorizations nor for billing. It all seems normal to me."

Normal? This guy should have been a comedian.

"In that case, why can't I access my page? Why was it disactivated?

"I have no idea, that is strange. Could you please hold, I'll generate a ticket for my colleagues in the technical department."

Another ten minutes of that irritating music followed. He finally came back on the line.

"Miss Blackstone, thank you for holding."

"Like I had the choice," I ironically though sotto voce said.

"Excuse me, I didn't understand."

"It's no big deal. Go ahead."

"So, there's something quite unusual in your case. A problem I never personally had before."

"Unusual? What's unusual?"

"Well, when we were trying to delve more deeply into the motive of why your page was blocked, my colleagues saw that it was disactivated by federal injunction…"

I sure wasn't prepared for that one!

"A federal injunction? You mean?"

"That's right, Miss Blackstone. The FBI ordered your page to be disactivated."

CHAPTER 35
Tchoubati

Darwin, Australia, July 2024

Little Darwin Airport was not far from the city center.

When she arrived in the domestic flight arrivals' hall, Suzanne Diggs didn't notice the man wearing sunglasses with a Bluetooth transmitter in his ear, holding a slate in his hands, pretending to be waiting for a fictional passenger. He, on the other hand, never took his eyes off the lady as she walked up to the car rental counter and followed her, seemingly peering at his phone.

And she hadn't paid attention either to the other man with his dark glasses who'd seen her embark on the plane in Brisbane, three hours ago.

After having gotten into her hybrid Toyota Corolla, she only needed about fifteen minutes to reach the little apartment she'd rented, in a small and peaceful building overlooking a lush botanical garden. She was delighted to see that tropical plants surrounded her room, which was on the ground floor.

She took a couple of minutes to unpack and hopped right back into her vehicle again, this time to drive to the minuscule and very cute Tipperary Waters Marina, which was surrounded by apartments and in whose waters lazily danced a few sailboats. She now was starving and following her nose, walked up to the Frying Nemo counter to order. She let herself be tempted by the Barra Burger, one of their specialties, which was a filet of barramundi fried in a beer batter. Looking at the menu she learned that the name of this fish, one abundant in that region, came from the aboriginal language and meant "fish with big scales," and that you shouldn't confuse it with tchoubabi, which was a type of catfish. She ordered a barquette of medium sized shoestring fries and a local beer to accompany her burger.

She sat down at a table by the shore, taking a buzzer that would light up and vibrate when her order was ready. She looked around at the apartment buildings behind the marina with their yellow streetlights giving a peaceful atmosphere. Then she looked up at the balconies. She took out her phone and looked at the photo she'd taken of Johanna Bolt's virtual business card, trying to find out where Ashley's sister lived.

After dinner she was planning on walking around the marina, below the arcades of the buildings, looking for number 23. For the moment, while coming back from the counter with her tray and sitting down, she was trying to guess what, if her intuition and deductions weren't playing tricks on her, the person who must be her daughter might look like. Okay, that wasn't the first time she had that impression, a strong and intimate one, but ever since she'd seen the photo of the young lady, she was convinced that Johanna was Lisa twenty years older. To convince herself even more, she opened her phone and stared at Ashley's sister's photos.

She suddenly nearly choked on a fry when she saw a slim silhouette, one with brown hair and an aristocratic bearing on one of the balconies. The young lady was leaning on her railing, looking out at the sailboats in the marina. She shook her head, ran her fingers through her hair several times, and then suddenly, as if some invisible and intangible force had taken over, seemed to be staring at the Frying Nemo patio, straight at Suzanne.

At that distance, how could anyone believe they were looking at one another? Spiritually, perhaps? Wishful thinking? Whatever, Suzanne felt her heart begin to pound, her mouth dried up, her hands started to tremble so much she had to put that delicious burger down. There it was again, that powerful feeling that truth was just at the tips of her fingers.

Her truth?

She had to get to the bottom of it. She quickly finished her meal, got up and brought the tray back to the counter, thanking the employees, and left the patio.

Her footsteps led her nearly automatically towards the balcony where the young lady was still standing, her arms leaning on the balustrades, her hands joined together, smoking a cigarette whose red-end guided Suzanne just like a lighthouse in the middle of a storm.

Suzanne felt like scolding her for having begun to smoke. A mother's reaction. Of course, the last image of Lisa when she was alive was when she was a child, not even three years old. Two decades had passed in their lives.

About thirty feet behind her there was a man with broad shoulders and a square jaw who was taking advantage of the darkness of the night and dim streetlights to follow her without being noticed.

CHAPTER 36
In the lion's den

NEW ORLEANS, *July 2024*

HAD I dreamed of a great first case for Blackstone Investigations, one that progressed rapidly, I would have been sadly mistaken. Up till now, I'd been treading water, running up against roadblocks and now, my problems had reached a whole different level. If the FBI was against me, I'd have to stand back and keep a low profile. No joking with the Feds.

But what the heck did they want? How could my little investigation disturb them? And why?

Had I put my foot in it? In a Louisianian jambalaya that was too spicey?

While walking along the Mississippi, annoyed, I couldn't stop dwelling on that. With my Facebook page blocked, now there was a whole window that had closed on the vast social networking panorama. A direct, easy to use and powerful opening to a host of witnesses who, like Josefina and Felix, were apt to help me travel back in time. Today's technologies facilitated access to the living memories of past years. So what could I do now? I could play it old-school: knocking on neighbor's doors, going through archives, all of that was possible but up till now hadn't given me a lot of results. Luckily, before they closed my Facebook page, I had been able to speak on the phone with two former Six Flags employees, and I still had their contact details in my phone, a tenuous link back to 2004.

While waiting to perhaps call them once again, I was trying to figure out what to do next. Should I play it cool so I wouldn't find myself under the FBI's radars, or else, in line with my investigative nature, trying to get to the bottom of this case, or should I contact them to find out why I was being blocked? Though that was a risky solution, my thirst for knowledge needed to be quenched.

Usually it's FBI agents who contact citizens, often when they're expecting it the least. It's rarely the opposite, except when you have a valid motive such as giving them statements or tips that could help catch a criminal. Which wasn't my case. I thought though that perhaps if the Gutierrez case didn't appear anywhere in Nola's police archives, perhaps it had caught the eye of the FBI back then.

Nothing ventured, nothing gained, as I always say to myself. I'd use my Facebook page to try to get through to the Bureau. How do you call the FBI? A question I certainly had never asked myself. I went onto the organization's website and looked for contact details of the New Orleans branch. And found a phone number which I immediately clicked on. It rang three times before a feminine voice picked up.

"New Orleans FBI, why are you calling? Please give me your name."

"Hello, this is Karen Blackstone from Blackstone Investigations. I'm contacting you about an incident on a Facebook page that I created about two missing persons in New Orleans in August of 2004."

She then asked me several questions and transferred me to one of the local agents in their "cyber" branch.

"Agent Maxim Callaghan, how can I help you?"

Once again I introduced myself, told him why I was calling, then after a few moments of silence, I heard him clicking on his keyboard.

"Miss Blackstone, could you come to our local office, 2901 Leon C. Simon Drive?"

I hopped into my car, without thinking for one fleeting moment that I'd be thrown to the wolves... Something I'd only realize much later.

CHAPTER 37
Child's play

Darwin, July 2024

STANDING BEHIND one of the poles under the arcades of the complex on the edge of the little marina in Darwin, Suzanne kept her eyes on the young lady on her balcony, holding a cigarette that she wasn't even smoking, looking out over the masts of the sailboats who were balancing slowly from right to left.

Hidden behind another pillar, the square-jawed man observed Suzanne.

A triangle of hunters and prey, each one paying attention to the others' next gesture. *The first one who moves will lose...* as the little kids sing in their nursery rhyme. *I hold you, you hold me, by the chinny chin chin. The first one of the three of us who moves...*

There suddenly was a movement on the balcony. A man had just appeared behind Johanna. He put his arms around her, put his face in her neck, and kissed her tenderly from behind. The young lady tilted her head, closing her eyes, a wide smile on her face.

She's not alone, Suzanne regretted. That would complicate her plans. She wouldn't be as easy to approach as her little sister in Hervey Bay had been.

A few seconds later, after the young man had whispered several words into Johanna's ear, the couple went back inside.

Suzanne sighed and left the shade of her hiding place. She walked down the dock back to her car parked behind the restaurant.

She didn't see the second vehicle in her rear-view mirror who was following her at about a fifty-foot distance and who stayed behind her as she drove down the streets in Darwin to her apartment, next to the botanical gardens.

As Suzanne was driving slowly in the parking lot, the man stopped his car across the road. He waited several minutes, got out, crossed the road that was dimly lit by several distant streetlights and went into the resident's parking space. He found Suzanne's car, took a picture of the license plate as well as the badge of the rental company, and with this information, got back in, and drove off to Darwin Airport.

They were open 24/7, and he went to the rental counter, chatted for a few moments with the car rental employee after having taken out a plaque that looked official, and then left with the copy of the contract that Suzanne Diggs had signed a bit earlier.

Carefully examining the signature, the man had trouble making out a first or last name, but what seemed sure to him, was that he couldn't recognize either *Suzanne* or *Diggs* in the hieroglyphs of the signature on the bottom of the page.

CHAPTER 38
At odds

New Orleans, July 2024

The offices of the local FBI branch were right next to Nola's second airport, Lakefront Airport.

A parallelepiped brown brick building with beige strips, surrounded by well-kept lawns opened its doors to visitors behind a metallic fence. It was a clean and I could nearly say bucolic complex, but still, it was a federal building, not some summer camp.

When I opened the gate, an agent checked my identity and recorded my visit in a logbook. You had to show a clean bill of health to get into the FBI.

Agent Callaghan came to meet me in the huge lobby and led me to his office.

He was a good forty years old, with salt and pepper hair cut at the regulatory buzz cut length, dark eyes that seemed to gaze right into your soul and a large straight nose that went well with his square jaw: a poster boy for law and order.

"Sit down, please. Go ahead."

"I'd like to know why the FBI disactivated my Facebook page which I'd opened to investigate a case that I'm currently working on."

I'd already spoken to him about this on the phone, so he knew what I was talking about, but his response didn't really surprise me.

"What case, Miss Blackstone?"

"The one about the disappearance on August 6, 2004, of Ricardo Gutierrez and his daughter, Lisa."

Callaghan now had a mocking grin.

"We don't have any cases with those names," he affirmed.

"But my client, Suzanne Diggs, Ricardo's partner, assured me that she'd gone to the New Orleans police about their disappearance."

"I know."

"How do you know that?"

"I know that you already went to see my colleagues who are in the police force."

"Really?"

"You can't hide anything from the FBI, I'm sure you know that... But if it's alright with you Miss Blackstone, I'm the one who's asking the questions here! So answer this one: why are you investigating a case that doesn't exist, up to publishing a call for witnesses on social media?"

"Because something happened that day at Six

Flags! My client isn't a crazy old lady! She was there, with Ricardo and Lisa. They were having a day at the park, just like thousands of other happy families. And then, in just a snap of the fingers, her partner and daughter vanished, and no one's ever seen them since. My client declared them to be missing persons. She's a wife and mother asking for someone to help her find them. How can you doubt that?"

"And how can *you* doubt what the police and FBI are saying?" Agent Callaghan bounced back. "Have you ever imagined that with the differences between versions, that your lady was making this whole *case* up? Should I put it this way, telling a *story*? Because there's no case at all here, but that Suzanne Diggs seemed to have spun quite a yarn to you."

The Fed's remarks cast doubts on something that had been simmering inside me for quite a while, as I had been struggling with Suzanne's quite strange attitude.

"In other words, you're telling me that my client had been lying since the beginning?"

"Have you even met her?"

"No," I pitifully confessed. "She's in Australia right now."

"You sure of that?"

There that Agent Callaghan pulled the wool from under my feet. And what irritated me the most was that he may have been right. Up till now, what guarantees did I have that Suzanne Diggs was actually there where she said she was? She'd affirmed to me she was vacationing on the other side of the globe, but nothing proved she wasn't closer. For example, here in New Orleans.

"I'm not sure of anything actually," I admitted. "But still, there's something here I don't get: if, like you're saying, all of that is just a tale that my client told me, why would she lie to me like that, why would she have hired me and paid me an advance?"

The federal agent spread his hands out as a sign saying he had no idea, and I subtlety could feel he was becoming impatient.

"My little lady, I don't know, and I actually don't give a damn!"

"Excuse me?" I gulped out, astounded by his sudden lack of tact.

"I mean, it's not my problem, it's yours!"

I immediately jumped on that opening.

"As it's not your problem, Agent Callaghan, and by extension the FBI's problem, why did you block my Facebook page and why not just let me continue my investigation? Including and especially if it's just a fantasy that my client has. How does that bother the police and the FBI?"

The man sighed, his hands laid flat on his desk, as if trying to contain something deep inside that was boiling over.

"Federal laws prohibit false disclosure or research using social media. My job consists in tracking down cybercriminal offenses and restricting false information and rumors that could harm American citizens. For that, your page has broken the rules. That's why."

I didn't understand his logic.

"Seriously though, all I did was borrow Billy Jensen's tried and tested method, and he's worked several times on cold cases, hand-in-hand with the police and the FBI! Why can't I do the same thing?"

"For a very simple reason, Miss Blackstone."

"Which is?"

"That your Mr. Jensen investigates *to support* the FBI and police in cases — perhaps cold cases — but *real ones*! There's a nuance there! As for yours, or should I say your client's, as far as we know it's neither a cold case, it's never been opened, it's not real... until proven otherwise!"

"I'm going to prove it otherwise, Agent Callaghan!" I proudly said.

"Even though we're telling you not to, Miss Blackstone? Be careful, it's never a good idea to be at odds with the federal laws of the United States."

"Is that a threat?"

"Consider it a warning, for now. Before you leave, could I give you some advice?"

"I'm always a taker for good free advice."

"I'd like to suggest that you ask the right questions, Miss Blackstone. Or better, ask the adequate questions for your client, that Suzanne Diggs, if that actually is her name."

CHAPTER 39
Her truth

Darwin, July 2024

Down Under, Suzanne's phone woke her up. In New Orleans it was only ten the day before. She saw the name Karen Blackstone on the screen in an SMS notification.

> Suzanne, I must speak to you immediately. I've got both important questions to ask you about some delicate subjects. Please answer my phone calls or even better, give me a video call. Thanks in advance. Karen.

> Give me a few minutes.

The lady put her cell phone on her bedside table

and sighed loudly. The day was certainly starting with a bang. Could she still postpone the moment she'd show herself to Karen? She couldn't keep on dilly-dallying like that without arousing suspicion. On the contrary, she had to preserve the trust that linked them in a common goal: finding Lisa — and Ricardo while they were at it — as well as the cause and *modus operandi* of their disappearance.

Before calling her back, she took time to take a shower while her coffee was dripping, drop by drop, a cup of coffee she peacefully enjoyed on her patio overlooking the botanical gardens.

Then she took care of her appearance, makeup, hairdo, before calling Karen.

She opened the application but had made sure that she was *presentable*, then with her index finger, pressed "Video Call."

Two seconds later she saw that Karen had accepted the call and then she saw her, with her face occupying the entire screen, and her own in a small square on the bottom on the right.

"Hello Suzanne," the detective began. "I hope I didn't wake you up. I'm not too good with time differences, I'm afraid. Speaking of which, what time is it in Darwin? You are in Darwin, aren't you?"

"Of course I am! Where did you think I was?" she asked, astonished. "Here it's almost nine in the morning. Do you want to see the inside of my apartment? Look, I'm right next to the town's botanical gardens, it's a great location!"

While speaking she showed Karen her apartment as well as all the tropical vegetation next to the patio.

"It is beautiful," the detective approved. "I'm delighted to finally meet you, not in flesh and blood yet, but at least see you. I can assure myself that I am actually speaking to the person that up till now, I only saw in a photo. That reassures me. But Suzanne, I must admit, there are several gray areas in our case."

"Gray areas?" asked Suzanne, frowning.

"Believe it or not, I just walked out of the FBI offices here in Nola, where I met with an agent who told me things I didn't like."

"Meaning?"

"He was categorical that there never was a Gutierrez case here in New Orleans. No one ever went missing from Six Flags on August 6, 2004. That is also what my police contact as well as my own research on the web and what I learned from a couple of people who worked in the park told me. None of them remember an event like that, though they did witness a couple of curious or at least unusual things."

"Like?"

"Something about costumes for the mascots that were missing that day as well as strange behavior by some of the mascots in the park. But that's not something that has allowed me to progress here. So, Suzanne, what's really bothering me here and excuse me for insisting, but it's this dichotomy between what you're saying and what I've been hearing here for several days, in particular from the police. What's the problem? I must admit that I'm finding it hard to believe everything you've told me."

Suzanne shook her head while the detective was listing her doubts. Then she sighed loudly.

"You're like all the others finally, Karen, even though I paid you!"

"Suzanne, it's not about money! You know that. It's about me trusting you."

"Just trust me then. No one wanted to believe me for twenty years. Even the cops didn't take me seriously! Why? I never understood why. Just like those who never understood my pain, my incomprehension of the events that took place so quickly, so brutally, without warning. One day they were there, the next day Ricardo and Lisa vanished, and people thought I had lost my marbles. Or should I say, they wanted everyone to think I was crazy, unbalanced, someone who made this all up. So Karen, I'm begging you, everything I have told you is the truth. I didn't invent a thing!"

On the other side of the screen, Karen Blackstone didn't say a word, trying to differentiate, in each of her client's words, accents of reality. *Her* reality, *her* truth.

But such is life, right? Each of us possesses our own truths, which are not always those of others. Does the strongest or the most common truth win against the less convincing or less popular truth?

Karen spoke again in that conversation that was interrupted by their respective cogitations.

"Okay. I'll buy into the principle that your truth is worth that of the authorities. So tell me then for example, what do you know about the nocturnal move from the property in Chestnut Street in the summer of 2004? That certainly isn't something ordinary!"

Suzanne was silent.

"Right, the move. It was a terrible, difficult moment, but an inevitable one! Ever since that day, I could no longer go there, it was absolutely impossible for me. That house, I couldn't even look at it without starting to tremble, cry, seethe. But I waited for them to reappear. I hoped. To no avail. I finally gave up. I watched the movers helplessly. Then I decided never again to return to that neighborhood in the Garden District that reminded me too much of Ricardo and of Lisa. I turned the page, looked to the future where the hope of seeing them once again, elsewhere, became my sole goal. And here, in Darwin, I can feel it on my fingertips. Lisa's here, close to me. Maybe Ricardo is too."

Karen jumped at that opportunity.

"Tell me a bit about Ricardo. Up till now, we've mostly talked about Lisa, hardly at all about her father, your partner. For example, would you be able to tell me if during the days, weeks or months before their disappearance, Ricardo's behavior had changed in some way that could justify him leaving? How were you as a couple during that time?"

"I see what you're getting at. You're insinuating that our relationship had gotten to a point where he wanted to flee? Run away from me and kidnap Lisa? I don't want to disappoint you, but Ricardo and I got along perfectly! Our romantic idyll was unique and full of passion! Nonetheless..."

Suzanne hesitated and Karen urged her to continue.

"Nonetheless?"

"Maybe in the weeks before the summer of 2004, Ricardo did seem to me to be more tense, less serene than usual. Maybe a bit more distant too... But that's something that happens to lots of couples, don't you agree?"

"A temporary distance in a couple doesn't systematically lead to a disappearance. Can you be more precise, Suzanne? Did you know why he was tense?"

"Not really. Ricardo was always very discreet, he never explained things. A true Latino, proud, vain, someone who never let anyone see his weaknesses or faults. Plus he wasn't the touchy-feely lovey-dovey type either. Anyway, that summer, when he would get back from work..."

"What kind of work?" Karen cut her off.

"A photographer."

"Nice job."

"It is, he was so talented, he had a way of looking at things, a vision. So, when he'd get back, he seemed annoyed, worried. Always looking over his shoulder, as if someone was following him or observing him. Being tailed. But I had no idea what or who was bothering him. I've always wondered about that, but he never gave me any clear answers. He was not a man of many words! As if, deep down inside, there was some unholy secret hidden. Sometimes he'd leave, and I wouldn't see him for days on end. But he always came back. Sometimes though in a state that worried me."

"Meaning?"

"Well, when he came back sometimes from his getaways, I called him my 'big alley cat,' he'd be coming back bruised, his hair in a mess and I could almost say, traumatized from inside. He'd come to purr next to me, I calmed him and did what I could to make things better."

"You said bruised?"

"Psychologically but yes, sometimes physically too. As if he'd been in a fight. Sometimes he had cut lines on him, scars like tribal scoring. At least that was what they made me think of. But he remained as silent as the grave when I questioned him. Like talking to the wall!"

"The day they disappeared, he was like that?"

"The days before he was really tense, yes. More than ever! He was the one that actually organized our outing in the park, sort of like an outlet that would do him good. But that wasn't very successful, was it!"

The two women talked a bit more before ending their video call.

. . .

As soon as she'd hung up, Suzanne Diggs took a deep breath and grabbed the dark-brown wig she'd been wearing, throwing it to the other side of the room.

Then she vigorously puffed up her hair.

Kaleidoscope

Sitting on the edge of the sofa, the patient's head was low, her hands crossed between her trembling knees. She needed nearly a minute of silence before she was able to answer the question Dr. Petrossian had just asked.

"If I know who my man really is? Who can affirm that they know their loved ones a hundred percent? Doesn't everyone have a part of shadow hidden inside? A percentage of our souls that we don't want others to see? Another self? Secret, masked, intimate? Good Lord! It's already so difficult to know who I am myself!"

"That's true, we did talk about this last time. Continue. That man, how would you describe him in a few words?"

The young lady sat back on the sofa, crossed her legs and uncrossed her fingers, putting her hands on her thighs.

"In just one word: complex. That's it, a complex man. But not one who had complexes. A man with *numerous facets, like a kaleidoscope. I'm sure that if we asked a hundred people to describe a man like him, we'd have a hundred different portraits."*

"The image that each of us projects to others is very subjective, that's true. Each person perceives others according to what they already experienced, their feelings, their expectations, their apprehensions, etc. Each person has a different glimpse of that kaleidoscope and its prism. Why does that man seem so complex to you?"

"Because he's not the same every day."

"Could you expand on that?"

The patient thought it over.

"One day white, the next black?" she proposed, asking herself the same question. "Yes, that's it. One day I understand him, the next day I don't at all."

"Why do you think so?"

"Because I often think he's hiding things about his past to me."

"Such as?"

"Sometimes he gives me the impression that he experienced terrible things. Sordid, sleazy things. Shameful things that he wouldn't like anyone else to know. Even his partner!"

"Could you be more precise, Miss, if you can?"

"Well, Doctor, if I believe my intuition, I'd say it might be something about drugs, or even worse, prostitution, and from there, I'd even think about something related to the Mafia..."

The psychiatrist nodded, which for him was how he accompanied a patient.

"Why did you say that?"

"Details I picked up here and there. A whispered conversation on the phone when I went into the hall. Messages I was able to read on his cell phone. Disreputable frequentations in neighborhoods to be avoided."

"How did you find this out?"

"Sometimes I followed him without him knowing… I was so worried about him then! What would you have done, Doctor?"

"I'm not in your shoes, Miss. That's why I'm seated here behind this desk and you're on the sofa. What did you see?"

"Things that were exchanged. Money for who knows what. I didn't get close to them and was afraid to ask him about it."

The doctor frowned before continuing.

"Can unsaid things like that persist in a couple? Is it healthy to hide things like that? Whoever is hiding them! One person who's hiding unlawful activities and the other who's hiding what they secretly saw?"

"No, it wasn't a good idea," the young lady admitted.

"Would you say that those secrets were what led you to what you referred to the other day as 'a separation?'"

"Yes, I'm sure that it did contribute to it, at least partially."

"It wasn't a voluntary separation then."

"No. He never would have left me like that. Something happened to him, that's the only thing that could

be possible. Something happened to him and... her. To them."

"*Them?*"

"*Yes, my husband. My daughter. I'm sure someone kidnapped them.*"

The doctor nodded, while taking notes, attentive and serious. He wrote silently for a few moments, seemed to circle a word or a sentence, before speaking.

"*This is the end of our session today. Do you have anything else to say?*"

CHAPTER 40
The gang

New Orleans, July 2024

After several days of investigation in Nola, I was reduced to wondering if I was heading in the right direction. It seemed that each path I went down ended up as a dead end. My client didn't bring me much food for thought, the few witnesses I'd seen only gave me some assumptions, nothing I could put my teeth into, and the police had told me nothing had happened. Just like a boxer, I'd been knocked out, was lying on the floor in the middle of the ring.

But behind all those incoherencies, I had the gut feeling that there was something important. I had two options: either this whole thing was a huge lie, or it was an imposing and impressive secret. Whether it was one or the other, I couldn't wait to shed some light on all those gray areas.

The tip about the nocturnal move that Mrs. Kellermann had told me about kept running through my mind. It seemed too strange to me that movers would work at night, especially when moving everything out of a large villa.

I now realized that Suzanne had eluded my question on that during our video call. She'd pointed me to another lead, that of Ricardo, and I'd jumped right into it. That investigation was becoming so bizarre that I'd forgotten the basics of any private detective: just like a dog, never drop what you've got your teeth in. I sent off a message to Suzanne.

> Suzanne, what do you think about the movers working at night? Didn't you think it was really strange? Did you ever wonder why?

Sitting in a café not far from my hotel with a steaming hot cup of tea, I opened my laptop and logged into the café's Wi-Fi. I began to search for companies who did that sort of work, targeting the largest ones, those equipped with trucks that had a hydraulic tailgate lift. There were a good dozen companies that I contacted.

Most of them hadn't even been open twenty years ago, except for the three largest ones.

I asked those three if, you never know, they would have conserved logbooks about the moves they'd done in the previous years, and most of them said that their archives only dated back to ten years. Once again, I'd run into a dead end.

But there was a glint of hope behind those shadows hanging over my investigation. I was on the phone with Nola Moving, a large private firm in New Orleans.

"You said that that nocturnal move took place when already?" asked Hector, the man on the phone at Nola Moving.

"In 2004, the summer before Katrina."

"Ah! Such a catastrophe! In 2005 that hurricane moved everything in its path. Over two hundred thousand houses were destroyed, do you realize that? Over a million inhabitants had to move out. And ever since, we've been rebuilding. But to come back to your question, Miss Blackstone, yes, in 2004 I was working with Nola Moving. I'll be retired in a year and a half, so things are looking up for me. So, like I said earlier, no I can't access any files from twenty years ago, that's for sure. But in my head, everything hasn't moved out yet, if you see what I mean. And I well remember back in those days, a case that was really strange."

He'd said *case*, I was on high alert.

"Yes? What kind of case?"

"About moving, which is why I remember it. Others would have forgotten all about it now. Not me. Believe it or not, for several months, maybe even a year there was a criminal organization terrorizing people in Louisiana and especially in New Orleans. They were nicknamed the Mover's Gang."

"Not a very moving name," I said ironically. "So what did that gang do?"

"Well, they sought out empty properties, vacation homes that were uninhabited for several months at a time or houses for sale but still with the furniture in them, or houses where widows had just joined their husbands in their final resting place, stuff like that. Their *modus operandi* was like this: well-dressed scouts went through high-class neighborhoods when not too many people were at home, when they were all at work downtown."

Hmm, why was I suddenly thinking of that mysterious lady sitting on a bench under a tree in Chestnut Street? That lady that Lucy Kellermann told me about, the one who observed the Gutierrez house behind her sunglasses and her newspaper? I nonetheless let him speak without interrupting.

"Once they were sure that the coast was clear, they drove in at night with trucks, with ten or so musclemen in each vehicle, and the houses were quickly emptied out. Or at least emptied of everything that had any monetary value. Objects, furniture, knickknacks, jewelry, stuff that could quickly be sold on parallel markets. Plus any loose cash, of course. And because they had the equipment to do so, they also took safes, hoping they were filled with valuables and carted them off on a pallet truck to be opened later. There you go. So, it's quite possible that the move you were talking about before was done by guys like them, who knows."

"Yes, you could be right," I said both for myself and for Hector. "And do you remember the name of that gang? I mean, outside of the 'Mover's Gang'"?

He hesitated for a couple of seconds.

"No, actually I don't. I always heard of them referred to as the Mover's Gang."

"Did the police ever arrest them?"

"Got me. But remember, right after, Katrina overturned the whole city soon. Maybe there wasn't anything else to move, like they all got laid off and then they were forced to find something else or go somewhere else. Outside of Louisiana. Guys like that always have good ideas. So I don't know if I helped you or not, but that's all I can say, Miss Blackstone."

"It's already a lot, thanks so very much."

As soon as we'd finished our conversation, I googled to see if there was anything about that "Mover's Gang."

That name was well-known in forums and blogs and there were links to several different organizations throughout the world.

I filtered by adding key-words such as *Louisiana* and *New Orleans* to get more targeted results.

By cross-checking various sources, I ended up concluding that the original gang was a part of one of the South-American mafia branches that had relocated to the States in the 80s, at first in Los Angeles, before spreading little by little throughout the country, including in New Orleans.

If my investigation was now going to stumble upon the underworld, I would be a sitting duck.

Plus the authorities weren't taking me seriously.

Would I be opening a huge can of worms?

CHAPTER 41
Shrinking

Zuccoli, July 2024

THE TWO VEHICLES followed each other with a fifty or so foot gap on Stuart Highway, a multilane boulevard that led to the center of Darwin, before turning south towards Katherine, and then, much farther on, towards Alice Springs. In the heart of untouched, desertic, aboriginal and sometimes hostile Australia, stood the famous and majestic Ayers Rock, a geological curiosity that was this island's icon.

The cars though weren't just two, rather three, with the last one lagging far behind Suzanne.

SUZANNE DIGGS HAD BEGUN to track Johanna Bolt that very morning, following her as soon as the young lady left her apartment overlooking Tipperary

Marina. Jo had led her, unknowingly of course, to the foot of the building where she worked, on Cavanagh Street. Suzanne, still not used to driving on the left side of the street, was following her presumed daughter's vehicle to the best of her ability. She parked her car, got out, and went to the building to look at the names of companies whose offices were located there. She saw the name of the company where the young lady worked, a name she'd already seen when she peaked at Ashley's cell phone at the restaurant in Hervey Bay while she had run off to the ladies' room.

The golden plaque said it was on the third floor. A deliveryman opened the door and Suzanne followed him in. Wearing a pearl-gray suit, she could easily have been mistaken for one of the employees who worked there. She took the elevator up with the deliveryman, who, during the few seconds of their ascension, looked her over from head to toe, with an approving eye. She exited the elevator first, relieved. When she got to the third floor, she walked down the hall and found the company where Johanna worked. It looked like a company that specialized in debt collection. That's not a barrel of laughs, Suzanne thought to herself. She'd imagined so many other things for her daughter... But after all, she was alive and she'd found her, what else could she ask for than getting to know her and going back to their life before? Before fate had separated her from Ricardo and Lisa.

Suzanne saw Jo leave the building for her lunch break with some colleagues, going to a little Indonesian restaurant that was nearby. As she wasn't alone, she couldn't introduce herself to her. Whatever, she knew how to be patient, and anyway, she was still hoping that the young lady would lead her to Ricardo, sooner or later. Fate smiled at her at the end of the day, and she was able to follow her in her car. They drove down the streets in the Northern Territory's capital city, streets with right angles. Johanna had stopped briefly to pick up the man with whom Suzanne had seen her on the balcony. They kissed each other passionately before Jo started off again. *Her daughter in the arms of a man, her daughter in love, her little princess who was now a woman*, she thought bitterly.

When they'd reached Stuart Highway, Suzanne was hoping her dreams would come true.

Which was the case twenty minutes later.

Driving down the highway at 60 mph, Suzanne was wondering where they were going so far from Darwin. Had Johanna decided to take advantage of that Friday during the dry season to spend a weekend at Berry Springs or at Nitmiluk National Park in Katherine? She instinctively glanced at the fuel gauge and was relieved to see she had a full tank, so she wouldn't have to quit tailing her daughter to fill up.

A few miles later, the couple put their left blinker on near Palmerston, signaling their intention of leaving the highway. Suzanne looked at the road sign and recognized the name that Ashley had pronounced on the boat: Zuccoli. She'd said that her parents lived there!

Suzanne thought the distance between her and her past was shrinking.

Zuccoli had all the characteristics of a dormitory town, a purely residential place, something that had recently been built. All the properties, with their carefully mowed lawns, their white walls, their dark gray rooves, most of them sporting solar panels, were on both sides of the straight roads with their still black pavement. All houses had only one story, one or two parking spaces in front of a garage where most of the families had hung a basketball hoop. There nonetheless were some tropical plants here and there in the middle of that modern and sanitized urban jungle.

Johanna's car slowed down, and Suzanne was especially careful not to be spotted tailing her. In all likelihood, Tindill Court, the road on which her daughter had turned, was a dead end. Suzanne drove past it, quickly glancing over and parked her car a bit further on, in an adjacent road. She quickly got out, put her sunglasses on, and began to walk towards Tindill Court on the opposite sidewalk.

She spotted the couple who were nearing the front porch of a house, though as it was starting to get dark, they couldn't see her. They rang the doorbell and waited a few seconds before a fifty-or-so-year-old couple opened the door, welcoming them with open arms.

She was able to make out a few sentences which broke her heart.

"Hi kids, so nice to see you again!"

"Hi, Dad. Hi Mom," Johanna Bolt replied.

Dad. Mom.

Suzanne's legs nearly gave out. Her head was spinning. Her heart, pounding. She was shaking.

That dad, if she was correct, that *dad* could only be Ricardo!

Yet, how could that overweight and nearly bald fifty-year-old – if you didn't count the crown of gray hair Cesar laurel style on his head – be her handsome Latino she'd loved, her Ricardo Gutierrez, the Latino sex-symbol who'd caught the eyes of the fairer sex? No, for Suzanne it was a shock to discover Johanna's *father*.

The shock though was even harsher when the woman, his wife, walked up to kiss Jo.

Though that man couldn't have been Ricardo, that lady, on the other hand, could only have been…

Impossible! Unacceptable!

She didn't believe her eyes! Even with a twenty-year-old distance, that silhouette was engraved in the depths of her memory.

Suzanne Diggs was convinced that she'd already seen her sitting on the bench in Chestnut Street's greenery…

The extra woman

For this new session, the lady had chosen the sofa, saying she preferred to lie down rather than be seated. Dr. Petrossian had suggested that she take her shoes off to be more comfortable and relaxed on the soft couch. He sometimes used hypnosis with some patients, a therapy that worked more easily when patients were extremely relaxed like that.

But it was much too early for that patient. Their dialog had to continue when she was fully aware. Perhaps later it would be the right time to dive deep down into the depths of her subconscious.

"Okay then, Miss. Firstly, how are you feeling right now?"

Her eyes closed, breathing peacefully, the woman could feel that soft couch against her back, her rear, her legs.

"I'm fine. Comfortable. Relaxed. Ready."

"Marvelous! What do you want to talk about today?"

Her eyes were moving quickly behind her closed eyelids.

"Her!"

"Her? Who is she?"

"The Other One. The Intruder. The Evil One. The Extra Woman."

The psychiatrist nodded, taking some notes.

"A lady you don't seem to appreciate, if all of this is true. But why did you say she was 'the extra' woman?"

"Because she's troublesome."

"And consequently?"

"She must be eliminated."

"What do you mean by that?"

"She must disappear..."

"I'm afraid I don't understand here. Have you committed or are you planning on committing some reprehensible act here? Remember, of course, that anything you say here shall remain a medical secret between us. Anything you tell me will never leave these four walls. Unless there are legal consequences? Is this clear?"

"Very clear, Doctor. Don't worry though. I'm not planning on killing anyone."

"That's quite a relief. But you have the right to wish someone were dead, to desire their death. Individuals can think whatever they want, even the darkest thoughts. On the other hand, an action, especially if it is premedi-

tated, is punishable by law. So, tell me, who is that 'extra' person?"

"A woman who's always skulking around us. Around me."

"Who is this 'us'"?

"Me. Ricardo. Lisa. Our family!"

"Do you know that woman? Her name?"

"I don't know her name. Just her face."

"What did you mean when you said she 'was always skulking around you?'"

"I've got the impression that she's always there, behind me, with each step I take. Whatever I do, wherever I go, wherever I am, I see her. Um, I don't always actually see her. Sometimes I just feel her presence. Behind my back. She's always there, behind my head, nearly inside it! Especially when I'm with Ricardo. That's when I feel that she's even more present, more pressing. Snooping. Spying on us. Snooping, spying, two words with the same root, don't you think, Doctor?"

"Probably. Can you describe her?"

The patient shook her head, her eyes closed, immersed in her memories and feelings.

"It's kind of hard, she changes the way she looks quite often. I'd say that she has long dark brown hair, that she's slim, svelte, and Latino typed. I remember I saw her once quite distinctly, one day when I was at home on Chestnut Street."

The doctor didn't interrupt his patient's logorrhea.

"Yes, I remember that day well. I was upstairs, in our bedroom, Ricardo's and mine. I was just killing

time looking out over the road, the comings and goings of people, and that's where I spotted her. I'm sure she was trying to be discreet, but I wasn't born yesterday. I kept my eye on her behind the curtains. She was sitting on the bench across from our gate, on the other side of the street, near the bushes and greenery. She was wearing dark sunglasses and pretending to read the paper, to mask her face probably. But Doctor, no one reads the paper by holding it right in front of their eyes, with their arms raised, and the paper almost touching their glasses! I'm sure she was spying on me."

"Did you go down to confront her?"

"No, I didn't budge. I was tetanized. She scared me. That's what I meant earlier when I told you I wanted her to disappear."

"Not kill her."

"No! I just wanted her to disappear from my sight, from my life, from my head! But I think that's impossible... She'll always be there, never far..."

CHAPTER 42
The multiple heads of a Hydra

New Orleans, July 2024

FINALLY! I had the impression that I'd moved a couple of my pieces on the chessboard of my investigation. After the black squares, now I seemed to be jumping from white square to white square.

My internet research on the "Mover's Gang" gave me a bit of interesting information. I still was not able to link that organization to the nocturnal move at the Gutierrez house on Chestnut Street, but at least I was working on something, not running up against a void, nothing, as had been the case up till now when I was trying to find more information on the double disappearance that took place on August 6, 2004. At least that was a small victory, wasn't it? I had to stop myself from cheering and fist-pumping right in the middle of the café next to my hotel where I'd just ordered a salmon club sandwich to appease my hunger pains.

I was also starving for information, scrolling down page after page, tab after tab, going from one site to another to learn more about that gang.

They said that gang began in Los Angeles in 2000, where the first illegal house movers came to the upper-class neighborhoods of Bel-Air, Beverly Hills, and Melrose. Then very quickly, the same type of criminal acts spread throughout the southern states, soon reaching Louisiana and Florida. That gang was terribly efficient, doing its dirty work for years without being apprehended, up until 2008. That year the FBI took over the investigations and caught them red-handed in Miami, in the middle of the night, while they were loading a safe on the tailgate lift of one of their trucks. Perhaps the same method they'd used at Gutierrez's, I wondered, looking for a photo of that van to no avail.

But that gang's methods must have been emulated, as even after those criminals were tried and sentenced, similar events sporadically took place now and then.

Another hypothesis the investigators had was that the gang was merely a small entity of a much larger organization, that it only represented one of the multiple heads of a larger and more formidable Hydra. That was their conclusion after they'd arrested one of the "movers," a man named Ignacio Galán, someone who wasn't unknown to them. That guy had a criminal record as long as your arm and had been found guilty of a series of wrongdoings for which up till now, he'd only spent a few weeks in prison in various states. That Galán, from El Salvador, belonged to a gang named "Mara Salvatrucha."

My notions of high school Spanish were too ancient for me to know what that meant, though I found the name quite nice. *Mara Salvatrucha*, it seemed like the Latin name of some exotic plant. Though I was quite sure that the crimes and misdemeanors they'd committed were far from being bucolic.

I kept on researching that organization, that Mara Salvatrucha, which was often referred to as the Mafia. It was also shorted to Mara, or simplified by the MS acronym, sometimes also MS-13, and had started in the 80s in Los Angeles. They had begun as a street gang to protect Salvadorian immigrants from other gangs, and rapidly grew to a membership of tens of thousands. And to think I'd never even heard of them! Then they transformed themselves into a criminal organization known for its cruelty, especially to an Angelino gang, the 18th Street Gang. Present in Central America, Mexico, Spain, and Canada, today it had over ten thousand members.

Its many activities, each as shady and underhanded as the others, went from drug and arms trafficking, facilitating clandestine immigration, aggressing the police force, money laundering, racketeering, juvenile prostitution, premeditated murder and hit contracts. Next to all that emptying houses was a mere hobby!

I wondered how the disappearance of Ricardo and

Lisa Gutierrez could be linked to that organization when I learned from an article that people from Central America were Mara Salvatrucha's most common and violent targets. Opposing gangs included the 18th Street Gang, the Juárez Cartel, the Tijuana Cartel, the Camorra, the Trinitarios and the Sombra Negra. Amongst their allies they cited the Mexican Mafia, the Medellín Cartel, the Golf Cartel, Los Zetas, and the Sinaloa Cartel. Friends sometimes became enemies and vice-versa depending on their various acts.

Gutierrez. A resolutely Hispanic name. From South America? Could be. And were Ricardo and Lisa targeted by Mara? The same thing for their Chestnut Street property? Did that gang cause them to disappear? Was Ricardo a member of an opposing gang? I'd have to ask Suzanne what she knew about that. During our video call, she'd told me about memories of not too Catholic activities he'd had or thought he'd had with shady or shifty people. But hadn't given me any names. Something here perhaps?

I sent Suzanne a new message. She hadn't replied to my last one.

> Does the "Mover's Gang" ring a bell with you? Have you ever heard of a criminal organization called Mara Salvatrucha? Did you ever hear the name Ignacio Galán?

But I never got an answer to my trilogy of questions.

CHAPTER 43
Her fantasies and nightmares

Zuccoli, August 2024

IN THE SOUTHERN hemisphere with its own time zone, July had just made way for August, which didn't change a thing for the climate. On the other hand, it was fatal for Suzanne Diggs.

WHEN JOHANNA and her boyfriend went into her parents' house, Suzanne waited a few more minutes before coming out from under the shade where she'd been hiding. She walked to the house and slowed down in front of their mailbox. She tried to read what was written on it without stopping so she wouldn't attract any attention. Luckily for her, their names were engraved sufficiently large enough so that she had no trouble reading them:

Pierce and Maggie Bolt
And their daughters Johanna and Ashley

Pierce Bolt, Maggie Bolt, Suzanne repeated to herself.

So that was the first name of that lady she'd recognized: Maggie. Up till now, she'd never known her name, and had only caught a few glimpses of her, intermittently. She'd come, she'd disappear, she'd come back, she'd leave. Like the time she'd seen her sitting on the bench next to the shrubbery on Chestnut Street.

The one spying on them.

The one running after her in her mind, her dreams, fantasies, and nightmares.

That bitch who undoubtedly had stolen Ricardo and Lisa!

And now, Maggie, that woman with long dark brown hair was there, behind the walls of that house in Zuccoli, with her husband and their two daughters.

Had she won? She'd succeeded! Yes, now Suzanne was persuaded: the woman who'd been spying on them was thus involved in the disappearance of the two people she loved the most. Maybe she wasn't the only one responsible for it, maybe she was a part of a larger organization that wanted Ricardo and Lisa to disappear. She was the beachhead, the one in charge of snooping, of infiltrating the family.

Her instinct hadn't been wrong! For two decades

Suzanne had felt deep down inside that Ricardo was in danger. But from what and why? Was it linked to his relationships? To his activities that didn't always seem clear and to his past that she didn't know much about? She no longer doubted that.

Nonetheless, that man, that Pierce Bolt didn't look like the Ricardo she'd known and loved. So, that Johanna? Could she really have been her Lisa? Or was all this just a part of Suzanne's fantasies, nourished for twenty years, exacerbated for the past couple of days, ever since the day when she thought Ashley was Lisa, then Johanna?

While theorizing, Suzanne continued walking along Tindill Court, going back to her car that was about fifty feet away.

She passed the Bolt property, where she could smell king prawns that were being grilled on a barbecue and could hear the voices of four people who were glad to see each other again. That domestic happiness sparked a muted anger inside her, a devouring jealousy. She wanted to turn around, walk up to their door, ring the bell and tell them everything she'd had in her heart and her mind for the past few minutes, few days, few years, for the past two decades!

What could she say though?

Hello, you are Ricardo and Lisa and that lady, Maggie, is an impostor, a usurper! She's lied to you for your whole lives, she stole my place, she took you away from me. Open your eyes, do something! The game is over, come back with me! I love you, you're mine, your life will now be with me!

Then she changed her mind. Saying things like that would have led her straight to the nearest police station. They would think she was crazy, and she'd be locked up in the looney bin for the rest of her life.

No, she had to be wiser, wittier, cleverer.

And why not tell Karen Blackstone about everything she'd discovered in just two days in Darwin? That would probably help the private detective in her own investigation in New Orleans. Yes, that was what she'd do: get her car and call her when she got back to Darwin.

She left Tindill Court and turned right towards her Toyota. She remotely unlocked the doors. Her lights blinked in the night, guiding her towards her car.

Behind her back she heard that characteristic sound of an electric vehicle that was coming slowly towards her.

Then right when she was about to open the car door, the car stopped next to her and its doors opened.

She didn't have enough time to turn around: a virile hand slapped itself over her mouth and a powerful arm pulled her back. Without realizing what was happening to her, she was dragged to the back seat of a car where two men sat on either side of her as the vehicle sped off like a whirlwind.

All three men were hooded.

Then one of them put a hood on her too.

CHAPTER 44
Enigmatic points

New Orleans, August 2024

We were now in August, which reminded me that the tragedy had taken place twenty years ago. Just a few days before the sixth, I could feel my tension increasing, a sense of urgency, some sort of moral obligation to solve that enigma that Suzanne Diggs had hired me for.

Speaking of which, my dear client had neither answered my calls nor my text messages. I had just tried for the umpteenth time to reach her, knowing that morning here in New Orleans was after dinner in Australia. Suzanne probably wouldn't be in bed yet and I had high hopes of speaking to her.

Hopes dashed.

I'd have to continue without her.

Without help. Alone.

And that was scaring me. My first important investigation was starting to look like a huge fiasco. Clues leading to dead ends, a client on the other side of the world who didn't have the elementary courtesy of picking up the phone when I called, and the feeling of being alone treading water in the muddy quagmire that the Louisiana bayou was famous for.

I suddenly wanted to, needed to hear Paul's voice, Paul who knew how to find the words to quell my doubts when I was floundering.

"Darling," he said with his sophisticated voice. "So nice to hear from you. How is your investigation in Nola going?"

"Not too good actually," I sighed. "I'm sinking in Louisiana's swamps."

"Watch out for the alligators!"

"I was speaking figuratively hun! Don't worry, I've got my feet on the ground but still, I sometimes feel like that ground is crumbling beneath my feet. Or, when I take one step forward, I find myself sinking into a sticky black mire. I'm sure you get the idea!"

"You're having problems then. Things aren't going as planned."

I told him about the little that I did know, and everything I still ignored. He listened to me attentively.

"What about taking a break and coming back to New York for a couple of days? Like your client waited for twenty years, she can wait a couple more days, can't she?"

"I would love to, you know that! But I've still got loads of things to do here."

"How about me coming down then, if it's okay with you, of course."

I began to smile, and a familiar warmth invaded my chest.

"You'd do that for me?"

"What a question! Of course I would, and right now! I'll just hop in my jet and fly down. I'll let you know, but I think I'll soon be able to be with you, right next to you, or even... Anyway, be prepared to thank me with effusion!"

"I am! Hurry up. Paul?"

"Yes?"

"I love you."

"Love you too."

After I'd hung up, I felt more apt to face that new day and my investigations with the hope of seeing my dear Paul soon.

It's always useful in an investigation that's not advancing well to recapitulate, to confront your certainties, doubts and open questions, so I began by listing the enigmatic points that I still was not sure of, at least on this side of the Pacific. What was happening in Australia for the moment only concerned Suzanne Diggs.

For each point, I added when applicable, who I'd

be able to contact to try to obtain some elements of a response.

Firstly, the nocturnal move on Chestnut Street. Did the Mara Salvatrucha gang do it? (Contact the New Orleans police)

Secondly, the costumes of those mascots that were missing on August 6th at Six Flags. Any link with the supposed disappearance of Ricardo and Lisa? If so, why the strange behavior that Josefina and Felix had told me about? (Contact Josefina and Felix, try to join other former Six Flags employees or even managers and owners)

Thirdly, what about the missing video footage shot in the park for August 2004? (Find the person in charge of surveillance)

Fourth, the message that Suzanne discovered in Chestnut Street: *The next time, it won't be Lisa's portrait that's missing...* Who sent it? The Mover's Gang? The Mara? The spy sitting on the bench? (Check with the cops if a complaint on this was filed or if it is more of my client's elucubrations)

Fifth, did Ricardo have any links with the Mafia? Was he a member? A victim? Was he kidnapped, sequestered, assassinated? Or was Lisa the target? (Police, FBI)

Sixth, why aren't there any traces of either of them, in the papers, on the web, nor in the archives of any law enforcement agencies? Not even the missing persons report that Suzanne filed. Or, *supposedly* filed, I suddenly thought. (Police, FBI? Though I already contacted them about that...)

Seventh, has Suzanne been lying to me from the very beginning? And if so, why? (Question Suzanne again, if of course she deigns contact me!)

When I'd finished writing that all up, I understood how many points I still had to check in my investigation. I still had a long way to go.

Before tackling those seven points, I tried to get through to Suzanne once again.

Unsuccessfully.

CHAPTER 45
Really crying out

Australia, August 2024

It was difficult, actually impossible for her to know where she was. Nor how long she'd been there. She had no idea how many hours had gone by since she had been dragged *manu militari* to the back seat of a car by two hooded men.

She was inside four totally nude walls, no decorations and especially no openings, plunging the room into an opaque darkness. She was seated on an uncomfortable chair with her hands cuffed behind her, causing a stabbing pain in her shoulders.

She was hungry. She was thirsty. They hadn't given her anything yet.

When she'd been in the car, she couldn't move in the back seat, squashed between her two heavy kidnappers who had put a hood over her head, masking the view. She was incapable of knowing where she was being taken. Plus, being a foreigner, she wouldn't have recognized anything anyway. So why the heck had they done it? To make it impossible for her to identify her kidnappers? Suzanne knew they weren't just taking her out for a drive, that she had been kidnapped, though she had never anticipated being kept prisoner after the kidnapping.

Sprawled on the chair in the middle of that empty room, the woman wondered with apprehension what would be next. An interrogation? Torture? Rape? What did they want? What had she done?

She couldn't remember how long the car trip had taken. Half an hour? An hour? Two, who knows? She'd lost track of time. Plus she thought they'd put her to sleep. She remembered feeling a sharp pain in her thigh, like a bee sting, and then a few seconds later, a black hole. No memories between that instant and the present time, where Suzanne had woken up on a chair with her hands cuffed.

Luckily or perhaps charitably, they'd taken her hood off. She could breathe easier now and see what little there was to see, as the only lightbulb in the room was off.

Her brain had now defogged a bit and was freed from that torpidity in which the sedative they'd administered had immersed her, and Suzanne suddenly thought of crying out. Shouting. But the voice that emanated from her dry throat sounded more like a crow cawing than a shout that could actually alert anyone.

"Is anyone there?" was what she wanted to ask, but the final result was just a mishmash of vowels.

The consonants ripped her larynx, and words died on her rugged tongue, one that was dry like a sheet of paper mâché. How many hours had it been since she'd not had a drop of water? She even had no saliva left.

The lightbulb suddenly came on. A pale-yellow light that allowed her to discover the nudity of the rectangular room. A small room made from concrete blocks with empty wooden shelves.

"Help!" she tried to cry out.

She heard footsteps from the other side of the only opening, a charcoal grey metallic door. A few seconds later the characteristic sound of a key being turned, then a narrow beam of bright light came in through the crack as the door opened.

Then she saw two huge silhouettes behind the door.

Two men wearing hoods, probably her kidnappers, came into the room, each with a chair. Suzanne instinctively tried to curl up in a little ball, but her position and her cuffed hands made that impossible.

They closed the door and walked to her. They brought their chairs right across from her and straddled them from behind, their arms crossed on the backrest.

They were silent. Waiting.

"Whoever you are, give me something to drink, I'm begging you," she managed to say.

A bottle of water miraculously appeared in front of her, and she tried to grab it. But couldn't because of the handcuffs.

"Unlock me!"

The words left her throat like craggy rugged gravel.

One of her jailers, instead of obeying her, opened the bottle and roughly placed it against her lips that she mechanically and avidly opened. She gulped down the liquid with little quick mouthfuls. For her it was a benediction, but, like an anatomical reflex, that intake of water reminded her that her stomach had been empty for hours, perhaps for an entire day, which she instinctively thought. Now she was gulping down larger mouthfuls until the man took the bottle from her. Water was running down her chin, neck, into her bra.

Neither of her aggressors had said a word.

"What do you want? What did I do? Why me? I'm an American citizen, you're taking a big risk here," she managed to say, hoping they'd understand the threat. "And who are you? Take your hoods off you cowards!"

"Who the hell are you lady?" one of the men with a powerful and authoritarian voice replied.

CHAPTER 46
My joker

New Orleans, August 2024

I was furious that I could no longer use Billy Jensen's method as my sponsored Meta account had been disactivated. I would have liked to use it for other research such as the nocturnal move at the Gutierrez place in the summer of 2004. I'm sure I would have learned something useful. I could have gone fishing for info on Mara Salvatrucha, as I knew that the gang had been active since the 80s in North America. Too many "*coulds*" and "*woulds...*" I'd now have to resort to more traditional methods.

I wanted to understand the link, if there was one, between Ricardo Gutierrez and Mara Salvatrucha or the Mover's Gang. But I'd run into a big problem: there wasn't any trace of a dude named Ricardo

Gutierrez anywhere! Not on the web, not in the papers. Nowhere! As if he'd never even existed!

Nowadays it's quite rare that you can't find any information about a name when you enter it into Google. Most people have at least Facebook, Instagram, Twitter, LinkedIn or some other social networking service profile. People exist, at least virtually! Of course, the Gutierrez case went back to 2004, which was the year that Mark Zuckerberg had created his photo gallery for his Harvard friends, and at the beginning it was only for students at that Ivy League university. It only opened, albeit in a primitive form to others in 2006. But Ricardo Gutierrez and his daughter disappeared in 2004 without any traces either in real life or on the networks. They didn't exist *before* 2004 nor *after*...

Except in Suzanne Diggs's memory, something I was sure of. But what if Ricardo and Lisa only existed in her head? If they were a fantasy of hers? Suzanne seemed to know the truth — *her* truth — defending it against anyone and everyone: the cops, the Feds, Ricardo and Lisa, and me. Was she against me and not with me? Was she alone against everyone?

If that was true, I had no reason to continue with my investigation. I could tell her I'd quit, break our moral contact, refuse any more money from her and start working on another case, a more traditional one, one where someone had *really* gone missing, with real people and not fantasies and elucubrations.

At the same time though, there were a few unsettling elements: that nocturnal move, the Six Flags mascots, what the old lady Kellermann had told me, and other little things.

Something had happened, but what?

With things like this, when my investigations lead me straight into a brick wall, an unsolvable problem, I take out my bag of tricks, my trump, my joker.

Spider!

When I can't find anything on the internet, when my police contacts or private colleagues have dried up, I always turn to my favorite hacker, my shadowy snitch. I know nothing about this guy except that he has an Eastern Europe accent. I have no idea of his real name, what he looks like, nor how old he is, but he was useful and often indispensable to me. He had a gift, and not one to be despised, of being able to surf on the internet's deepest and darkest layers, what he called the deep web, and below that, the dark web. There where drug or arms dealers do their nefarious deeds. There where financial hackers, 2.0 terrorists and cybercops chase each other, the first ones winding their ways through the holes in the net held by the second ones, in a constant cat and mouse game. Spider was at ease in that universe where he was able to access unexpected resources for me, files that normal people like me could never reach, secret defense and things like that.

While calling him, I was hoping he'd be able to help me out of that dead end where I seemed to be and give me a helping hand.

"Hey! Miss Karen Blackstone, it's been a while!" he

said cheerfully when he picked up. "What's up? Miss me? Looking for a good tip again?"

"Spider, you should do comedy! If you weren't so useful to me I don't know if I'd even have a cup of coffee with you..."

"You know I never leave my four walls, so for the coffee, it's just not gonna happen! So tell me what I can do for you this time even if you don't like me."

I gave him an outline of my investigation.

"But the person named Ricardo Gutierrez, and his daughter Lisa Gutierrez, seem not to exist anywhere except in my client's mind. I can't find anything about either of them. I thought that maybe, you'd be able to find something in your secret hiding places, in the abysses of internet where you spend all your time."

"Maybe I could," he croaked. "*Nothing ventured, nothing gained*. Anything else?"

"Yes, if you find some new information about a Mover's Gang and an organization named Mara Salvatrucha, I'll take that too."

"It's noted. That's it?"

"That's already not bad, because in my humble opinion, this is going to cost me, as usual..."

"*Hard work deserves a fair reward*, you know that better than anyone. I'm on it. You need that for when? The day before yesterday?"

"You're cracking me up, Spider. As soon as possible, thanks. Ah! There's one more thing. Can you see what you can find on my client? Her name is Suzanne Diggs."

"Consider it done. You can pay me like you usually do."

"Which I will."

"I'll send you an SMS."

I hung up and in the following minute I received a text message from a hidden number with the bank details of an offshore account for the wire transfer, with the amount in Spider's message. And it was a hefty one. But that time I wouldn't be giving an expense slip to Myrtille Fairbanks, my former boss. This time Blackstone Investigations would be paying with its own money! Not quite the same thing!

CHAPTER 47
The insanity

AUSTRALIA, August 2024

"I'm starving," Suzanne Diggs implored. "I'll only answer your questions after I've had something to eat."

The man across from her, straddling his chair, shook his head while making little irritated noises with his tongue.

"Tsk, tsk, tsk, you're not the one who decides here. You don't have anything to negotiate with."

When he said that, he made a mocking move with his chin towards the handcuffs, something Suzanne of course noticed.

"Unlock me!" the prisoner ordered once again. "You don't have the right. You'll regret this."

"Little lady, you're mixing up the roles here. Did you even wonder for a second what your rights are?

What are you doing in Darwin? What are you doing in Australia?"

"I'm on vacation! You don't allow tourists in Australia? I know that your government is very protective of its citizens, but still, you're going a little too far here."

"Don't try to be cute, Suzanne."

"I see you know my name," the lady said bitterly.

"Of course we do. We've known it for ages. For too long, if you want to know. And now it's time to put an end to all this. And we think we also know what you're doing in this country. We've had an eye on you ever since you set foot here, Mrs. Diggs. In Hervey Bay, we were never far from you…"

When he said those words, images and scenes came back to Suzanne.

"When someone snatched my purse and put that threatening note inside it, that was you then."

"Not me personally, but probably one of our guys. I don't have the gift of ubiquity!"

"Your guys? What organization do you belong to?"

"I'm not answering that question. You can guess. I'm sure you've got a couple of ideas in that little head of yours. But don't worry about that, it's not important if we belong to X or Y. What is important is that you stop playing your little games."

"My little games? My conscience is clear. Which is not the case for everyone in this room. What do you want? What are you going to do with me?"

"I think you'll find the answers to those questions

all by yourself. All you have to do is rewind the roll of film of your memories."

"You are crazy!" shouted the prisoner. "Let me loose and give me something to eat!"

"We're the ones who are crazy? You got some nerve, lady!"

The man sitting across from her sighed and gestured to the other guy.

"Go get her something to eat so she'll shut up."

The second jailer obeyed. So there's some hierarchy here, thought Suzanne. While he was gone, the questions continued.

"What were you doing last night in front of the Bolt's house in Zuccoli? We followed you there. Why were you spying on them? Why did you follow their oldest daughter? And why did you approach their youngest daughter in Hervey Bay? What have you got against that family?"

That time it was the lady who laughed ironically.

"I think you know just as well as I do because you tried to prevent me..."

"Mrs. Diggs, this deaf man's dialogue is getting on my nerves. You know we're both playing a con game. I know perfectly well what you're up to and you know that we know. Like we know that you know. So what's important now is that you stop."

"Stop what? With who? What are you planning on doing with me? Eliminating me?"

"I can't answer those questions now. I'm waiting

for orders from above. Till then my role consists in keeping you away from the Bolts. And vice-versa."

Right then the other hooded man walked in, a plate in his hand with a measly sandwich in it. He put it down at the foot of the prisoner and unlocked her handcuffs.

"Don't do anything stupid," he ordered.

Freed, Suzanne vigorously rubbed her aching wrists and greedily grabbed the sandwich.

Then the one who had been sitting got up and both turned around and picked up their chairs. Before leaving the one who seemed to be the boss had one more thing to say.

"Take advantage of your stay her to think things over."

"Think what over?" Suzanne articulated, her mouth still full and not caring that crumbs were falling from her lips.

"To the insanity that led you to this, let's say, unpleasant situation."

Then the heavy door squeaked on its hinges and closed in a muffled noise. A few seconds later, the lightbulb was turned off, leaving Suzanne alone in the dark.

CHAPTER 48
Old-school

New Orleans, August 2024

IN THE EVENING of that new August day in Nola, I still hadn't had any news from Spider. On the other hand, I was overjoyed at the wheel of my rental when driving to New Orleans Lakefront Airport, a much more intimate one than Louis Armstrong International where I'd disembarked a few days ago. Paul had an ETA of five pm. My fear of flying made it complicated for me to hop on a plane, and I admired the courage that my boyfriend, if I could use that term, had, an experienced pilot though he was still young. He had his own private jet, one he'd inherited from his parents, and it allowed him to fly much easier and faster than taking commercial flights. He felt as free as a bird in the sky when he was in the cockpit. As for me, a tiny plane like that scared me even more than a big Boeing or Airbus. Who knows, maybe I was wrong.

Paul knew that I'd never set foot in his little plaything. The only time I had was right at the beginning of our story, a short trip from Long Island to Manhattan. A round trip at night, one that ended in our first kiss.

When I saw his plane from the arrivals' terminal bay windows on the taxiway, I was relieved that he'd landed. I was already trembling at the idea he'd be hugging me in a few minutes, after he'd filled out the paperwork.

Finally, a few minutes later, I rushed up to him and hugged him tightly.

"Oh! I can't tell you how good it feels to smell you," I whispered.

"Honey, do you like the way kerosene smells?"

"Don't be silly! Come on! Let's get out of this place, I'm taking you to dinner in the Vieux Carré!"

THE VIEUX CARRÉ, or more simply the French Quarter, was Nola's historical district. The ideal place for a romantic meal, and that evening we'd walk up and down the streets with their Creole architecture and atmosphere, something that was quite a change of scenery for a New Yorker used to huge glass and steel buildings in Manhattan. We finished our little walk in Rue Saint-Louis where I'd reserved a table at

Antoine's, a Creole restaurant said to be the oldest one in the entire city.

We sat down and I decided to have a grilled Louisiana redfish served with an oyster white butter sauce over pilaf rice with fried mushrooms and onions. As for my dear Paul, he was tempted by a beef stew in red wine sauce with shallots served with homemade mashed potatoes. All of that accompanied by a divine bottle of Chardonnay.

I felt like forgetting my ongoing investigation during our romantic meal. Yet, I couldn't forget Suzanne "and company" though the meal was mouthwatering and the wine delicious. Despite myself, I brought up the subject.

I gave Paul a short version of my progress and setbacks, small victories and heavy frustrations, when he interrupted me.

"Seeing's how new technologies are closed for you, why don't you try to work old-school style then?"

"Old-school? From door to door? I already did that on Chestnut Street."

"I'm talking about doing the same thing on a larger scale, in a larger neighborhood."

"That takes ages and it's far from guaranteeing results, especially when you think that all this happened twenty years ago."

"Exactly. That's why I'm suggesting a cheap method - one that's cheap moneywise and cheap timewise: distributing and posting flyers! You stuff mailboxes in the whole neighborhood, and you stick little posters up on every streetlight or stop sign in the roads around your target. You explain what you're looking for briefly, you leave your phone number, and you wait until something falls into your lap, like ripe apples falling from trees. I'll help you, I love playing tourists! Before social networking, that's how we did things. Your cat didn't come home at night, someone stole your bike, you found some keys, stuff like that and it usually worked."

"You're right, it's simple and cheap and I don't understand why I didn't think of it myself."

"Because you've got the detective 2.0 mindset! I'm more down to earth. Okay, I'm younger than you, but still I'm sometimes old school! Plus you put an ad in the local paper, and *voilà* !"

Like he said, *voilà*, that's one of the reasons I love him: his complementary way of seeing things. That's why I felt so much lighter since he arrived in New Orleans: I knew I could count on his support and priceless help.

I took a long sip of my Chardonnay, appreciating it.

"Paul, what would I do without you?"

"You'd still be the most beautiful woman on earth, but probably for other eyes."

Then I heard a "ping" on my phone, that I'd forgotten to turn off when we entered the restaurant, something I usually do as I hate hearing phones ring when I'm dining. I took my phone out and saw that Spider had sent me a text message. I couldn't prevent myself from reading it after having apologized to Paul, who nodded in acquiescence.

A few words, leaving me speechless.

> I found your Ricardo!

CHAPTER 49
A divine apparition

Australia, August 2024

Her throat burning, Suzanne Diggs wondered if there was someone that could hear her behind that horrible metallic door. Lying down on a mattress that they'd seen fit to bring her a few hours ago and that they'd put in a corner of her jail, as that's how she referred to it, she was tired, but above all, hungry and thirsty.

"I have to pee!" she shouted for the umpteenth time, when she finally heard the door creaking on its hinges. There was a beam of light that came through at the same time as the lightbulb in the empty room was turned on.

One of her kidnappers, his face dissimulated by a mask, walked up to her with firm and determined footsteps, his massive and powerful silhouette in the shadows.

"Can't you shut up?" he shouted to her. "It's late."

"Dammit I have no idea what time it is!" the prisoner burst out. "I have to go to the bathroom and now, or I'm going to wet myself."

"Your wish is our command, Ma'am," replied the man cunningly putting down a pail. "Your portable toilet."

"I'm not going to go in that!"

"You'll wet yourself then. I personally couldn't care less. Do whatever you want. Don't worry about me though, I'm not going to look. I'm leaving. Don't panic, I'll leave the light on, I'm a nice guy actually. I wouldn't want you to pee on the floor!"

He left, snickering to himself while Suzanne rushed to the pail, forgetting any modesty, quickly dropping her slacks and panties to finally go to the bathroom.

She sat there quite a while, pants down and her bladder finally emptied out, letting her mind flow back to distant souvenirs. A prisoner with nothing to do, all that was left was that typically human occupation: recalling memories. Going back in time, back to the origins of her life. At least for that life she was still fighting for: her relationship with Ricardo Gutierrez, the only man who had counted for her.

Sitting on her makeshift toilet, she remembered the day they'd met. It was impossible to forget that date, it was Independence Day.

New Orleans, July 4, 1988.

The very first time she saw him, it was like a divine apparition. To that starry-eyed young girl, it was as if he had a halo above his head. Though there was a crowd surrounding him, he was the only one who she saw. She was subjugated by his jet-black hair, his dark eyes and his sparkling smile.

Just like many other Louisianians, they'd gone to the banks of the Mississippi to admire the traditional fireworks display that would be shot off from two barges. Fate had brought them together on a grassy spot in Woldenberg Park, right on the riverside, whereas others would be watching from the French Quarter or for those who were really lucky, from the Creole Queen dock, a paddle steamer where jazz musicians would be playing all evening.

Above them there were red, blue and white fireworks illuminating the sky over Nola. Spectators were clapping and shouting out admiratively in front of that stunning pyrotechnical achievement over the peaceful Mississippi River.

Suzanne suddenly lost her balance, because her head was turned towards the sky, and fell against the shoulder of that very man whose presence had her tingling that whole evening just as much as the fireworks display.

"Excuse me, I'm so sorry," she said before pulling away from him.

"No problem, you can lean against me if it's more comfortable for you."

"No, really, I don't know what to say."

Though she certainly had some ideas. She would have sold mother and father to put her head up against his powerful yet tender shoulder.

When the firecrackers and fireworks had ended, they continued the late evening together, walking through the French Quarter where there were a host of impromptu concerts and amateur shows. That atmosphere summed up the Cajun motto: "Let the good times roll." And the times were good. Everything was rolling for them.

He'd left his friends to be with her. She was flattered. For her it was the first time that a man — a real man, not a pimply faced teenager — seemed sincerely interested in her, at least not just for her body. And he incidentally behaved as a perfect gentleman, only wanting to spend a pleasant evening with her, almost a sleepless night, to celebrate Independence Day.

After that memorable evening, he'd hinted that he'd love to see her again and asked her for her phone number, so he'd be able to set something up soon.

She accepted, and he found her lips. She allowed him to kiss her, instantly intoxicated by happiness, pleasure and hope.

Those moments had been the very first ones of a

life of tormented feelings, one that would end a few years later in the worst possible way.

CHAPTER 50
A whole new life

New Orleans, August 2024

Paul and I quickly finished our dinner. I couldn't wait to answer Spider's message. Even better, to actually speak to him, which was what I did as soon as we left Antoine's.

In the lively French Quarter, I jumped as soon as Spider answered.

"Spider, you're a lifesaver! You really found Ricardo Gutierrez?"

"Ah! I knew I'd be hearing from you soon. And to be honest, I had fun arousing your curiosity with my short message. But strictly speaking, I neither found nor located Ricardo. Let's just say that I was able to, just like a modern bloodhound, find out more about your rascal. And let me tell you, quite the rascal he certainly is!"

My head was spinning. Was it from what he had just told me, or the bottle of Chardonnay that Paul and I had downed? I urged him to continue.

"Spit it out Spider! What did you find?"

"So, you know that the web has several different layers. The everyday web that everyone uses, then the deep web and after that the dark web, and for us, our research goes back twenty years. At that time, the internet was far from being what it is nowadays, you probably remember names like Netscape, Yahoo, and AOL. Or to put it otherwise, it's like trying to unearth a diamond at the very bottom of a mine. So Karen, with your research, you hit the first layer, the web everyone can access and where your Ricardo guy can't be found. Neither *before* nor *after* 2004. But on my web, I found Ricardo Gutierrez. On the other hand, I didn't find a single thing either *before* 2004 or *after* that date, which tends to prove that something did happen, and that date was a turning point."

"His disappearance at Six Flags."

"Maybe. But I couldn't exhume anything precise about that. It is like Ricardo Gutierrez ceased to exist after 2004."

"That's virtually the case," I agreed.

"That's the right word, Karen. Virtually. Because I personally can't affirm nor infirm his physical presence."

"Nonetheless, that's what my client is affirming. That Ricardo and her daughter Lisa physically disappeared in 2004. As if they were dead."

"They are," Spider stated.

That answer took my breath away. That answer, though it did confirm one of my hypotheses, was devastating.

"You're sure about that?"

"Not at all," my 2.0 snitch quickly replied. "To some degree I can affirm that they are dead. Or should I say that their names are dead. As of 2004, they no longer exist anywhere. If you want, I can give you my own personal opinion on the question, as I've already seen cases like that before."

"Of course I do. Spider, you're playing with my nerves here, that's not very Christian."

"That's good, I'm an atheist. Puns aside, I'll tell you what I think without charging you. I'm quite the philanthropist, aren't I Karen?"

"You're really getting irritating now Spider. Spill the beans, dammit!"

On the other end of the line I could hear him burst into laughter so loud it nearly exploded my tympan. I could imagine him bent over in front of his multitude of computer screens. I imagined him as a young man who was an eternal teenager, with a baby face and quite overweight because he never budged from his seat. Of course I could have been totally wrong, but right now, that was the least of my worries.

"Yes, ma'am! You're not gonna have to clean up after me. Here's my theory. In similar cases to this one, it's been proved that the name of the person who suddenly disappeared was just an alias."

"An alias?" I repeated stupidly, though I had understood.

"A pseudonym, in other words. A first and last name used for a specific purpose, that after the end of a given event, are suddenly no longer useful. That's why that pseudonym isn't used anymore and thus you can't find it anywhere. In a nutshell, it's not the *person* Ricardo Gutierrez who vanished, it's the *pseudo* Ricardo Gutierrez that's disappeared. There's a nuance there! After 2004, either that person went back to using his real name, or else he changed it once again, and he's living a whole new life now!"

CHAPTER 51
As silent as the grave

AUSTRALIA, August 2024

HER KIDNAPPERS WERE the ones who decided when it was day and when it was night for her. They lit or turned off that lightbulb whenever they felt like it, which in that makeshift prison without any windows, left Suzanne completely disoriented. She'd lost track of time. How many days had gone by since she'd been kidnapped in that peaceful little town of Zuccoli? And who were those kidnappers who kept their faces hidden? She had wondered about that, going back to what had happened in the past weeks, months and years, without however reaching a satisfactory conclusion. She did know she was bothering some people. Those men visibly were members of the same organization that had snatched her purse in Hervey Bay. She'd been followed.

Suzanne was intimately convinced that she wasn't the prey of some tiny Australian group. She'd been tracked. Every movement she'd made she'd been spied on, ever since she'd set foot in Australia. At least from the moment she'd gotten close to Ashley after she spotted her at the ice cream shop.

All she could do there was think, so the prisoner unbridled her mind and memory. She remembered some signs years before that had troubled her, without being able to put her finger on what was bothering her or its origin. Like she was being watched or followed. That was especially true in the first months after Ricardo and Lisa had vanished. Like an individual was watching her at each intersection. When she was at her window looking outside, sometimes she thought she'd noticed the silhouette of that man, one of the men following her. Someone had had their eyes on her.

Were they afraid of her?

One thing led to another and using an original and unusual association of ideas, her thoughts went back to that blessed era in her relationship with Ricardo. Blessed up to a point, Suzanne thought bitterly, back to one day where she'd dared ask him something.

∼

New Orleans, January 1999

. . .

Their romantic idyll had already lasted for six months. They saw each other intermittently, generally speaking when Ricardo initiated it, when he wanted to and when he was available, as he was a busy man, often absent, "on business trips" as he always said. What business? He'd never told her.

He was the one who decided when they'd go out, often in the French Quarter, to the iconic places where they'd first met. On the banks of the Mississippi or in the Vieux Carré, as long as it wasn't raining. When it got colder, they'd generally go to a hotel, or later on, to her place. She'd opened the doors of her home, her heart and her body. Suzanne quickly trusted that man who reassured her, knowing she could rest her head on his large shoulders.

But there quickly was a breach, like a stab wound, in their relationship. One afternoon in January, they were lying nude on her bed, in her little apartment. They'd just made love with a mixture of zeal and true affection when, taking advantage of his dreamy post-coital state, she dared ask him a question.

"Don't you think it's time for us to think of living together? What if I moved to your place? You never took me there."

Suzanne was undoubtedly both very naive and innocent. She was head over heels in love with Ricardo. A six-month up-and-down liaison for her was a total of intense moments she wanted to increase by adding them together, multiplying them until the moment her man would only be hers, hers alone, every day, every second. She needed him, she couldn't get by without him, without his caresses, his kisses, his warmth, his attention, his words, without everything that made them a real couple.

But the dark glint she'd seen in Ricardo's eyes after her suggestion scared her. And his scathing answer, even more.

"No way! Don't even think about it!"

At first she was as silent as the grave, her mouth gaping, incapable of pronouncing a single word. She got her breath back after an apnea due to her stupefaction.

"But Ricardo... come on. Why? I love you. You love me. We love each other. I thought we were a couple now..."

The man sighed, remained silent for a moment, before replying, this time in a kinder voice.

"Yes, we *are* sort of a couple. Yes, I love you. But Suzanne, I can't live with you. It's impossible."

"Why?"

"Because... I'm not a man you want to get attached to. I need my freedom and solitude too, sometimes. I'm not someone you want to be seen with!"

"Of course I do! I sincerely appreciate being with you. I feel so good when I'm with you."

"Suzanne, you don't know who I am. You don't know anything about me!"

"Well, tell me then, tell me everything" she begged, putting her head on his brown-haired chest.

But he pulled away, as if nauseated by her contact.

"Suzanne, shut the fuck up! I'm telling you I'm not someone you want to be seen with. All I'd do would be to get you in trouble."

CHAPTER 52

A couple of extra bucks

New Orleans, August 2024

I STILL HADN'T GOTTEN over what Spider had just told me on the phone. I had sort of thought that there was a possibility he had been using a pseudonym, but now it was confirmed.

"A whole new life," I repeated, pensively. "With a new name. But which one?"

"That, I have no idea of. I couldn't get an answer. What's your client's name again?"

Suzanne Diggs, with two Gs. Why?"

"What if Ricardo Gutierrez had become Ricardo Diggs?" Spider suggested. "I'll try to dig around, ha-ha, pun intended."

"I don't think that'll work. What I'd like you to do would be to follow a lead that might seem crazy to you at first sight, but when you think it over…"

"What?"

"So like I told you when I first called you, my client, who's in Australia right now, hired me when she thought she recognized her long-lost daughter, Lisa, as the girl selling ice cream and who was named Ashley Bolt."

"Twenty years after she went missing."

"That's right. But it turns out that Ashley was only nineteen, so she couldn't have been Lisa. However, her older sister, a girl named Johanna Bolt, could correspond to a twenty-two-year-old Lisa today. So, to come back to the beginning, Spider, maybe Ricardo is now named Ricardo Bolt and lives in Australia?"

"Why not?" admitted my secret informant. "We could look at it that way. And have you done anything about that yet, Karen?"

"Nope. But I've only got partial elements on that subject," I humbly recognized. "The last time I was able to talk to talk to my client, she was getting ready to leave for Darwin where Johanna Bolt is supposed to be living. But that doesn't tell me where her parents live, or even her father's first name. Nothing proves that it's Ricardo under a new identity. That could be anyone!"

I could hear Spider clicking away on his keyboard. Then he stopped.

"Would you like me to do some research starting on what I've got, meaning Hervey Bay, Darwin, Ashley and Johanna Bolt?"

"Well, knowing your resources, much better than my humble ones, I'm sure that you'll get better results than me. And more rapidly. Would you take on this supplement?"

"My pleasure, Karen!"

"I'd assume you'd be wanting a couple of extra bucks for that?"

"You're getting to know me well. Isn't there an old saying that says *all work deserves to be rewarded*?

"I'm sure there is. How much?"

"Two hundred. In advance. Same account as last time."

"It's a deal!"

Spider was an efficient guy. Ever since I'd begun using his services, I'd never been disappointed. He worked quickly and was a professional. He continued.

"In the meanwhile, I still owe you some info about my previous research. About the Mover's Gang and the Mara Salvatrucha gang too. I cross-checked data with what I'd obtained on Ricardo Gutierrez, and it matched!"

"Really?"

"More or less. There isn't much data left, at least not on your ordinary web, but the dark web has spoken, and the name of Ricardo Gutierrez comes up every once in a while, not necessarily directly linked to Mara Salvatrucha, but with occurrences that lead me to think they're sort of *parallel*. I'll explain, Karen. So I'll start with a short history of the gang — or the mafia — whatever you want to call it. The Mara Salvatrucha gang began in 1970 in Central America, in El Salvadore precisely. And Ricardo Gutierrez also was born in 1970 there. After that the Mara moved to Los Angeles in the 80s, with the goal of protecting Salvadorian immigrants from other gangs in the region, Mexican, Asian or African-American ones. Ricardo Gutierrez lived in Los Angeles for several years, from 1985 to the middle of the 90s. Age fifteen to twenty-five or so. That criminal organization enrolled young people, teens, sometimes even earlier. Then the Mara spread into different states in the USA, especially in the south of the country and it reached Louisiana in 1995. Ricardo Gutierrez moved to New Orleans in... 1995. See where I'm going with this?"

I didn't believe my ears.

"That is troubling," I confirmed.

Paul and I were seated on a bench on the banks of the Mississippi, a place much calmer than the noisy streets in the historical center of town. With my phone cornered between my shoulder and ear, I was taking notes in my notebook while Spider was giving me information. My brain-fog, stemming from one too many glasses of Chardonnay, had cleared. I could now think straight. He continued.

"There's nothing that allows me to affirm however that he's linked to Mara Salvatrucha, but you have to admit that they seem to have a parallel path."

"Undeniably so."

Before concluding our phone call and starting a new investigation, Spider advanced another of his pawns.

"So, to conclude then, I looked for any information about an event that had taken place in Six Flags in August of 2004, but once again, I ran up against a wall of empty pages. Nonetheless, there was a little something that pinged in my tiny brain when I read articles about Mara Salvatrucha's range of actions: I read that some of their militant groups had been suspected of or even arrested and sentenced in the 90s and 2000s for kidnapping of children and demanding ransoms. Did you think of that hypothesis for Lisa Gutierrez?"

"I did but couldn't find anything to back it up. Do you think that because we haven't found anything about a kidnapping and ransom gang that it means that it wasn't the case?"

"Nothing's impossible," Spider said laconically.

CHAPTER 53
Her real place

Australia, August 2024

It seemed to Suzanne that at least a week had gone by — second after second, like an IV drip — since she'd been kidnapped in Zuccoli. Yet it had just been forty-eight hours at the most.

But how can't you lose track of time in conditions like that? And what did they want from her? All she was doing was looking for her partner and daughter. Her family. And why were they hiding their faces? Who were those people who, though keeping her a prisoner, didn't seem to hate her? If she was a problem for them, why didn't they just eliminate her? It would have been easy, there weren't any witnesses, she was abroad, no one except for Ashley Bolt and that detective she'd hired had any idea where she was. On the other hand, Ashley believed she was in Sydney as she'd lied to her about her destination when leaving Hervey Bay!

When she thought of Karen Blackstone, she had a bit of hope. Maybe she'd be able to find her! That private detective would move heaven and earth to pinpoint her client. Too bad they'd taken her cell phone, the prisoner bitterly regretted. At least Karen knew, after their last phone call from Brisbane Airport, that Suzanne was leaving for the capital of the Northern Territory.

Suzanne sat up on her poor excuse for a mattress they'd given her earlier, her back aching. When they had the goodness of their hearts to leave the lightbulb on, she'd pace back and forth in the thirty square feet of her room to get the circulation going in her legs. She'd quit screaming and shouting to be released a long time ago. She was now resigned, and as they'd told her to think things over until she knew what brought her here, that is what she did. That was even all she did! She went upstream in her memories, just like a salmon swimming back to its origins, and remembered the years before she was separated from Ricardo and Lisa.

She suddenly recollected those difficult months that had followed that day when Ricardo had dissuaded her from moving in with him.

∽

New Orleans, December 1999

The year 1999 wasn't a good one for Suzanne. Since her little spat with Ricardo last winter, their relationship was both tense and stretched.

When he'd told her to "shut the fuck up" – those were his exact same words, words that hurt her deeply –, at first she obeyed, was docile. As he considered himself as someone you wouldn't want to be seen with, it was better for her to distance herself. Except that was only theory! It wouldn't work with her ideal lover. She couldn't get enough of him... She undoubtedly was still just a starry-eyed young girl. They didn't have the same background. She didn't have the Latino blood that flowed through the veins of that Salvadorian, with all that it implied of pride, courage, and violence. She didn't share his troubled past that she guessed by snippets when he consented to give her some hints about it or when she was spying on him.

Because Suzanne sometimes did spy on Ricardo. She had such a thirst to see him, feel him next to her, that she couldn't help but follow him right up to his home. He lived in the Garden District, one of Nola's most expensive neighborhoods, right next to the river. A sumptuous villa, surrounded by impenetrable walls. She'd often followed him and regularly sat on a bench in the foliage of the street to watch him live his life... his life without her. She often was nearly physically sick with pain, with her stomach in a knot, when she'd see him at the wheel of a sports car, sometimes accompanied by a woman. A woman she of course instantly hated.

A woman who had taken her place, the one she should have had! She should have been the one seated on the leather passenger seat in that car! She should have been the one living there. She should have been Ricardo's wife.

She should have been the one he loved!

From time to time he met up with her in the afternoon in a small hotel in the French Quarter they both liked, because it reminded them of their very first time. The room, with its wrought iron balcony overlooking the Mississippi, was where they feverishly had first made love. Of course, maybe they saw each other less, but they loved each other even more, like famished animals.

But Suzanne still wanted more, more from him. It had become an obsession.

Months went by and 1999 wound to an end, and on that day in December, right before Christmas, Ricardo and Suzanne were strolling down Canal Street where all the palm trees in the street were illuminated with Christmas lights and topped with crowns. It was nice out, they had their arms around each other, they were admiring the Christmas decorations. Suzanne could feel that that day Christmas magic had made Ricardo even nicer, even more loveable.

They made love that night in their hotel room with its balcony decorated with lights.

That was the beginning of a whole new era in their chaotic relationship.

An era of happiness, one where Suzanne finally had the place she deserved.

Her place.

CHAPTER 54
Curriculum

New Orleans, August 2024

Our night, though interrupted by tender moments, was a restorative one. Both Paul and I needed some rest. My investigation was advancing step by step, characters were becoming a bit clearer than they were the first days I'd arrived in Nola. But each day that passed without any news from Suzanne despite my numerous calls worried me more and more. The last time I called, it went directly to her voicemail, as if her battery was dead.

After a hearty breakfast, I created a flyer on my laptop and asked the person at the front desk to print out fifty of them. I admired the results when they brought them to my room, already cut in a 4"x 6" postcard size.

Call for witnesses

For an investigation into missing people

We are looking for information from neighbors, friends, merchants, anyone who knew the Gutierrez family — Ricardo, Lisa and Suzanne (Diggs) — who lived on 1253 Chestnut Street until August 2004.

If you can think of anything, though it may seem insignificant to you, please contact us — ask for Karen — 212-509-6999.

Each clue could save someone's life. Or that of several people.

I CUT and pasted that ad and ordered it to be published on the website of the local paper. Don't always put all your eggs in the same basket (or same can of worms?).

After that I bought what I needed in a drugstore not too far from the hotel and then Paul and I drove to the Garden District to start putting those posters up. That reminded me of back in the day, when I was a student we'd go around our university putting up posters for events or programs at our theater.

After we'd put glue on the back of the flyers, we firmly pressed them against each available stoplight or streetlight, hoping that they'd be visible. We did the best we could so they wouldn't drown in the midst of other tracts which nauseated me, most of them with a feminine first name and a phone number only.

"Prostitution today," regretted Paul.

"Often students who need money for living expenses after having paid out a fortune in tuition."

"And who are known as escorts, for the politically correct. I hate stuff like that. I can imagine a father, a mother, or a brother happening upon an ad like that..."

"They're just pseudos'! You think they're all named Lolita, Almira or Tenebra?"

"I think that's disgusting," Paul said, ripping off a couple of those foul ads to replace them by my call for witnesses.

Once we'd finished, all that was left to do was to check my phone with the hope that I'd soon obtain some hypothetically useful information.

A few minutes later my phone rang!

"Karen? Spider here. You're gonna be proud of me."

"Wow! You never sleep?"

"I don't have an exhausting lifestyle," my hacker eluded. "So, if you're still interested, I've got the curriculum of the whole Bolt family."

"Of course it does. That's what I'm paying you for!

Give me a couple of minutes so I can find a place to sit down and take notes. I'll get back to you."

Paul and I walked down the street until we found a nice bench located in the shade with bushes at the back of it. By a malicious act of Lady Luck, that bench was right across from the house the Gutierrez's formerly owned, now owned by Mr. and Mrs. Clark. I called Spider back.

"I'm all ears."

"Here we go. The Bolt family is a family of four. The father, Pierce, born in Perth in 1968. The mother, Maggie, born in Brisbane in 1972. The oldest daughter, Johanna, born in Perth in 2002. And Ashley, the youngest daughter, born in Darwin in December of 2005. You already heard of the last two, right?"

"Exactly, those were the names my client gave me. Keep on going."

"The parents have lived in Zuccoli since 2010. It's a little commuter town in the suburbs of Palmerston, in the south-west of Darwin, Northern Territory. It's a new city that was built officially in 2007, as Darwin was spreading at the speed of light, a dynamic city. You wanna know where that cute name of Zuccoli came from?"

"Sure. Why?"

"The town was named after a guy called Guido Zuccoli, a pilot who was specialized in acrobatics in the air, also a businessman in aeronautics, someone well known in the Northern Territory because that's where he crashed in 1997. Can you imagine something like that? The dude he crashes then ten years later there's a town with his name where he splattered! You think Charles Lindberg crashed in Bavaria?"

"I have no idea. But Spider, does that have anything to do with our investigation?"

I could hear him chuckling.

"Not at all, but Zuccoli makes me think of Italian pasta... You know, farfalle, cannelloni, rigatoni, tortellini, conchiglioni, fettuccine and zuccoli! Makes me laugh, maybe 'cuz I'm not Italian!"

"Spider? I'm not paying you — quite well I must say — to listen to your one-man-show inspired by as non-exhaustive list of pasta. Get down to business!"

"Yes, boss! So, anyway, let me look at my notes again. The parents live in Farfalle, no, I'm just kidding, in Zuccoli. Johanna lives in Darwin, in an apartment overlooking the Tipperary Marina. Ashley lives in Hervey Bay. She works in an ice cream shop, but you already know that. Johanna works in a debt collection company. Maggie, the mother, is a nanny at home. And Pierce is a culinary photographer."

"A culinary photographer? He's specialized in taking pictures of leeks and apricots?"

"You're pretty close, Karen. He works freelance for quite a few culinary magazines and he sells his photos to illustrate their articles. Plus he's employed by a bunch of food-processing companies that he sells pictures to for packaged food, you know what they call 'presentation suggestions.' Those photos of recipes where everything looks delicious, everything's laid out carefully, and all that. But when you try to do the same things, you end up with a sort of yucky blob with an uncertain color and texture."

"I do see, yes," I agreed, thinking of the few times where I actually tried to cook something more elaborate than just reheating a dish in the microwave.

"You know that those photos are generally fake? It's not even real food! It's stuff made from plastic or cardboard with food coloring and paint. That's why it never looks like what we get on our plates! So that's what your Pierce Bolt does: he makes us believe, with his photos, that we can all become great chefs. Smoke and mirrors, that's what his work is!"

"I didn't even know jobs like that existed. After all, if he can make a living from it…"

"Guess so."

With all that we'd forgotten about the Gutierrez family. I asked Spider for confirmation.

"And nothing there that indicates that the Bolts knew the Gutierrez's?"

"Nuttin'! I dug, looked, cross-checked, multiplied my sources of information but the Bolts were born as Bolts — except for Maggie who was a Barty before she got married — and they remain Bolts. I was able to access confidential administrative files, from Maggie and Pierce's wedding certificate in Brisbane in 1988, everyone's birth certificates, what schools they attended and all that. All this little family has been

Australian for dozens of years, no doubt about it! You want my personal conclusion?"

"Sure, though it's probably the same thing as mine."

"I think that your Suzanne Diggs made this whole thing up..."

CHAPTER 55
A flabbergasted spectator

Australia, August 2024

Suzanne currently could no longer tell day from night, and the same thing was true for her memories and reality. When was she *dreaming* and when was she *thinking*? When was she recalling the past and when was she thinking of the present? Dates were getting mixed up in the mind, as were faces and names. Had it always been like that? She was beginning to have doubts about her certainties. Between two brief visits of one of her kidnappers who brought her food and changed her "commode," the prisoner returned into the past.

She relived those years from 2000 to 2004, which for her, which for her heart, had been the best ones in her life. This period began with a key event, one of the most moving ones in anyone's life…

New Orleans, September 2000

Two hundred and eighty-five days.

That was how long it took Suzanne to become the person she'd always dreamed of being.

Forty weeks and five days.

The incubation length that transformed the old Suzanne into the new Suzanne.

Nine months.

Like for women all throughout the world, that was the time it took to conceive... a daughter.

Nine months after that date at the end of December 1999 when Ricardo had joined her in that little hotel on Canal Street, the one with the wrought iron balcony, decorated with Christmas lights.

For nine months, she'd observed, like a flabbergasted spectator, the birth of a new life.

She'd seen her silhouette change.

She'd seen her stomach with its baby bump. Her tender breasts beneath her ample flowered dresses.

That was it, that was what she'd seen.

She'd also felt the very powerful sensations that only pregnant women can feel during that unique time. Hot flashes, nausea, heavy legs, difficult digestion, unexplained tears, mood swings, the passage from melancholy to euphoria, to sadness to pure joy.

At first, Ricardo refused to believe her. It wasn't

possible, not him, not them. He finally had to face the facts and ended up being overjoyed. He was going to be a father! Even though he was disreputable, even though his existence was piecemeal and dangerous, his future not always very clear, his progeniture quickly made him proud, and had become one of his reasons to live.

And best of all, it would be a baby girl! They'd name her Lisa, it was a sweet name, one that was like honey in your mouth.

After a few weeks and out of necessity, Suzanne was finally in her place: in that villa in Chestnut Street!

Now she was the one standing behind the curtains in the bedroom upstairs.

She was the one sitting in the leather passenger seat in that sports car as it left the property through the automatic gate.

SHE WAS THE ONE WHO, her hand on her taught stomach, would glance out at that unknown woman who for hours on end, would be seated on a bench in the shade across from their house.

CHAPTER 56
Running after ghosts

New Orleans, August 2024

THE DAY HAD GONE by like sand slipping through our fingers. Between the preparation of the flyers and putting them up all over Garden District, as well as Spider's call and what we were able to deduce from it, Paul and I hadn't seen it go by. The afternoon was winding to an end, and we were walking along the banks of the Mississippi, in the neighborhood near where the Gutierrez family used to live. My mind was confused, my soul was sad.

"This investigation is tiring me," I admitted.

Hand in hand, we were both walking, our heads lowered, or sometimes turned towards the paddle boats on the river. We felt like we were starring in an episode of Tom Sawyer.

"I understand," Paul sympathized. "This case is a

real headache. You want to know what I think? Your client, that Suzanne Diggs, she's not being frank. I've got the feeling that she's having you chase ghosts, ghosts who inhabit her mind."

I sighed.

"You're right. I'm starting to think that ever since the beginning she's been making this whole thing up. I'm chasing her crazy fantasies. And that's making me as crazy as her! Sometimes I even think that maybe she's the one who killed her husband and daughter and then she got rid of their bodies by tossing them into the bayou where they turned into alligator food, and ever since that day she's been insane. There are lots of cases where murderers mentally occult their acts and then say they're victims. Suzanne Diggs, who the heck are you?" I said out loud, looking over the peaceful waves on the Mississippi.

I suddenly had another idea. I took out my phone and clicked on a number.

"Spider? Karen. You've got nothing against a couple more bucks?"

"I was thinking of spending a year on vacation in Barbados, but I can put off my departure for a couple of days. What do you need?"

"I want to know everything about Suzanne Diggs. Maybe she's the key to this mystery. Can you get that info for me quickly? And how much is it going to cost?"

"I'll start right away and even give you a discount! We're friends now, aren't we! I'll do it for a hundred bucks instead of two hundred. Pretty soon I'll be working for free for you!"

"You're becoming a philanthropist, Spider! Thank you."

"I'll get back to you."

My phone rang just an hour later when we'd returned to the hotel. Unlike what I'd been hoping, it was neither Spider nor Suzanne, who I still hadn't heard from for days now.

"Is this Karen?"

"Karen Blackstone, yes. Who's calling?"

"Hi. My name is Melvin Fuss," said a voice that I figured must be coming from someone at least seventy. "I saw your poster on the corner of the road where I've got a grocery store; it's perpendicular to Chestnut. I think I can give you some information."

"Perfect! Thanks for calling. Go ahead."

"Could you come to my grocery store? I'll be closing in half an hour. I'll wait for you, the shutters will be closed about halfway, just knock when you get there."

"We'll leave right now then. Thank you."

I jotted down the address he'd given me and followed by Paul, hopped into my rental car.

It only took us twenty minutes to get to Mr. Fuss's shop, which was not far from Gutierrez's former home. I parked right in front of the iron shutters that were effectively half closed and knocked to tell him we'd arrived.

"Mr. Fuss? Karen Blackstone!"

"Coming!" said a tremulous voice from the back of the shop.

With a metallic creaking the shutters rose, and we went in. A little man who must have been all of five feet tall let us into his shop which was much more like a delicatessen than a convenience store, and I was salivating just looking at his products. From the road, it wasn't much, but once you were inside it was a true Ali Baba's cave for those who enjoyed fine food. The shopkeeper looked older than his shop. I felt he had been born there and that was where he'd end his time on Earth.

"This is Paul Nollington, my partner. Thank you for your help," I said, following him into the back of the store where we all sat down around a little Formica table with wooden chairs around it.

He served each of us a cup of hot mint tea.

"You were looking for information about the Gutierrez family, right?"

"Exactly, and anything you could tell us could be of invaluable assistance. Did you know them?"

The old man, who should have been retired ages ago, nodded his head for a few seconds and half closed his eyes.

"Of course! Everyone around here knew them! You

couldn't miss them. They were powerful people in the neighborhood. Unavoidable."

"What do you mean by that? What made them powerful? A bad reputation? Their fortune?"

"I really can't say they had a bad reputation. But a reputation, yes, they did have one. What was his name again, Eduardo?"

"Ricardo," I corrected him.

"That's right! Ricardo Gutierrez. El Rico*"

"His nickname?"

"Exactly. That's what everyone here called him. A guy with guts, everyone respected him, believe me. And he didn't need a bodyguard to defend himself either... So, yeah, though he looked like your ideal son-in-law, he had the reputation of being someone you wouldn't want to hang around with, but I can assure you it was better to be his friend than his enemy."

"Meaning?"

"You see this shop?" asked Melvin Fuss with a circular movement of his arm. "Who knows what would have become of it without Rico Gutierrez's support."

This guy was getting interesting.

"He helped you out financially?"

The man laughed, with a throaty sound that seemed to come from his atrophied lungs burned to a

---

* El Rico: could be a nickname for Ricardo, but also means "The Rich Man" in Spanish.

crisp by decades of tobacco as I could tell from his yellowed fingers.

"Not exactly like that. Money didn't really flow in that direction."

I thought I understood.

"He was racketing you? Threatening you?"

"Quite the opposite! Without him, in 2002 or 2003, my shop would have been the victim of organized gangs who were terrorizing New Orleans back then and I would have had to close. Those gangs were El Rico's competitors. He protected us from them, in exchange for a little monthly sum. A small effort so there wouldn't be any problems in the neighborhood, he told us."

"That's a type of racket, just like the Mafia, Mr. Fuss. They say they're protecting you in exchange for money."

"But we were glad, us shopkeepers around here, to be protected. Because if you could count on the police to protect citizens, everyone would know that. Plus Ricardo wasn't a bad guy. He respected us. And his family was adorable too. I don't understand why they disappeared so suddenly."

"So you're saying that Ricardo and his daughter Lisa disappeared? On August 6, 2004?"

"I couldn't give you the exact date, but it was around then. I only know that all of a sudden I never saw them again. That was tough. For me and my store. I suddenly didn't have anyone to protect me. The other gangs came back, but then that other organization that Rico belonged to kicked them all out."

"What was the name of that organization, Mr. Fuss?"

"We called it Mara Salvatrucha, or MS-13."

My eyes popped wide open. I turned to Paul who also had his ears peeled.

"You're sure about that? Ricardo Gutierrez was a member of Mara Salvatrucha?"

"Positive! That was the organization that protected us. And incidentally, to prove that he was a member of it, once he showed me a tattoo he had on his nape. The number 13."

"The number 13? Do you know what that means?"

"I forgot, it was twenty years ago. But I'm sure it was one of the MS-13 symbols. You can check for yourself."

"Do you think that Ricardo's disappearance is linked to him being a member of Mara Salvatrucha?"

"Got me, probably though. A vendetta between various mafia groups. I remembered that there had been a rumor in the neighborhood that Ricardo got what he deserved. Just like little Lisa, who undoubtedly was a collateral victim of that rivalry between organized gangs. Poor kid."

"Did you know her mother? Did you see her again after they moved? I know she left this neighborhood, but did she ever come back to your store? When you're used to a store, sometimes it's no big problem to drive a few more miles."

"Ah! No, I never saw that nice Maria again either," Melvin Fuss said regretfully.

I thought I'd misunderstood.

"No, that's not her name, Mr. Fuss. Ricardo's partner — they never got married — was named Suzanne, not Maria."

The old man energetically shook his head.

"Ah! No, not at all. Maybe I don't got all my marbles anymore, but I'm a hundred percent sure that Lisa's mother was named Maria. Plus, I knew her. She was a good customer here at my store, one of my best ones, but even more, one of the nicest ones I had. And I even remember her last name. Rivera. Maria Rivera. I thought it was such a pretty name, like a diva!"

CHAPTER 57
The queen

California, 2004

"They really fucked us over," said the prisoner in his orange jumpsuit. "What the hell did El Loco do? I trusted him, I thought he was the best one to succeed that time. But he fucked everything up, how could he have done that?"

"Me too, I trusted him," said the lady on the other side of the armored glass window, a phone in her hand, speaking softly just like he was. "Something unpredictable happened that day at the park."

The inmate clenched his jaw, his maxillaries whitening the tense skin of his cheekbones sticking out over his straight beard.

"Unpredictable, tell me about it! Everything got all screwed up! I didn't believe in that Six Flags op," he said bitterly. "Who had that stupid Daffy Duck and

Bugs Bunny idea? Huh? Right from the beginning I said no. And it fucked up and look where I am now! Dammit! You think I belong here? All this fucking concrete, armored glass and quenched steel," he continued talking about the tiny room he was in, with a window behind him where a prison guard was seated with a machine gun slung over his shoulder.

Tears that had been held back for too long were welling in the eyes of the lady on the other side of the window. Just like every wife of a chief, she had to be strong, infallible, untouchable, just like her man. But it was now clear that her man would never be setting foot outside the prison. No one had ever left Pelican Bay alive since it was created back in 1989! There of course had been serious "incidents" like the Vaughn Dorch case, or the riots in 2000 or the Madrid vs. Gomez case. But prison breaks, never!

Yet they both felt that this game wasn't yet over. All the pieces hadn't yet been moved. In chess, the king can falter, but as long as the queen is still standing, there's hope.

She broke that deathly silence between them.

"I can try to take care of them personally."

"You?"

There was a veil of disdain or at least a tad of skepticism in that word.

"Yes, me. Ever since we've been together, you and me, ever since then I've only been hanging out with people like you, and I think I've learned quite a lot.

Sort of like I'm starting to be a pro in your line of work. Plus I can always ask El Loco if I need help."

"He's worth nothing!"

"Let's give him one more chance. See if he can get it right this time."

The Christ-like inmate thought that over. He finally made his decision.

"After all, why not? Do whatever you want my beautiful lady. Get me the revenge I deserve, whatever it takes! That won't get me out of this dump, but it'll ease my pain."

"I at least owe you that."

"Find them, dead or alive, but preferably... dead!"

CHAPTER 58
Like a dog with a bone

New Orleans, August 2024

WE'D JUST LEFT Melvin Fuss's grocery store, our minds still confused and upside down by what he'd told us. He'd confirmed the hypothesis stating that Ricardo Gutierrez was a member of the Mara Salvatrucha or MS-13 mafia gang. He had that tattoo, that number 13 tattooed on his neck, plus a nickname — El Rico, the rich man.

Plus the old man had affirmed that Ricardo's partner, Lisa's mother, was someone named Maria Rivera.

I thought about something else and rushed back to the shop. I pounded on that iron curtain that the shopkeeper had just lowered.

"Mr. Fuss! Mr. Fuss! Can you open up again for me? It's Karen Blackstone again, I've got one more question for you."

A few seconds later, the iron shutters rose with a metallic creaking. I saw that little white-haired man in front of me.

"You forgot something?"

"Just a precision or a confirmation. You affirmed that Maria Rivera was Ricardo Gutierrez's partner. His official partner? His wife?"

"No, they weren't married, but yes, he shared his life with her, or if you prefer, she lived with him in their villa on Chestnut Street. I'm sure of that because I often delivered groceries there at the end of the day. When Ricardo was away on business and she was alone with Lisa, Maria often phoned me to place an order and then I delivered it to her. So yes, no doubt about that. Unless she was their maid," Melvin Fuss joked.

"And Lisa was Ricardo and Maria's daughter?"

The old man squinted for a few intense seconds.

"To tell you the truth, I can't really answer that question. I always saw that little girl with Ricardo, or Maria, or all three of them together, but I never asked to see her birth certificate! I'm sure you'll understand that I didn't need it for them to buy some ketchup or a can of beans!"

"I understand. Thank you."

"But I must say that the little girl looks a lot like her dad. The same dark brown hair, same dark eyes. Nearly his spitting image."

"Thank you, Mr. Fuss. Could I get back to you if I have any other questions?"

"Of course, if I could be of any help."

I left his shop and sent off a message to Spider.

> Spider? How about another little bonus? Anything you can find about a lady named Maria Rivera, presumed to be Ricardo Gutierrez's partner and Lisa's mother. Thank you. How much will this set me back?

> Gotcha! 50.

> Good for me! Thanks for the discount :-)

> I'll get back to you soon about Suzanne Diggs. I think I've got something.

AFTER WE LEFT THE SHOP, Paul and I kept on walking in the Garden District, still talking about the case. I wire transferred money to Spider for the umpteenth time.

"All that is making me see this case from a different angle," I began. "If Suzanne Diggs is neither Ricardo's partner nor Lisa's mother, who is she?"

"I have no idea," thought Paul out loud. "And why did she hire you to find them with the pretext they'd disappeared? A disappearance we didn't find anywhere else except in what she told you."

"She's been lying since day one," I seethed. "Lies about facts, lies about people, lies about herself, about them, about everything! She says she found her daughter who never was her daughter... Shit!"

I kicked a piece of wrapping paper on the ground before picking it up with the tips of my fingers and throwing it into the nearest bin, next to a streetlight.

"But why the heck isn't she taking my calls? She hired me to investigate a false double disappearance and then she goes missing too. What's going on here?"

Paul was thinking things over. He shook his head.

"I don't like this story about the mafia and street gangs. There must be some link: things like that don't happen to ordinary people. When you lead a healthy, honest and ordinary life, you don't have problems like that. Karen, let this one go, it's scaring me."

"Let it go? Did you ever see me abandon a case?"

"No, unfortunately. But I've got bad vibes on this one. It stinks to high heaven! Plus those behind it are dangerous people and I don't want anything to happen to you."

"What could happen to me? All I'm doing is investigating."

"You step in a mess like that and when it's too hot, you get burned. And also, as your client went missing, let's be practical, she's not gonna pay you. You're going to work for free? You think Blackstone Investigations is a philanthropic association?"

I sighed, knowing he wasn't mistaken there. But just like a dog with a bone, once my teeth were in it, I was incapable of abandoning it if there was still some meat on it.

"I want to know the truth. I want to unmask Suzanne," I concluded before entering the car.

I'd just turned the key when the audio system of the car, linked to my phone by Bluetooth, said I had a call. I picked up my phone, remaining parked.

"Karen? Spider here. Got the goods on your client."

"Perfect! I was getting impatient. Go ahead."

"Suzanne Leanne Diggs, born on October 13, 1975 in Des Allemands."

"Des Allemands?" I asked, astonished. "What do Germans have to do with anything?"

I could hear him chuckling.

"Des Allemands and you're right, it does mean 'The Germans' in French, is a little town of about two thousand, south-west of New Orleans. Its French name is sort of like Des Moines, or The Monks, the capital of Iowa. You wanna know something funny? Des Allemands was proclaimed as the Catfish Capital of the Universe in 1975! You could never invent something like that!"

"What's that got to do with Suzanne?"

"Nothing at all, but it's a funny anecdote. Anyway, my sources told me, and you know they're always right, that Suzanne was never married and never had a child. At least she never declared one: no birth certificates. Last known address: Canal Street in the French Quarter. Must be nice, I'd imagine. She studied sociology at Louisiana University. She's never been to jail, just a couple of speeding tickets, but we've all had those. No police record. To sum it up, nothing notable on her curriculum, except, except…"

"Except?"

"Exceptional? Exceptions? Accept this? Just joking, I'm crap with word games. So I was saying: except that she was often interned in the psychiatric ward at Beacon Behavioral Hospital in New Orleans from 1999 to 2004."

"Um hum," I said to myself.

"Where there's smoke, there's a fire someplace," Spider said philosophically. "If you want, I've even got the name of one of her doctors who she saw when she was there, both in the hospital and in his private practice. A Doctor Sacha Petrossian. And he still works sporadically in that same hospital."

I mentally heard a little "ding" in my mind.

"Petrossian? That name rings a bell."

"I see you appreciate the fine life, Karen."

"Why?"

"Petrossian is one of the most prestigious brands of caviar in the world. But this psychiatrist doesn't have anything to do with that family who made a fortune selling sturgeon eggs. I'll text you his details. That'll be all for today Miss!"

Spider hung up, and it was once again silent in the car, except for the purring of its motor. I put the blinker on and slowly drove down the streets in Garden District.

"Suzanne Diggs in the psychiatric ward for years… Why does that not astonish me?"

CHAPTER 59
The worst company

AUSTRALIA, August 2024

SHE WAS afraid she was going crazy, locked up between those four walls where she only had the worst company: her own!

Alone with herself, alone with her worst enemy.

Alone with her memories, her fantasies, her ghosts.

A terrifying trilogy that she constantly went back into, as she had nothing else to do, nothing else to think of.

Thus now Suzanne was no longer in her Australian jail, she was in the bayou in Louisiana. Her voyage back to the past took her to that day when they'd decided to take a trip to the bayou, that iconic landscape around New Orleans. It was in the spring of 2004.

* * *

New Orleans, April 2004

All three of them were waiting, hand in hand, with Lisa between them. They were impatiently looking for the airboat that would take them into the bayou, that separate world, that unique place with its specific odor of untamed humidity.

"We gonna see 'gators?" the child asked, apprehensive.

"Of course sweetie," her mother replied.

"Don't worry, honey," her father reassured her.

It was crazy to think that ever since they'd been living in New Orleans together, they'd never taken that trip to the Cajun country, something that was always on the A-List for tourists. But the same thing was true for New Yorkers who had never gone up to the top of the Empire State Building or Parisians who had never gone up the Eiffel Tower. Most people don't appreciate the beauty surrounding them.

So after those complicated months they'd had, this day for them was a very special one.

Those months where there had been strange disappearances of photos in their house on Chestnut Street. As well as the unexplained apparition of an anonymous threat concerning Lisa.

Lisa's birth had paradoxically drawn Ricardo and her apart. As their daughter grew up, she found him more distant, rarely available for her. He always told her he had other fish to fry. That he had a life without her.

She suffered terribly, told him that over and over again, but he never listened.

They nonetheless were reunited that spring day.

They got on the airboat with a guy named Carl at the helm, a country boy dressed like a ranger, with combat fatigues, a wide-brimmed hat and reinforced boots, who warmly welcomed the twelve or so passengers on that three-hour cruise on the green and waveless waters of the swamp.

The skiff soon hit forty-five miles per hour in the midst of that lush vegetation with its thousand and one shades of green and brown.

He slowed down and it didn't take them long to see alligators, snakes, beavers, and nutrias, those river rodents also called coypus that Cajun people trap to make pâté from.

That outing was punctuated with cries of joy and surprise. The little family, reunited at the front of the airboat, never paid any attention to a lady with large sunglasses seated at the back of the boat.

Her melancholic eyes were dissimulated behind her smoked glasses, and she seemed to be staring more at the passengers than at the flora and the fauna in the bayou.

. . .

After that day, they had a very tormented period of several weeks, during which she also had to leave.

The last time they were united having a good time was on August 6, 2004, at the Six Flags amusement park.

CHAPTER 60
A double pathology

New Orleans, August 2024

Beacon Behavioral Hospital was ironically located only half a mile as the crow flies from Six Flags, separated by I-10. Located on the southern bank of Lake Pontchartrain, the hospital with its typical Louisiana-style architecture tried to be a place where professionals could listen to their outpatients and help them relax for those who came for an appointment, as well as for more serious cases where patients were interned for several days or weeks.

I was able to get an appointment with Doctor Sacha Petrossian quite quickly. He said he'd see us between two patients. He'd politely accepted my request, and Paul and I were now seated on two wooden armchairs in a hall decorated with potted plants, across from the door with the psychiatrist's plaque on it.

A few minutes went by before the doctor came out, accompanied by one of his patients.

"You must be Miss Blackstone," he said, holding out a hand.

"Thanks for fitting us in, Dr. Petrossian."

The man must have been close to a well-deserved retirement, with his white hair surrounding a bald head covered with brown spots. He was tall and svelte, with an aristocratic bearing. He showed us into his office and closed the door behind us.

"Please sit down."

I looked around the room, saw a couch where Suzanne Diggs had perhaps been lying on years ago and decided to take the chair in front of his desk.

"I'm logically bound by the oath of professional secrecy," the doctor began as he also sat down, "but in this case which dates back quite a while, I think I'll be helping justice and the law if I tell you what I know about Miss Diggs and her pathology."

"Was she a long-term patient with you?

"Oh! Quite a few years I'd say, though intermittently. I was able to find her file," he said pointing at a thick archives box where he took a folder out. "I first saw her in 1999 and then up until 2004. After that, it was as if she'd vanished!"

Every time I hear that word I shiver.

"She vanished?"

"Yes, she suddenly quit coming. She didn't come to

the appointments, she didn't warn me and didn't cancel the following ones. I hope nothing serious happened to her."

As I no longer had the faintest idea about the protagonists in my investigation, whether they were dead or alive, had disappeared or had been found, were themselves or someone else, using the name they'd been born with or a pseudo, I thought that perhaps Suzanne Diggs had died in 2004, and my client wasn't the person she'd said she was. Perhaps it was identity theft, who knows? In which case...

Was my client Maria Rivera, Ricardo's real partner, Lisa's mother, who was pretending to be Suzanne Diggs? Why would she do that?

Ah! Now I was going crazy too, good thing I was sitting in front of a shrink! I mentally shook myself so I could answer the psychiatrist.

"As far as I know, and last I heard, she's alive and is vacationing in Australia, probably in Darwin."

"That reassures me."

"Why did Suzanne come to see you? What was she suffering from?"

Dr. Petrossian took a minute to reread his file. He sometimes would emit a muffled growl or nod, then he finally looked up.

"I remember that it took me quite a while to succeed in understanding my patient," he carefully said. "I'd like to say that that stemmed from the fact that she didn't understand herself either, she didn't know who she was. Little by little I was able to diagnose her. I must say though, but it's not to make an excuse that Suzanne Diggs's problems were quite hard to diagnose, as they were ever changing. Which was why it was so difficult for me to establish adequate therapy. To tell you the truth, this patient was suffering from a double pathology. Two psychiatric disorders had collided with each other inside her, sometimes simultaneously, sometimes successively, forming a huge psychic maelstrom! Quite the can of worms inside her brain, that I can assure you of!"

"I believe you easily," I agreed thinking of the headaches I had from trying to figure her out. "And those pathologies must have a name, I imagine."

Petrossian nodded and placed his crossed hands below his chin, like a picture-perfect doctor, before beginning an explanation that he tried to simplify as much as possible so that laymen like Paul and I could understand it. He cleared this throat and began.

"The first stage of Suzanne Diggs's troubles was easier to diagnose. Have you ever heard of Adele, one of Victor Hugo's daughters, the legendary French author?"

"I think everyone's heard of Victor Hugo. But I don't know a thing about his daughter, I had no idea that she existed. Why?"

"Because Adele Hugo and Suzanne Diggs shared one common feature: they both suffered from erotomania!

My eyes popped wide open as it was a word I'd never heard in my life.

"Is that related to nymphomania?"

"No," Dr. Petrossian replied categorically. "I understand that the similarity of these two words could confuse neophytes, but the pathologies are totally different. In erotomania, there's Eros, the god of love. And here we're talking about love. At least in one of the two partners. But nymphomania is hyper-sexuality, also known as 'compulsive sexuality,' a type of behavior characterized by the continual and persistent research for sexual pleasure. Often with numerous partners as soon as they're interested. Erotomania, on the other hand, will be focused on only *one* object of desire. This is also known as Clérambault's syndrome and is characterized by an individual's illusory delusions of another person being infatuated with them. And Suzanne Diggs often said in our many sessions that a very handsome, important and powerful man loved her."

"Did she ever pronounce his name? Does Ricardo Gutierrez ring a bell, Doctor?"

"No, my patient never gave me a name. She always referred to him as *my husband* or *my man*. She often spoke of *her daughter* or of both of them, in which case she'd say *them*."

"I understand and I think that she was referring to the person named Ricardo Gutierrez. Was this a relationship totally invented? Nothing at all ever happened between them? Even Mr. Gutierrez had no idea about it?"

The psychiatrist consulted his notes.

"I'm persuaded that at the beginning, there was something between them. An adventure. One day, it was —wait a sec... — in January of 1999, my patient told me that during one of their dates, that man told her he wanted to, and absolutely had to put an end to their relationship. He said, and I'm quoting here: 'Suzanne, shut the fuck up! I'm telling you I'm not someone you want to be seen with. All I'd do would be to get you in trouble.' She took that really poorly. For her, the whole world — *her* world, the one that she'd build in her mind — collapsed. And for me that was the moment that her erotomania began, when he brushed her off like that. Suzanne was extremely possessive, invasive. I think that she was infatuated with a married man."

"He wasn't married, but he was living with a partner."

The specialist in mental pathologies nodded his head and mumbled a couple of words I didn't understand.

"In this case, now I better understand a few things about Suzanne's erratic behavior. To begin with, considering her obsession with that man, she couldn't admit that he wanted them to break up. Obsession and possession are close. While their 'love,' and I can put that in quotation marks, was shared, she accepted that. But when he wanted to break up with her, Suzanne Diggs loved him only unilaterally and secretly. While believing he still loved her. And imagining their 'reciprocal love.' Pure erotomania."

In my head I was putting all the little pieces of the information I'd gathered together.

"Did you keep on seeing Suzanne in 2001 and 2002?"

"I did, and she never missed one of our monthly sessions. Why?"

"Because her 'daughter,' as she called her, Lisa, was born in the beginning of 2002. Could Suzanne have gotten pregnant from Ricardo before they separated?"

"No," replied Dr. Petrossian. "Or she had an abortion. In 2001, I never saw Miss Diggs pregnant. And I never saw her pregnant during the whole time she consulted. And that is precisely what led me to diagnose the second pathology of my patient, undoubtedly the most formidable and difficult one for her mind."

"What is that, doctor?"

"In our medical jargon, we call it depersonalization-derealization disorder."

CHAPTER 61
She lived her life

Australia, August 2024.

In the harsh light of the lightbulb hanging from the ceiling of her Australian jail, Suzanne tried to cling to her last memories, that long period of several months, several years, in which...

~

New Orleans, 2001-2004

... their couple was having serious problems, something she could feel deep down inside.

Ricardo wasn't just distant from her, but absent, horribly absent, morbidly absent!

Ever since he's rejected her violently,

"Suzanne, shut the fuck up! I'm telling you I'm not someone you want to be seen with. All I'd do would be to get you in trouble..."

she'd languished each day a bit more, drowning herself in the obscure abyss of her thoughts.

She could no longer separate her dreams from reality, her desires and the cruel truth of her life. Sometimes she was herself, she existed, but other times, she became the Other One, The One Who.

The One Who possessed Ricardo.

The One Who'd given birth to Lisa.

The One Who shared their life.

The One Who was pushing her away from that life.

She sometimes was that woman who, behind the curtains in their bedroom, was looking down at that unknown woman sitting on the bench across the street on Chestnut Street. Other times she was once again that woman sitting on the bench, spying on the life of the other family that was taking place behind the walls of that villa that she often thought of as hers.

And when the couple went out, she'd hide herself behind the trunk of the tree and slip into their property before the electric gate closed.

She was able to enter the house using a spare set of keys that she'd had made one evening in the French Quarter, when Ricardo was sleeping soundly after they'd made love, passionate love.

She lived *her* life between those walls.

For those few minutes or hours of solitude, she was far from being alone! Was she living *her* life or *her* life?

Whatever. She enjoyed those instants, making herself a cup of coffee, sitting on the sofa, taking her shoes off, putting her feet up on the coffee table in the living room and smelling the air and atmosphere of the house.

Other times she dared lie down in *her* bed, smell *his* odor, *their* odor.

Or else she'd enjoy a bubble bath in *her* bathtub. Dry herself off with *her* towel. Spray a bit of *her* perfume on. She'd put *her* earrings on her ears, try on several of *her* necklaces and *her* rings. She'd do her hair, so she looked like *her* portrait, the one she contemplated in the huge mirror in *her* bathroom.

Other times, nude after a bath, she'd find herself walking around in the house without shame nor scruples, and she'd take time to rummage around in *her closets*. She'd admire *her* dresses and suits, holding them in front of her, her arms stretched out or pressing them against her, standing in front of the mirror. Sometimes she'd even dare put on *her* underwear, *her* dresses, *her* skirts and she'd look at herself, satisfied. She thought she was beautiful, more and more beautiful!

Each time she took a few minutes to go into *her* daughter's bedroom. At first, an infant's room, then a little girl's room with Mookie, her stuffed monkey on her pillow. Then Suzanne would lie down on that little bed and sing nursery rhymes, rocking Mookie Monkey in her arms.

. . .

But she always finally left, albeit reluctantly.

But before leaving, she'd take a picture or two of them, she was so tempted to do so and regularly gave in to that pleasure. Yes, during her last visits, she'd never leave without a photo of *her* husband, *her* daughter, *her* couple, or *her* family.

Once she'd even left them a little souvenir telling them she'd been there...

> *The next time, it won't be Lisa's portrait that's missing...*

CHAPTER 62
In her skin

New Orleans, August 2024

"I'll try to be as clear as possible so that you'll understand what a depersonalization-derealization disorder is," Dr. Sacha Petrossian told us. "Generally speaking, it's a dissociative disorder."

"You already lost me," said Paul ironically.

"Well, a person suffering from a dissociative disorder can totally forget what they're doing for several minutes, hours, or sometimes even longer. They sometimes feel they've skipped over a part of their lives. Besides that, they can feel disconnected or detached from themselves, meaning from their memories, their *identity*, their thoughts, their emotions, their bodies, and their behavior. They can also feel detached from the world they live in. Suzanne accumulated all of that, quite an astonishing and huge psychic cocktail! But what was the most severe for her was her dissociation of identity. She was unconsciously someone else."

"Maria Rivera," I added.

"Ricardo Gutierrez's real partner?" the psychiatrist deducted.

"Exactly."

"For her, I did note here an extended time of disassociation from her own body and her mental functioning. Patients suffering from a disorder like that have the impression that they've become an outside observer of their own existence and that they're not attached to their own environment. They often feel disconnected from their own souvenirs and are incapable of recalling them clearly."

"Now I better understand some of the things Suzanne Diggs described to me. When she was recalling souvenirs she thought she'd had, but that actually were just a projection in her mind, as if she were in Maria Rivera's skin. For example when she said that she was behind some curtains and she'd observe a lady sitting outside on a bench in front of their house: in her sick mind, she'd become Maria who was observing Suzanne, and not the contrary. And the same thing was true when she affirmed that she'd found her missing daughter in Australia not too long ago. Probably Maria and Ricardo's daughter, after all, but certainly not hers."

"You understood everything, Miss Blackstone," the psychiatrist affirmed. "As months and years of that ambiguous and troubled relationship went by, Suzanne developed a possessive and vindicative jealousy. Jealous of her rival, Maria, and she vindicated Ricardo as being hers. The mixture of her depersonalization-derealization disorder and her erotomania led her to fantasize and imagine things during her entire life. But the worst thing for her was that suffering from erotomania, she couldn't understand why Ricardo wanted to break up with her. When Ricardo shouted out 'Shut the fuck up' and rejected her, without realizing it, he triggered the founding act of Suzanne's ultimate and higher level of insanity! You must understand that the delusions of a depersonalized erotomane can lead to harassment and then degenerate into a crime of passion!"

"A crime of passion?"

"That's right. Those suffering from erotomania are rarely cured. It's a severe and long pathology, a chronic paranoic psychosis. Up to the point that their entire lives are built around it. Until the climax."

"That day of August 6, 2004 at Six Flags," I finished up Dr. Petrossian's sentence.

"That could be true as that was right when Suzanne quit consulting me. To make a long story short, this condition plays out beginning with a conviction in four stages. Firstly, the *assumption*: the erotomane begins by believing that the other person 'is secretly in love with them,' that the other person began by making sexual advances to them, but they can't or are afraid of admitting it, or that they're just dissimilating their love. Secondly: *the hope stage*. This is usually longer and the erotomane hopes they'll be loved or hopes the other person will openly declare their love. The patient is optimistic. They remain stuck in this stage as long as their hope isn't dashed, and it sometimes can last for an entire lifetime. Thirdly, *the frustration stage*. The erotomane usually becomes depressed and draws away from everyone. They sometimes become aggressive or suicidal. And that can lead to a fourth stage, *resentment*. The patient's aggressiveness now targets their loved one and can actually lead to murder. The patient finds it totally natural to destroy the object of their love, just like that person had previously destroyed them."

Both Paul's and my mouths were hanging open. In my mind, all the wires were now connected. Those false leads Suzanne had given me, the absence of a police file on the disappearance of August sixth, the doubts I'd had about the true identity of my client. I summed up my thoughts.

"And had Suzanne lied to everyone, including myself? What if no one actually disappeared, meaning it wasn't reported, but on the contrary, there was a murder? A double murder disguised as a disappearance. Dr. Petrossian, could Suzanne have killed Ricardo and Lisa? Or at least hired someone to do the deed?"

"Considering her pathologies and her anterior acts, the answer to that question is undeniably yes."

CHAPTER 63
Her place

Australia, August 2024

Suzanne had dozed off.

Her dreams and souvenirs had blended together. Only one thing remained clear in her memory: that day at Six Flags Ricardo had organized to give a last chance for them as a couple.

∽

New Orleans, August 6, 2004

During the past few months she phoned the residence in Chestnut Street more than she should have. When Ricardo picked up, she begged him to see her again, even if it was for the very last time. Their final date.

When the Other One picked up the phone, she remained silent, never responding to her "Hellos" and just sighing hatefully and angrily.

Ricardo, after many phone calls, finally gave in. The Other One was in Denver for a seminar. The coast was clear. She could remember every word.

"Okay, Suzanne. Let's give ourselves one timeless day together with Lisa. What about going to Six Flags?"

"Oh! Yes, that would be wonderful!" said Suzanne, applauding just like a little kid. "We'd get much closer, all three of us. Like the family that we are."

"Suzanne..." Ricardo sighed, and then started to take care of the logistics.

He'd come to pick her up, so they'd be able to arrive as soon as the park opened, to make the most of that day.

When they got there, Ricardo showed *her* daughter a hut with a sign on it saying *Lost Parents*.

"You have to remember where this is, okay? This is where you should go if unfortunately you can't find *Suzanne or me*."

Suzanne was seething internally. Why hadn't he said, "*Mommy* or me?" But she couldn't demand so much of him so quickly and hadn't objected so as not to confuse the little girl.

That's how they played the fake couple. All three were holding hands, all three were laughing. He called her "my darling," even when Lisa was there, and the little girl didn't think anything of it.

They'd gone on the Ferris wheel, they'd watched Lisa try to catch those little ducks in the water, she'd had some cotton candy.

That day had gone by just like a fairy tale. Suzanne thought they'd returned to their true love. Now, she'd finally have her place in that family...

Then, in the middle of the afternoon, she had a sudden urge to go to the bathroom, and they'd walked to the closest restrooms.

"Do you have to go too?" Suzanne asked Lisa.

"No, I already went before."

"We'll meet you back here," said Ricardo, pointing at the entrance to the hall. "Take your time, honey. Lisa and I will be studying all the different flavors of ice-cream in the shop over there."

She had no idea when she rushed into the ladies' room that their paths would be separating forever.

When she left the restrooms and didn't see them waiting for her, she asked at the ice cream stand if the employee had seen them, then she ran to the "Lost Parents" hut, and had an announcement made for Ricardo and Lisa.

She'd never seen either of them again.

She'd run up and down the parking lot without finding Ricardo's car.

She'd felt she was going crazy, kneeled on the pavement in the lot, screamed her wounded and abandoned soul out, while behind her, the Ferris wheel was still spinning round.

Then she'd taken a cab to the police station where she filed missing persons' report for *her* husband and *her* daughter.

CHAPTER 64
A Blunder

New Orleans, August 2024

Upon leaving Dr. Petrossian's office in Beacon Behavioral Hospital, I suddenly felt lighter, as if the weight of my doubts had finally lifted. Knowing that Suzanne Diggs had suffered from — and this probably still was the case — severe psychiatric disorders shed new light on what had happened twenty years ago and what my client had told me. Her absence and silence for the past two days also now made sense.

Nonetheless, the response of the practitioner to my question of whether her double pathology could have led her to commit a crime was still deeply troubling. Before going back into the car, I spoke about that with Paul.

"I really can't imagine that Suzanne was capable of kidnapping and or killing Ricardo and Lisa."

"Even nuts like she was?" he replied. "The shrink said that it certainly wouldn't have been improbable."

"But in that case, why would she hire me to investigate their disappearance, if she had caused it? She paid me good money to do this. That doesn't make any sense."

"Maybe it made sense to her, but you must admit that with her psychological profile, she's not a logical person. Or maybe she's simply innocent, has nothing to do with that case. Or else she can't distinguish her illusions from reality. But at the same time, you don't even know her," Paul objected.

"You're right, we only talked a couple of times on the phone and had one video call. I imagine that's not enough to have a precise idea about a person who's psychologically ill."

We drove for a couple of minutes along Lake Pontchartrain on our right, heading towards the center of Nola. Paul brought the subject up again, after having thought over his deductions.

"I'd say it had involved an outside intervention."

"Continue."

"We know, the grocery store guy, Melvin Fuss, and Suzanne, both told us that Ricardo Gutierrez, nicknamed El Rico, was a member of that MS-13 mafia gang."

"That's right."

"And we also know that it's a gang that's capable of lots of wrongdoings, from racketing people to assassination, without forgetting kidnapping kids, demanding ransoms, etc."

"Affirmative."

"And we know that Mara Salvatrucha-13 had several enemies, gangs and rival mafias."

"That they did."

"So, why couldn't Suzanne have, with her erotomania at a peak, hired one of the members of a rival gang to eliminate the elusive object of her desires, her infatuation? Mafia type organizations just as brutal as Mara."

"You're talking as if you'd been reading that from a book, my dear," I gently mocked him. "But I must say that you're not wrong. She could have hired someone to kidnap and eliminate Ricardo, *her* main target, as well as Lisa, collateral damage and her secondary target in her desire to become a mother. We have to consider that as a valid hypothesis. But then again, what surprises me is that I didn't find a single thing in the papers or on the internet about that. Same thing, not a single mention of the Gutierrez name, nowhere!"

"That is disconcerting."

"Same thing about the absence of any police files. And what about my Facebook page on their disappearance that got axed. What the heck could that mean?"

"You want to know what I think? All that makes me think of something not nice at all. Sometimes the authorities eighty-six cases to camouflage malfunctioning in their departments."

"Like?"

"A police blunder, for example…"

CHAPTER 65
A farandole

Australia, August 2024

SECONDS NOW SEEMED LIKE WEEKS, minutes like months, and hours like years.

In that anxiogenic context, Suzanne could no longer differentiate where she was from where she'd been and now from before. As for after, could she even imagine an after?

As it seemed to her that it had been ages since anyone had come to see her, despite her calling out and complaining, and she'd now even believed that no one would ever come. That she'd die here, between those four walls. Where was she anyway? She had no idea. She vaguely remembered a trip, a long plane trip. But she suddenly visualized whales, she was swimming with them. Crocodiles too. What was a mere dream and what was true?

Her eyes closed, Suzanne let a century or maybe just a minute go by, to concentrate. But nothing came.

What had she done? What crime had she committed?

Why was she being punished like that?

She'd die here.

Just like a tornado, she was suddenly invaded by a depressing sadness.

Katrina.

Who the heck was that Katrina? A friend? A rival? A family member? What family? Had she ever had a family?

Sacha Petrossian.

A man's name. Her husband? Was he her family?

Ricardo. Maria. Lisa.

How many other names?

Pierce, Maggie, Johanna, Ashley.

A slew of them, a farandole of names dancing around in her mind.

Karen. Suzanne.

Amongst all those names, one of them would finally think of her. One of them would deliver her from the trap she'd fallen into.

The one you rushed into yourself, she heard herself think.

In a bolt of lucidity, the prisoner was sure that help would end up coming. They couldn't keep her locked up for years, that was something no longer possible in today's world.

Natascha Kampusch.

Never heard of her.

Yes, someone would come for her. Cops. Yup, men in uniforms with arms would save her. They'd be shouting: "Police! Police!" They'd shout her name. "Suzanne, are you there? Talk to us, Suzanne!" She would scream, she'd shatter her vocal cords if she needed to so someone would hear her, someone would come to her jail. Then she'd hear the muffled and characteristic sound of gunshots behind the heavy armored door, she'd know that her kidnappers had just been killed, they'd break the door down and the police squad would rush in, picking her up in their powerful arms and they'd take her away, far away from that endless nightmare, finally!

Yes, that's what would happen.

But what did happen was far from what she'd hoped for.

No gunshots were fired, but the door was opened, and a group of men walked in. They weren't wearing uniforms and didn't have guns, at least none that she could see.

But they were all wearing hoods over their heads. She'd seen those guys before.

Her kidnappers. She wasn't exactly thrilled…

Two of them remained behind while the third one walked to her, lying down on her mattress. She could make out his beer belly gut in the light. That must be their boss, bosses are always overweight, because they no longer run, they're not active anymore, they remain seated for hours on end behind their computer screens or counting all the money that others made for them.

The man managed to kneel, his gut hanging between his thighs that he was forced to spread. She could only see two dark eyes in his hood when he approached his face to hers.

The cloth covering his head didn't go all the way down his neck and Suzanne could make out a tattoo that she was sure she'd recognized.

The number 13.

When his lips were close to her ear, he whispered something that she at first didn't understand, but she quickly assimilated it calling upon her souvenirs.

"When the hell are you gonna finally leave us alone?"

CHAPTER 66
The first one to find it

New Orleans, August 2024

Back at the hotel, Paul and I sat down in the large but cozy lobby and ordered Darjeeling tea while logging into their Wi-Fi network with our laptops.

"You're going to have to reformulate your previous web searches. Find the right keywords to get results. Bypass that forbidden subject, delve into peripheral resources that will be able to bring us, through correlation, to the main subject. Find coincidences of dates, names, places, etc. Then cross-checks, deductions, and conclusions!"

"Um, Paul, are you thinking of working for Blackstone Investigations? You seem to be doing pretty well as a super sleuth."

"Careful Miss Big Boss, I'm expensive!"

"Do you accept payment in kind?"

"It all depends on what type of payment," my sweetie replied with a chortle while leaning towards me to kiss my neck. "Time to get down to business now! The first one who finds something gets to ask whatever they want of the other…"

"Deal."

We both started off in a feverish race, looking for even the tiniest element that could help us progress and find some eventual lead about a kidnapping or an organized murder that was either committed by the MS-13 or some rival gang.

As for me, I keyed in words such as *gang wars in New Orleans, Mafia vendettas New Orleans, MS13* paired up with the names of other local gangs in 2004. All that did was to show articles linked to minor offenses: assaults, shoplifting, police custody, fights between rival gangs, or racketing. Of course Mara Salvatrucha was often quoted, but never linked to the Gutierrez case. A case, we now knew, never existed!

Some results gave us the background of MS-13, which originated in El Salvador back in the 70s, came to the United States via troubled Los Angeles in the 80s, and then little by little had spread throughout the North American territory, including of course New Orleans.

I was ready to give up, despondent to be stagnating once again. I'd already given Spider that subject to look into and didn't know what else I could do.

"Gotcha!," Paul suddenly shouted. "I'm first! I got something!"

"What?"

"I landed a big one."

"If you're talking to me about tuna fishing or the biggest barracuda they pulled out of Lake Erie at the beginning of the 2004 season, that doesn't interest me."

"Not at all my dear! My fish doesn't have any scales, and I don't actually know if it's still alive, but I can assure you that it was pulled out of the depths back in 2004, right after Ricardo Gutierrez went missing. Maybe it's just a huge coincidence of dates though. But what you have to do is expand your research, not just focus on Nola. Here, take a look."

He turned his laptop towards me so I could read the article he'd exhumed. It was dated September 15, 2004 and was from the well-known *San Francisco Chronicle*.

Big Salvadorian Mafia catch in the States.

We have just learned from the judicial authorities that Isidro Vegas Paladar, nicknamed El Cristo, the number one in the Mara Salvatrucha gang in the United States, has been incarcerated.

This man is the head of a network

of several thousand members in America and is responsible for multiple crimes and misdemeanors. This huge haul, followed by a closed-door trial that took place in San Francisco for five weeks beginning on August 20th, took in, outside of El Cristo, several of his lieutenants — which we could also call, as they do, his "apostles", as there are twelve of them — who accompanied their leader behind bars.

El Cristo had special treatment from the federal justice system: he was incarcerated in the Pelican Bay penitentiary, located in the extreme north of California, not far from Crescent City and near the border with Oregon. This high-security prison already houses gang members such as those in the Mexican Mafia, the Nuestra Familia, Black Guerrilla Family, Aryan Brotherhood, etc. It now will have one of Mara Salvatrucha's directors in the States between its walls. Quite the honor!

This is a Supermax prison (for super maximal), where its inmates can only leave their cells for an hour per day and are mostly held in solitary confinement. They exit their cells with their hands cuffed behind their backs and their feet fettered. Meals are served to them through a "serving hatch" installed in their cell door. Prisoners are often excluded from any activities or work. The openings are electronically controlled and in most cases, opaque, so that inmates cannot see outside. Living conditions are extremely spartan, with furniture made from concrete and integrated into the walls. The walls, like the piping and doors, are phonically insulated so that prisoners cannot communicate with each other.

With conditions like that El Cristo will certainly not be able to run across any of his old friends.

The majority of Pelican Bay's inmates are sentenced to maximum sentences, and Isidro Vegas Paladar was sentenced to a total of two hundred and sixty years of imprisonment.

The other twelve members of the police haul, El Cristo's apostles, who managed the gang's affairs in several different states are, for

```
reasons  of  security,  imprisoned  in
other  penitentiaries  in  the  United
States. They have been sentenced to
between  fifteen  and  forty  years  of
prison.
```

"So?" asked Paul proudly when I'd finished the article. "What do you think, Sherlock Blackstone?"

"Maybe it's a coincidence. Or maybe not. But it is troubling. You think that Ricardo Gutierrez could have been one of El Cristo's twelve 'apostles' and that he's been rotting away in some American prison since 2004?"

"And what if he were that infamous El Cristo himself, Mara's big boss?"

CHAPTER 67
Sending me packing

New Orleans, August 2024

Being incarcerated in a state prison, a super-maximum-security prison to boot, was something that could justify the brutal and permanent disappearance of a man like Ricardo Gutierrez.

But what about little Lisa? You don't lock up a kid who's not even three in jail and then throw away the key!

Yet, the hypothesis of El Rico, maybe being one of El Cristo's twelve apostles, or at least his representative in Louisiana, was logical and could well explain quite a few loose ends in this case that was entangled like a ball of yarn.

There was one little detail though that kept on bothering me.

"That still doesn't explain why we can't find

anything on Ricardo Gutierrez, neither before nor after 2004. Why his name disappears though he's a mere lieutenant, when El Cristo, that Isidro Vegas Paladar, the head of all this, was thrown under the bus as a public scapegoat?"

"To hide some police blunder, like we thought earlier? Or maybe we're just totally wrong about him?" Paul proposed.

"Could be," I signed, leaning back on my armchair.

I remained in that position for a minute, eyes closed, then suddenly sat back up, went to my computer and typed in Isidro Vegas Paladar.

I wasn't about to hold my breath though. That inmate, if he was still alive, would never leave Pelican Bay and I wouldn't be allowed to interview him. Unless I completed tons of administrative paperwork, too time consuming. Time I didn't have. I couldn't forget that somewhere, on the other side of the world, my client was now also missing. Speaking of which, maybe I should alert the authorities? But I could well imagine how the cops would welcome me with open arms, same thing for the FBI who'd not up till now been very cooperative with me, and that's putting it mildly.

In the meanwhile I found out that El Cristo had been married to a lady named Isabel Raya, born in 1970, also from El Salvador. I found the Facebook profile of a fifty-four-year-old lady who seemed to correspond and contacted her. If she could speak to me about her husband — his past, his background, his relations —, who knows, maybe she'd be able to give me a few tips about Ricardo too. That was what I wrote to her hoping that she'd write back. And also, if El Rico had been one of El Cristo's apostles, she perhaps had known him. *Nothing ventured, nothing gained*, like my favorite old saying goes. At the very least, her answers could confirm or invalidate an eventual link between the various players here, as well as the coincidence in the dates.

WAITING FOR A HYPOTHETICAL ANSWER, I texted Spider.

> Dear friend from the shadows, could you please locate ASAP the GPS signal from the number 33 75 402? That's Suzanne Diggs's phone. Thanks a million. Karen.

At least he wouldn't be sending me packing.

"I'm going to take a shower, I'm knackered," I said, folding my laptop and giving Paul a sexy wink.

"I'm knackered too," he affirmed with a bawdy look, following me to the elevator.

TEN MINUTES LATER – our shared shower must have perked us both up –, I felt like my brain had been kickstarted again.

Especially as I'd had two notifications.

The first one was from Isabel Raya, via Messager.
The second one was signed Spider.
I read his message first.

> Hi Karen! This number hasn't pinged for 48 hours. The last time was in Zuccoli, which is in the suburbs of Darwin. I was able to track it from the municipal airport where your client rented a vehicle from Hertz, a hybrid Toyota Corolla licensed YLC 76C. NT Outback Australia. The car has anti-theft tracing. And curiously the car drove around for a day in Darwin before driving south-east towards Zuccoli, where the phone stopped pinging and then it returned to Darwin. As if your client had lost her phone in Zuccoli... (This one's a freebie).
> Spider P.S. Here are the exact coordinates of the last signal.

"Lost her phone forty-eight hours ago..." I repeated pensively. "Nowadays, who could live so long without their phone?"

CHAPTER 68
Los Apostoles

NEW ORLEANS, August 2024

IT WAS TRUE, nearly no one in 2024 could survive without their phone. Even if she'd lost her phone, Suzanne Diggs would have found a way to inform me about the progress she'd made in Darwin and ask me about what I'd found in Nola. After all, I was being paid for that. But there had been nothing for two entire days.

I was starting to fear that she'd had a problem, or even worse. How could you explain that her phone remained mute in Zuccoli, while her rental car was still moving?

Another hypothesis: Suzanne was consciously fleeing me and ignoring me. Did she have something to hide from me or fear?

That's where I was in my thoughts when I clicked on the Messager notification to read Isabel Raya's message.

> Hello Miss Blackstone. You're right, I'm the partner of poor Isidro, who's been incarcerated in Pelican Bay for the past twenty years already. You have no idea how terrible this is! Each day that goes by is like torture for me as his wife. Knowing that he'll never leave those inhospitable walls, that his days will slowly go by in horrible prison conditions... And just imagine what our children feel, children who their father has never seen growing up! Anyway, I'm available to speak to you. Let's call each other, here's my number.

Her phone number followed, and I clicked on it to call her. She immediately picked up. I could visualize her, holding her cell phone, impatiently waiting for what I'd tell her.

"Isabel Raya," she said.

"Karen Blackstone here. Hello Mrs. Raya. Or should I say Mrs. Paladar?"

"Isabel is fine. You have no idea what your message did to me. All these empty and senseless years, my lifeless days, without my Isidro. I raised my twins alone. They were only eight when their father was arrested and thrown in jail. It's terrible, believe me."

Her voice was cracking with emotion. Even twenty years later you could feel that the pain she'd had when her husband was put behind bars was still there. I sympathized. Yet, in a corner of my mind, I never forgot the clear notion that her dear Isidro had been a formidable head of a mafia-type gang with his hands full of the blood and fear of hundreds of victims. He undoubtedly deserved to be in prison and rot there.

"I understand your affliction, Isabel. And I share it. Nothing's worse than not being able to see your child grow up. I went through that too..."

"Thank you, Karen. You wanted to know more about a certain Ricardo Gutierrez, is that right?"

"Yes, he was also called El Rico. Unless it was El Cristo."

"No!" she cut me off. "El Cristo is my husband. And yes, El Rico was Ricardo Gutierrez's nickname."

"You knew him then? He was a member of your husband's organization?"

I heard her sigh deeply and sadly.

"What a story," Isabel Raya deplored. "If I could do it over, I'd do whatever I could to prevent the errors — the horrors — of the past. You know, us women in Mara Salvatrucha, no one listened to us at all. It was — and it still is — only for the men, the *machos*. Even for the wives of the bosses like me or Maria, Ricardo's wife."

I noted that Isabel had now confirmed the true identity of Ricardo's partner, Maria Rivera. Suzanne was thus an impostor, a fraud.

"What happened in 2004, Isabel? What led to your husband being arrested? What do you know about that memorable net cast over the MS-13 organization?"

"Good Lord, it still makes me tremble twenty years on. The police came to oust my Isidro at the break of dawn, on our property in Los Angeles, with heavy weapons. There were dozens of them, with sharpshooters, antiterrorists, and there was even a helicopter! The grand *armada*, you could say. Our children were screaming, crying. Me too, I must admit. Isidro was dignified, his jaw was clenched with rage, he didn't resist them. He allowed himself to be arrested and taken away calmly, so he wouldn't frighten the children anymore. Then there was the trial, and he was sentenced to two hundred and sixty years of prison. Two hundred and sixty years, Karen! Two hundred and sixty years in that horrible prison in the middle of nowhere in California, in the woods, between four walls, in inhuman conditions!"

She began to sob loudly before regaining control and continuing.

"Isidro was arrested as were all of his trusted colleagues, the ones he referred to as his apostles, *Los Apostolos*."

"Ricardo, El Rico, was he one of them?"

"Absolutely. He was the head of the Louisiana sector."

"So he was also arrested, had a trial and was put in prison like the others?"

There was a silence before Isabel Raya answered.

"Karen, I can't certify that, I'm sorry. Each apostle went to trial in a different courtroom. I don't know what happened to all the others. Some of them, yes, others no, and I don't know for Ricardo Gutierrez. But in your message you said that you thought that Ricardo and his family could have escaped prosecution?"

"It's a hypothesis, yes. Someone who knew them affirmed that was what happened."

"That is incredible, what news! I feel like saying 'good for them,' at least they're not suffering like I've been suffering for thousands of years... If you know where the Gutierrez family is, I'd love to know, because they're people I really appreciate. Maria is such a lovely lady. Knowing they're free would make me so happy. By procuration I mean."

"I understand. If the info I have is useable and correct, it would seem that the Gutierrez family now resides in Australia."

"So far?"

I briefly told her about Suzanne Diggs, her peregrinations and suppositions Down Under.

"I don't know that lady," declared Isabel Raya. "But if all of that is true, I'd love to see them again. I'd love to talk about the good old days with them! I mean, before they got caught. Knowing they escaped, it's... I don't know what to say! Can you tell me where they live? Give me their contact details? That would be fantastic."

I could feel Isabel's overflowing enthusiasm with

what I'd just told her. But still, there was one little detail niggling at me.

"Mrs. Raya, if you were that close to them, what astonishes me is that you two didn't stay in touch, even after they departed from New Orleans."

"Do you think I didn't try? Of course I had their phone numbers, their emails. I called Maria, Ricardo, I sent them emails. And you know what?"

"Tell me."

"They'd become absolutely unreachable. Their phone numbers were no longer in service, and my emails came back with a message that the address was unknown. As if they had up and vanished, evaporated from the surface of the Earth! Gone AWOL suddenly. So yes, please, Miss Blackstone, if you could tell me where they now are, I'd be eternally grateful."

"To tell you the truth, I was hoping that you'd be able to give me more information about them, or even point me to where they are or help me contact them. So right now, all I can give you is an address: Tindill Court in Zuccoli, Palmerston County, south-east of Darwin, which is the capital of the Northern Territory in Australia."

"Marvelous!" exclaimed El Cristo's wife, the most famous prisoner of Mara Salvatrucha in the United States.

I was about to hang up.

"Ah! I almost forgot. The Gutierrez family changed names. Now I think they go by the name of Bolt. Pierce and Maggie Bolt. Ever heard of them?"

Isabel thought that over before answering.

"Not at all. But for me it's logical that they changed identities to escape the American legal system!"

I couldn't contradict her on that point.

CHAPTER 69
Que tal, guapo?

San Francisco, August 2024

When Isabel Raya, alias Isabel Paladar, the wife of Isidro Vegas Paladar, alias El Cristo, finished talking with Karen Blackstone, that private detective who was tailing the Gutierrez family, she closed her eyes and took a deep breath.

When she opened them again, she had a huge smile on her face.

A smile that showed two pointed rows of teeth, just as sharp as the fangs of a hyena.

A smile that soon transformed itself into a sneer and snigger that she couldn't stop when her chest, shaken with hiccups, took her breath away.

She finally calmed down and the first thing she did was to call Pelican Bay to obtain a visitation with her husband.

After that she picked up her land line and with her beautifully manicured index finger, clicked on one of the many contacts of her favorite list, which was none other than El Cristo's list he'd given to her. As the king was behind bars, his queen was in charge of business...
— "*Holà Isabel. ¿ Aún me extrañas?*"*
— "*Holà, El Loco. ¿ Que tal, guapo ?*"†

---

* "Hello, Isabel. You missing me already?"
† "Hello, El Loco. What's up, handsome?"

CHAPTER 70
Tiny Devils

New Orleans, August 2024

After my conversation with Isabel Raya Paladar, I spoke to Paul who'd only heard my side of the discussion.

"Little by little I'm starting to wonder if Ricardo Gutierrez went to Australia to flee the Americans and avoid jailtime while implanting Mara Salvatrucha over there."

"But under a different identity."

"Like Pierce Bolt, a perfect identity, a good father, an irreproachable culinary photographer. Talk about a cover! Wait a second, I just thought of something."

I grabbed my laptop and started to search for information by entering *Mara Salvatrucha + Australia* in Google. One of the headlines popped out, a 2017 article published in the *New Zealand Herald*.

The deadliest gang in the world, Mara Salvatrucha, is starting to infiltrate Australia

I READ through the columns written by the New Zealander journalists, reading out loud the most interesting sentences.

"They say that there was graffiti that MS-13 had revindicated, though it was signed with names like 'Tiny Devils' or 'SPS-13.' The organization targets the Australian drug market, a booming and very lucrative one. Listen to what they say next, that really scares you."

Often terrifying to look at, gang members often cover their faces with tattoos.

They're known to be particularly cruel and violent towards *people that don't respect them*.

Throughout the world, this gang has over 100,000 members. Some of them have been found guilty of rape or murder, crimes motivated by *revenge*.

Others are no older than eight and each new potential member must endure an initiation that consists of receiving brutal kicks and a beating.

"That is scary," Paul agreed.

"And that's not all. Listen."

What the gang values above all is loyalty, and if one of the members is disloyal or unfaithful to them, they're punished. They're either assassinated, or they cut their hands off.

Many gang members now live in El Salvador and they're so cruel that they had to build a separate prison for them.

"A little farther down, this is what I found".

It is chilling to realize that MS-13 is doing its utmost to become the gang that has the largest number of murders throughout the world and that it has perhaps been sneaking slowly and secretly into Australia for quite a while.

Reports say that highly tattooed members are seeking "clean skins" to join their group and commit crimes more discreetly.

Their presence in Australia was noted for the first time in 2015, in Bondi, on the outskirts of Sydney, where their name was tagged on a garage door.

Mailboxes and walls have also been

```
covered   with   bright   blue   graffiti,
and     inhabitants     are     becoming
frightened.
```

"Doesn't surprise me at all," Paul commented. "It's understandable."

"The Tiny Devils," I said again. "Or the SPS-13."

I typed those names associated with that or Ricardo Gutierrez, El Rico and Pierce Bolt.

Nothing came up. Then my sweetie asked another good question.

"If I follow your line of thought, you're thinking that maybe Ricardo succeeded in slipping through the cracks of the American judicial system when everyone else was caught?"

"It seems plausible to me. And then he fled to the other side of the world to set up and head the Australian branch of MS-13, under a new identity, maybe a more Anglo-Saxon one. Leading to radio silence on that subject because the authorities never caught him."

"But all that supposes that Pierce Bolt is really Ricardo Gutierrez," Paul added.

"I've got a bad feeling you're right. I'm persuaded that Suzanne, who's been delusional for the past twenty years, has never stopped looking for the object — or the subject — of her fantasies. I don't believe in coincidences. If her road led her to Australia, up to Ashley and then Johanna Bolt, and to Zuccoli where her phone suddenly went dead, that must mean something. All of that added to what we both know, that's too many coincidences to be coincidental…"

Paul was nodding while following my logic. He looked at me.

"And if Suzanne got a little too close to Pierce Bolt, perhaps she put herself in danger," he said grimly.

"She walked right into the lion's den…"

CHAPTER 71
Perfectly ripe fruit

San Francisco, August 2024

The situation now had to immediately be addressed.

They'd been chasing them for twenty years now. Twenty years since that cursed August 6, 2004 when everything went belly up.

Where everyone got screwed too, Isabel Raya Paladar thought bitterly. That day when dozens of protagonists fell into that deep pit. There were no winners that day. Except…

But with hindsight everyone always has twenty-twenty vision and now she had to focus on the essential and crucial hours to come.

How ironic was that! Just thinking of what that lady, Suzanne Diggs, the name the detective had given her, had suddenly spoon-fed them. All they had to do now was pluck the perfectly ripe fruit off the tree.

Isabel repeated to herself that she had to address the situation right now. Pick the fruit before it rots.

To do that, she didn't care about the time difference! Australia was too far to send El Loco quickly. No big deal, she had to strike while the iron was hot!

El Loco gave Isabel, also known as La Reina*, the name of their representative on the other side of the Pacific, a certain Pablo Ortiz. He was nicknamed El Cocodrilo, the crocodile, and was feared by everyone Down Under. Just like the saurian, one of the symbols of untamed Australia, Pablo had that yellow reptilian look in his eyes that went right through you, and he never blinked. He was patient and resolved, cruel and bestial. He'd been in Perth since 2017 and it would only be a four-hour flight for him to Darwin, where he'd be close to Zuccoli.

Isabel briefed him on the phone, telling him everything he needed to know about the situation, the players and stakes. He already knew some of the players, at least from reputation. A good little soldier, El Cocodrilo would obey her every word. His mission in Australia had begun a few years ago, firstly under the name of SPS-13 which poorly masked his allegiance to

---

* "The Queen" in Spanish

MS-13. The tats he had proved that better than words could do. The number 13 he had tattooed on his neck was clear, as was their sign of recognition between members: one hand pointing down, fist closed, index and pinkie fingers stretched to form the letter M of Mara.

"You call me when you get there, Pablo, okay?"

"Will do."

El Cocodrilo hung up and dialed another number.

When the plane landed at Darwin Airport, his contact was waiting for him in the arrivals hall for domestic flights with a sign that had a fake name on it, one they'd both agreed on. He was the trusted contact who'd be driving him to Zuccoli. Much quicker and safer than taking a cab or renting a car. Also much easier to recover the semi-automatic pistol and micro-serrated knife as well as a few more toys that generally customs agents and security gates didn't appreciate.

CHAPTER 72
Two birds with one stone

Zuccoli, August 2024

"When the hell are you gonna finally leave us alone?"

That was the question Suzanne Diggs couldn't get out of her mind. It had come from that masked mouth behind the black cloth of a hood where the only thing she could see were two eyes shining with rage.

That distorted the voice of course, but it seemed to her that she'd recognized its inflections. That unforgettable tone, its nuances that her ears could never forget.

That voice that she'd loved for a day, adored all night, and that she still dreamed of.

Like everything else of course. Voice, body, heart. The only sticking point of the person she'd venerated before was that she'd only recognized his voice. Everything else, that overweight silhouette, that paunch, nothing else matched the image that was engraved in the marble of time and her memory.

Was she still delirious? Was her sick brain playing another terrible trick on her? As it had done for twenty years, losing her on the path of her perception, that path that split into two: reality, on the one hand, and fantasy, on the other.

She decided on the second.

"Ricardo? Is that you my love?"

In the harsh light of that empty room, there were two protagonists: her, on her knees on the cold concrete and him, standing in front of her. The two men who had come in with him were standing arms crossed, on both sides of the only door. The only escape route for Suzanne.

Yet did she still want to escape, and did she have the energy? She'd been imprisoned between those four walls for an eternity and seemed to have given up all hope of leaving one day. After all, that was logical, she thought. Imprisoned between four walls just like she'd been for nearly her entire life, in the stranglehold of her sick brain.

Imprisoned inside and imprisoned outside.

The man slowly nodded, seemingly with pity.

"You haven't understood a single thing despite all the years that have gone by. You never give up, you insist, you still believe in your dreams, in your delusions. Poor Suzanne."

"But Ricardo. If it's you, take your mask off sweetie!

"Stop calling me that, dammit!" shouted the hooded man. "I'm not yours! I don't belong to you!"

Then with an angry gesture, he grabbed the cloth from the top of his head and ripped it down uncovering his face.

"You're just as crazy as you were twenty years ago, Suzanne," Ricardo said bitterly. "I'd warned you. I'd told you to leave me alone, that I wasn't someone you wanted to be seen with, but you never let go."

Suzanne opened her eyes just as widely as two roulette balls in a casino. The balls inside her head were spinning. What number would they stop on? Red or black? An even or an uneven number? Unless it would stop on the green square, the zero, the nothing, the void, the emptiness of her existence?

Tears were slowly welling up in her eyes.

"But, that perfect day we had at Six Flags," the prisoner pleaded.

"Shut up! You don't know what you're talking about. You don't even know everything. I never told you everything. Why should I have? I didn't owe you a thing."

"But Ricardo, we were happy! We were a family!"

"You never realized that the problem was right there, Suzanne? That family, that couple, you and me, all that only existed in your sick mind!"

"That's not true," she sobbed. "That's not true. There really was something between us."

Ricardo sighed, resigned.

"Okay, maybe there was. I lost my way for a moment with you."

"A moment? Months, years," Suzanne corrected him.

"I thought I was clear with you from the very beginning. I was married, I loved my wife. You knew all that. You were only a pastime, Suzanne. A mistress, a folie, something that lasted too long for me."

"That wasn't what you said when we were together in my apartment or in our hotel on Canal Street."

The man paced back and forth in the narrow empty room, his soles clacking on the concrete floor, as if he were counting down meaningful seconds.

"That was at the beginning," he conceded. "After that, I wanted it to be over. I understood that you weren't in your right mind. I could feel that you represented a danger for me, for my family. My real family. I had a daughter. Maria had given birth to Lisa, and we were happy, all three of us. But you wouldn't give up, would you? You were sticking to me like a mussel on a rock. And that's when things completely went off track for you."

"Ricardo, what are you talking about?"

"I said you went off track. You were scaring me! You think I never noticed your little outings?"

"What outings?"

The man stopped pacing and snorted through his nose.

"See? Suzanne, you didn't even know what you

were doing. What was going through your head when you were sitting on that bench in the street, right across from our villa? What were you thinking of for hours on end, lurking there in the shadows, trying to see what was going on at our house?"

"At our house, that's right, Ricardo, at *our* house!"

The man pounced on the woman who was kneeling, threatening, his arm raised, fingers ready to choke that miserable person trembling at his feet, hands joined on her thighs, her head lowered while she continued to sob.

"Jesus Christ, it wasn't at *our* house! Once and for all are you going to stop that bullshit? That was Maria's and my house, with our daughter Lisa."

"Our daughter, Lisa, yes, our daughter."

He was just able to contain himself before committing something irreparable. He wanted to reply to hurt her, to hurt her soul, but he remained silent for a few seconds. Long seconds that seemed like hours to Suzanne. He continued though.

"You were spying on us. You'd come into the house when we were gone, you'd lie down on our bed, on Maria's and my bed. You'd drink our coffee, you'd take baths, I could smell the bubble bath when I'd come back in. You ever dared enter Lisa's room, her sheets were wrinkled when we'd get back, sometimes her favorite stuffed animal was on the floor. You stole photos, pictures of our family. And that ridiculous note you left, that threat you left us: *Next time, it won't be Lisa's portrait that's missing...* Maybe you thought I wouldn't recognize your handwriting? You at least could have made the effort to type it. Luckily I saw it first and put it in my pocket. I didn't want to scare Maria. Are you able to imagine for one second how you could scare people? You were openly threatening to kidnap my daughter, Suzanne! I had to protect her, I had to protect us from you, from your insanity. I understood what was going on in your mind. I had good friends who were doctors and psychiatrists. Your erotomania, your depersonalization, all that, I understood it all. Complete insanity! And I had to get us away from your insanity."

Suzanne was now crying harder, soon sobbing uncontrollably, while Ricardo was summing up their last months of their cursed relationship in New Orleans. Before slowly drying up. A long silence now inhabited the makeshift jail. Now the man was pacing once again, going around the slumped body of his former mistress. She started up again.

"But Six Flags? That doesn't count? You accepted me, you let me hope! It was such a marvelous day... At the beginning..."

"That disk is scratched," Ricardo deplored. "And here you go again with the same old thing. My poor Suzanne, Six Flags was just a stratagem. A strategy I imagined to permanently get away from you."

Suzanne didn't believe her ears.

"You sacrificed all that just to leave me?" she asked, astonished.

Ricardo sneered.

"No, don't think you're that important! In reality, I had more urgent reasons to disappear. A threat, something even more dangerous than you, was hanging like the sword of Damocles above my head… Let's just say that that day, in the park… I killed two birds with the same stone!"

CHAPTER 73
The right conclusions

New Orleans, August 2024

As soon as I'd shed light on the danger lurking in Australia and well aware — not to mention very relieved — that it would be much too long to fly there, I looked up the phone number of the police station that was the closest to Zuccoli. Something that wasn't complicated, their number was on their web page and all I had to do was to click on it.

"Palmerston Police Station, Sergeant Tricia Sharpes, how can I help?" asked a pleasant feminine voice with a strong Australian accent. "Could you please tell me who's calling?"

"Hello, Sergeant. My name is Karen Blackstone from the Blackstone Investigations Agency in New York City. I'm an American citizen who was hired by a client who I believe is in danger in your region."

"Hmm, and what's that person's name?"

"Her name is Suzanne Diggs and she's also an American. I have very strong presumptions making me think something serious has happened to her. I've been in contact with her until forty-eight hours or so ago, and since then, I haven't been able to get through to her. I know that her cell phone was last localized in Zuccoli, which is why I called your station, because I think it's the one that's the nearest to that town."

"You're right and Zuccoli is in our zone. As far as you know, what was she doing in Zuccoli before you lost contact with her?"

"Well, it's a very long story, but to make it short, she was looking for a young lady that she thought, though she was wrong, was her daughter. And that young lady in question is Pierce Bolt's daughter, a Zuccoli resident. Have you heard of him?"

"I should have?"

"Um, probably not. What about Ricardo Gutierrez? Or El Rico?"

"Not either, but my Spanish is pretty rusty."

"Then," I continued, "have you ever heard of a mafia gang originally from El Salvador, Mara Salvatrucha, also called MS-13? Maybe they're better known in Australia as SPS-13 or the Tiny Devils."

"Yes, I have heard of the last two," confirmed Sergeant Sharpes. "Miniscule mafia-type groups who have been trying for the past couple of years to gain some foothold in Australia. Mrs. Blackstone, do you think they could have been involved in your client's lack of communication?"

"Yes, I do. And my investigation led me to link that guy named Pierce Bolt to the Salvadorian mafia. And he's probably in the Australian branch. He could actually be one of its leaders. I'm afraid he's kidnapped my client, or even worse. If you could send someone over there, I can give you the Bolt's address."

"Please do."

"They live in Tindill Court, a cul-de-sac, in Zuccoli."

"I've got it. I'll send a squad car over. In the meanwhile, you can hang up. But please keep your phone on so we can call back. Thank you for calling."

"I do hope it's not too late," I concluded both for the sergeant as for Paul and me.

I was biting my bottom lip, an indubitable sign that I was becoming nervous. Blaming myself for not having realized how dangerous and serious the situation was. I'd let Suzanne Diggs, and her lies pull the wool over my eyes, I'd run up against the skepticism of police and authorities and I hadn't reached the right conclusions. In other words, I felt pitiful, like I was a total loser.

"I think I completely screwed up the first investigation for Blackstone Investigations!" I said to Paul.

My dear boyfriend put a soothing hand on my forearm.

"Karen, stop beating yourself up. It's not your fault. You were far from where that took place, your client is a pathological liar, you came up against forces stronger than you: the Mafia, the police, the FBI. You can't blame it all on yourself. You did as much as you could. Even right now, when you called the cops in Australia. This case is out of your hands now. You just have to wait, be patient, and turn the page."

"Turn the page," I mentally repeated, holding my head between my hands. "Easy to say!"

All the easier as the near future would make it impossible for me to let go.

Someone knocked loudly three times on my door.

"Karen Blackstone, open up! FBI!"

CHAPTER 74
Salvadorian cumbia

DARWIN, August 2024

THE PERTH-DARWIN FLIGHT was right on time. Holding only a small carry-on, El Cocodrilo didn't have to wait at the baggage claim and in just a few minutes he joined his colleague who was waiting for him in the arrivals hall.

A few minutes later, they were both sitting in the car driving down the large highway and strictly respecting the speed limit so as not to be noticed, towards Zuccoli.

The chauffeur had put the car radio on a Latino station that reminded him of home. El Cocodrilo was nodding and slapping his thighs in rhythm with his palms. You could tell he was both relaxed and serious about the job he'd been entrusted with.

"I still can't believe we're the ones who are gonna kill this asshole," he repeated every two minutes.

To which the chauffeur invariably answered, "Yeah, crazy isn't it?" while looking at the road.

While keeping time with the song, El Cocodrilo played with his semi-automatic pistol — a black Walther PPQ 9mm Parabellum — that had been awaiting him in the glove compartment. He was having fun inserting the charger, taking it out, putting the sight to his eye, pretending to shoot saying "Pow! Pow!" to the rhythm of a Salvadorian cumbia Grupo Algodón was playing, without paying any attention to the other cars. So excited by the stakes that he forgot the measures of caution and discretion that were recommended.

The chauffeur, a good driver, told him five minutes later that they were leaving the highway and put on his left blinker to take the turnoff to Zuccoli.

A few minutes and a few roundabouts later, the vehicle with its dark windows was driving slowly in a calm and well kept up neighborhood towards Tindill Court to the address they'd entered into their GPS.

They soon saw the house, and El Cocodrilo now was nearly drooling.

"Here's to us, *hijo de puta*!"

CHAPTER 75
Cabrón!

Zuccoli, August 2024

Suzanne Diggs had no idea what to think anymore.

"Ricardo, what threat are you talking about?" she stammered, her mouth dry. "What happened at Six Flags?"

Her swollen tongue gritted against her palate, as if it was now a piece of sandpaper.

"Yes, it's true. I accepted that day together at the amusement park as an adieu. I wanted to mix things up. I could no longer stand knowing you were there, that close to my wife and daughter. Suzanne, you'd become much too cumbersome, too dangerous, much too... crazy. Do you understand that?"

Her tears were his only answer. Suzanne had never understood that and never would. Behind Ricardo, the two giants with their musclemen biceps crossed their arms on their chests, listening to the conversation of the former illegitimate couple. Attentive and ready to intervene if needed.

Ricardo continued with a harsh voice.

"Oh! I don't even know why I'm wasting my time justifying what happened. After all, I don't owe you anything, except for a part of my past and present problems. But what the hell! It's actually doing me good to get this off my chest. So, back then, I was in a very uncomfortable situation. Up shit creek without a paddle, you could say. In the years before that damned 2004, I'd made myself a huge list of enemies, plus some of my allies had turned their backs on me and... and the cops started flying around me like vultures. I was cornered, Suzanne. I *had to* disappear, flee Nola, I didn't have a choice! It was either that or spend the rest of my life in jail. Or get myself killed by one of my enemies. Or friends, who knows! You're never wary enough of your friends. Anyway, one day I was awakened at the crack of dawn by individuals that I'd hoped I'd never see at my house. And in a blink of an eye I was cuffed and taken to a very unhospitable place."

∽

New Orleans, July 2004
  The FBI facilities

Recording of official interview N° 1

(*Noise of a door being closed, metallic chairs being dragged on a tile floor for a few seconds*)

Federal Agent John Collins: Okay, starting now, everything we say will be recorded. I'm Agent John Collins from the FBI. I'll be leading this interview accompanied by Inspector Philip Cairn, from the New Orleans police. Make yourself comfortable, Mr. Gutierrez. Or would you prefer to be called El Rico?

Ricardo Gutierrez: Call me whatever you want, Agent Collins. I'll see whether or not I like it. But I have to tell you my Spanish is far from being fluent.

Federal Agent John Collins: Of course. And I'm the queen of England! *No me jodas, cabrón!*[*]

Inspector Cairn: Let's stop playing these little games, Mr. Gutierrez. You were born in El Salvador on April 17, 1970 from two Salvadorian parents. I'm sure you are fluent in Spanish. And your nickname El Rico isn't a fluke I'd say. So just answer our questions.

Federal Agent John Collins: You are here today to respond to different charges brought against you, Mr. Gutierrez.

Ricardo Gutierrez: I don't see what I could have done wrong. I'm a respectable American citizen.

---

[*] To be polite: "Don't fuck with me, bastard!"

Federal Agent John Collins: Nonetheless the local representative of a mafia-type organization that is quite a bit less respectable. Here are some very interesting files on you as well as a detailed report about your very lucrative activities, if I can judge by the monetary value of your property in the Garden District or your many sports cars or luxury vehicles. For example, let's see...

(*Noises of papers being manipulated for twenty or so seconds*)

Federal Agent John Collins: Let's start by this one, the one about intimidation and extortion attempts, or in other words, racketing many respectable shopkeepers in New Orleans, Baton-Rouge, and Lafayette. Quite a scope there, congratulations.

Ricardo Gutierrez: I don't know what you're talking about, Agent Collins.

Federal Agent John Collins: That's quite strange as I have here the official statements of people tired of being forced to pay your 'contributions' as you liked to call them.

Ricardo Gutierrez: I don't believe you. Gimme their names!

Inspector Cairn: That's not the way it works, Mr. Gutierrez.

(*Sound of the palm of a hand hitting the desk*)

Federal Agent John Collins: Don't bother, Inspector. (*New noises of papers being gone through)* Let's have a look at the next file then. What about the Mambo Club in Nola?"

RICARDO GUTIERREZ: Never heard of it. What is it? A discotheque?

FEDERAL AGENT JOHN COLLINS: Almost. I'd personally call it a gambling joint, a hole in the wall. A titty and pussy bar!

RICARDO GUTIERREZ: I can't help you, I've never been there.

INSPECTOR CAIRN: That's strange as our sources have informed us that you own that joint.

RICARDO GUTIERREZ: Erroneous sources, Inspector. I doubt that you'll find my name on the organizational chart of that Mambo Club.

FEDERAL AGENT JOHN COLLINS: I agree with you on that point, Mr. Gutierrez. Your name is not in the articles of association of that place. On the other hand, there's someone named Lola Menendez, probably a figurehead, who's named as manager of the Leisure Ltd. company, owners of that bar. A company registered in Delaware[*]. And just look at this! And this company is a subsidiary of another entity whose head office is in the Cayman Islands[†]. And look at this too. Anyway the financial package of this company is huge

---

[*] Delaware is often considered to be a tax haven because of its pro-business laws and low taxes. Roughly 50% of American companies in the New York stock exchange have their head office in Delaware, supplying about a fifth of the state's revenues.
[†] The Cayman Islands are one of the world's largest tax havens, with a multitude of offshore shell-companies registered there.

and very well imagined but at the end of the day, you, Ricardo Gutierrez, you're the one who reaps the benefits.

Ricardo Gutierrez: I admire your analytical spirit, Agent Collins. Congratulations, you'll do well in your next annual assessment.

(Noise of feet of a chair squeaking then a chair falling over)

Federal Agent John Collins (*who is speaking to Inspector Cairn*)*:* If he keeps on making fun of me I'm going to punch that son of a bitch in the face.

Inspector Cairn: Probably not the best solution, Agent Collins. He's being ironic, don't pay any attention to it. Poor guy, he's grasping at straws.

Ricardo Gutierrez: Hey! I'm right in front of you.

Federal Agent John Collins: Just wait, *Rico de mierda*.

Inspector Cairn: To continue then with this file, it seems that between the four walls of the Mambo Club, when it's dark outside, people have been known to exchange a few greenbacks for sachets of white powder or miracle pills. See what I'm getting at, Mr. Gutierrez?

Ricardo Gutierrez: No idea. Blue pills that increase… the popularity of men? Stuff I personally don't need. What about you, Agent Collins?

Inspector Cairn: Don't answer that, Agent Collins. Mr. Gutierrez, you know what I was alluding to, but if you want me to spell it out for you, you're suspected of heading a drugs traffic network in the whole of Louisiana. Am I clear?

Ricardo Gutierrez: If I listen to you, I'm a complete pervert! What else?

Federal Agent John Collins: A prostitution ring, for example. Camouflaged there once again in the Mambo Club. Your dancers don't just dance, and your waitresses don't just serve drinks... A practical club if you need to launder money.

Ricardo Gutierrez: Nice! Anything else, Agent Collins?

Federal Agent John Collins: So, let's see, what else do we have?" (*Pages being nervously turned*) Illegal trade in weapons. Assassination contracts, ones executed using a machete. Illegal immigration. Aggressions on policemen. Rape. Armed robbery. Probably still missing a few here, and I haven't even touched on violent crimes. Your file is as long as my arm, Mr. Gutierrez. You're looking at serious time!

Ricardo Gutierrez: I don't believe you'll be able to prove anything against me. I'm not denying that there's delinquency in the streets of New Orleans just like in all the other cities of our dear country, but there's no way you can personally involve me in that.

Federal Agent John Collins: That's where you're sorely mistaken. Right here I have sufficient and overwhelming evidence to put you in jail. Of course, you're not one of the minor players in all of this. On the contrary, you're one of the leaders! One of Mara Salvatrucha's pillars. The tattoo you've got on your neck proves that. And by the way, sentences are much heavier than they are for little dealers, whores or various middlemen. Just with what I've got here, I'd say you'd be released from prison in about 2186, when you'll be 216 years old, if my math is right. You've got a daughter, don't you, Mr. Gutierrez? Lisa, a cute kid.

Ricardo Gutierrez: You keep my daughter out of this, you son of a bitch!

Federal Agent John Collins: As for me, you can stop insulting my mother... Of course, I wouldn't harm a child. But what's sad is that you won't see her grow up. Or maybe half an hour per month in the visitation area of a high-security prison. That's not much!

(*Long moment of silence, only broken by some coughs, someone clearing their throat and sighing*)

Ricardo Gutierrez: What do you want?"

Federal Agent John Collins: I'd like you to be more cooperative, Mr. Gutierrez. I'd appreciate that. We're not trying to catch small fish here. What we're interested in are the organization's leaders. Big game fishing. Sharks with long teeth...

CHAPTER 76
Igniting a fire

New Orleans, August 2024

The two federal agents who came to take me in from the intimacy of my hotel room didn't say a word to Paul and me about their motives. They drove us, luckily without cuffing us — we opposed no resistance —, to the FBI's head office in New Orleans, exactly where I'd gone myself just a few days ago.

They actually pleasantly led us to Agent Maxim Callaghan's office, that man who'd rather cooly received me after he'd shut down my Facebook page.

"I was sure we'd be seeing each other again one day, Miss Blackstone," he said with a hint of a smile. "You seem to be a person who's too curious and too stubborn to abandon your investigations when told to do so, even when it's the FBI telling you to. You think you're above the laws? Sit down," he ordered us.

Which we did.

"I have no idea who this young man is."

"Paul Nollington, I'm Miss Blackstone's partner."

"You work for Blackstone Investigations?" Agent Callaghan asked.

"Unofficially, I guess you could say," replied Paul proudly.

"I wouldn't be proud of that if I were you."

"Why not?" I shouted, feeling hurt both for my partner and my company.

Callaghan sighed.

"Oh! Just calm down, will you! You have made a complete mess of things in just a couple of days, and you'd be better off keeping a low profile, okay?"

"But what did I do?"

"You and your so-called client, that Suzanne Diggs, have trampled that proverbial anthill. Now that The Queen has been awakened, we don't know what'll happen. You've reactivated powers we've been trying to curb for years."

"I don't understand a word you're saying, Agent Callaghan. Just be clear, we'd gain time and effectiveness."

"Just as ironic as usual I can see. I'll be clear then. The last time we saw each other, we had just deleted access to the Facebook page you created about the double disappearance of Ricardo and Lisa Gutierrez. But that didn't stop you from continuing your investigation. Your quest for truth about the subject."

"I thought you said there was no subject," I continued ironically. "What's the truth then?"

Agent Callaghan made some guttural noises with his mouth, so I'd shut up.

"*Tsk, tsk, tsk*, if it's all right with you, Miss Blackstone, I'm the one asking questions here. I was saying that you're stubborn, and with your client Suzanne Diggs, you've been trying to shed some light on a case that's much bigger than both of you. You have no idea what you've stuck your nose into, Suzanne and you."

"True, I don't have any idea, but I can see clearly enough to know that my client is in danger. I'm fearing for her life now, and here we are, just wasting time!"

"Watch it! Slow down there. If there's anyone here making us waste time, it's you. So just calm down. You're going to listen to me and I'm going to explain why you and your partner are here. Without meaning to Miss Blackstone, you ignited a fire, and it's now up to me and other people involved to put it out. We know exactly what you've done recently. We tapped Suzanne Diggs's phone and we've been following her, ever since she arrived in Hervey Bay."

My eyes suddenly popped wide open with surprise and a sudden comprehension.

"That purse snatch and grab act was you then?"

"Let's just say it allowed us to hack into her phone. We had to control her comings and goings and her conversations. From there, we also could check her messages and calls with you, amongst others. That also allowed us to track your communications."

"But that's illegal! You don't have the right to do that! My phone is private property!"

Federal Agent Callaghan slowly shook his head while Paul, sitting next to me, was nodding.

"Miss Blackstone. You must know that private law is subject to common and public law, and this is true whenever the interests and security of the Nation are at stake."

The Fed's words were getting me worried, my hands began to shake. I just stammered.

"And how did my acts interfere with the security of the United States?"

Agent Callaghan clapped his hands.

"There you go! That was the right question! You have no idea what you triggered. Those you've endangered."

"Then quit beating around the bush and tell me once and for all what the problem is!"

"We know you contacted La Reina."

"La Reina?"

"Exactly. Isabel Raya Paladar. El Cristo's wife, Isidro Vegas Paladar, married to the highest-ranking man in Mara Salvatrucha's organizational chart in our country and who today is behind bars in Pelican Bay Prison, in California. You gave Isabel Raya an address in Zuccoli. And you're persuaded, — Suzanne with her intuition, luck, and stubbornness, and you with your deductions and cross-checks —, that Ricardo Gutierrez and his family live there."

"That's what we think, yes. So what?"

"So what? Your stubbornness, your thoughtlessness, your nose that you stick into everyone's business, all that's about to wreck twenty years of efforts by the FBI to combat organized crime."

"But..."

"I'd bet anything that right now Mara Salvatrucha is heading straight to Zuccoli. Miss Blackstone, have you ever heard of the MS-13 National Gang Task Force?"

CHAPTER 77
Win-win

Zuccoli, August 2024

"Mr. Bolt," said one of the hooded men standing with their arms crossed at the door. "I think you've said enough. The lady doesn't need to know what happened after that."

"That's true," continued the second one. "What she needs is to be locked behind the doors of an insane asylum. She's dangerous. For herself. For you. For the safety of..."

Ricardo — or Pierce, depending on who was talking to him — shook his head thinking about what the two giants who looked like bodyguards with their huge biceps, their rounded pecs, and sculpted thighs in their cargo pants were saying.

"I know," he sighed. "But I feel like I have to express myself. I've kept this inside me for way too long. These secrets have to be told sometime. Twenty years like this, it's not a normal life!"

"For sure!" one of the men added.

"I understand you," Ricardo admitted. "I owe you, we owe you, my family and I all owe you a lot. I know that you're sacrificing your existence for us. So I don't want to antagonize you, but Jesus, I have to get this off my chest! This lady who, in a certain way, did count a bit in my life — my previous one of course!— is completely crazy, I know. But she deserves to know. To understand."

Ricardo turned towards the lady kneeling in front of him.

"Suzanne. What happened on August 6, 2004 in the Six Flags parc was premeditated, and you were kept in the dark on purpose. It was the completion of a process that had begun a few days earlier in accordance with the FBI and Police."

∽

New Orleans, July 2004
The FBI facilities

Recording of official interview N° 2

(NOISE OF CHAIRS, *people clearing their throats, a glass being put down on a metal table*)

FEDERAL AGENT JOHN COLLINS: Ricardo Gutierrez's interview continues after a short pause. Mr. Gutierrez, are you going to cooperate with us?

RICARDO GUTIERREZ: Do I have the choice?

FEDERAL AGENT JOHN COLLINS: Like I said a bit earlier, of course you have the choice. Life in prison. Or cooperating with us. Win-win. Totally win-win! It's up to you.

RICARDO GUTIERREZ: But if I talk, if I give names, they'll kill me. And my family too!

FEDERAL AGENT JOHN COLLINS: The American government has logistical, legal and financial resources to protect you in these circumstances, Mr. Gutierrez. You and your family. You won't be the first nor the last to take advantage of this arrangement.

RICARDO GUTIERREZ: I'll have to leave New Orleans?

FEDERAL AGENT JOHN COLLINS: Yes. No doubt about that. Unless you want to continue living next to those that you'll be having arrested.

RICARDO GUTIERREZ: I'll do whatever it takes to leave and protect my family. And at the same time, flee a person who's a bit too... cumbersome.

FEDERAL AGENT JOHN COLLINS: I told you that it was win-win!

RICARDO GUTIERREZ: So specifically what happens?

FEDERAL AGENT JOHN COLLINS: We're going

to set up a sting operation for Mara Salvatrucha's leaders. A trap with bait in it.

Ricardo Gutierrez: Bait?

Federal Agent John Collins: Yes, Lisa, your daughter.

Ricardo Gutierrez: No way! I'll never do anything to endanger my daughter!

Federal Agent John Collins: We have to pull out all the stops and take tough action, catch them red-handed. This will take place in two stages. Firstly, your statement with names, facts, dates, details. From then on, that can of worms will be wiggling. You'll become the target for your former friends, and they'll do whatever they can to punish you for having given up their names. And Mr. El Rico, you know better than I do that one of MS-13's golden rules is clear: internal traitors are punished by death.

Ricardo Gutierrez: Yes, that's one of the worst things about our organization… Traitors must die. And their families too.

Federal Agent John Collins: So we'll set up an outing at Six Flags with your daughter. Before that, you'll make it known that you're going to the park with her. Your former friends, at least those we haven't yet arrested after your statements, will be forced to try something there. They'll have their eyes on you 24/7. Ready to take you down as soon as possible. And beginning today, you, your daughter Lisa and Maria your wife will be placed under our active, constant and deliberately visible surveillance. The only window of opportunity we'll give them, if I can put it that way, will be that day at the park, where we'll be discreet, even invisible. After which, we'll exfiltrate you... forever.

Ricardo Gutierrez: Are you sure of your men, Agent Collins? You're sure it'll work?

Federal Agent John Collins: There are always risks when you take on a mafia organization that's been stung. You know that very well, you know that MS-13 is very well organized, heavily armed and has a reputation for violence and even cruelty. But on our side, we know how to take down MS-13, that scourge that's becoming omnipresent in the States. And this will be thanks to you, Mr. Gutierrez. You'll be our beachhead for this huge sting! I'll be risky, dangerous, but if you escape from the back door, it'll always be better than spending the rest of your life in prison. Don't you agree?

Ricardo Gutierrez: Let's do this.

(*Follows a long list of names given by Ricardo Gutierrez, alias El Rico, head of MS-13 in Louisiana. Amongst those names, that of the biggest fish in the lake of Mara Salvatrucha's predators: El Cristo, Isidro Vegas Paladar*).

CHAPTER 78
An extensive program

New Orleans, August 2024

"No, Agent Callaghan, I have no idea what the MS-13 National Gang Task Force is. But I can feel you're chomping at the bit to tell me."

The federal agent nearly smiled.

"Not that I'm chomping at the bit Miss Blackstone, believe me I've got a heck of a lot of better things to do rather than setting a too curious detective straight. But it's part of the job. Like I told you, you threw a monkey wrench into the mechanics of something that you didn't understand, a case that is top secret. I have to tell you that the Gutierrez case, we can call it that, was an extensive and complicated program at the beginning. Shortly after we put together the MS-13 National Gang Task Force, right after we organized their disappearance. In December of 2004 more precisely. The task force is a decision-making group put together by the FBI in Quantico, where their headquarters is located. I'm a part of it, by the way. Besides its range of actions in the US, the MS-13 National Gang Task Force coordinates investigations at an international level and gives intelligence to State and local police in each country involved in combatting Mara Salvatrucha. Now do you understand what you did?"

I was biting my lower lip, just like a little kid being scolded.

"I understand," I said pitifully. "What can I do to try to put this... blunder right?"

"A blunder? Yeah, sure! A huge mistake and I'm being polite! You're just an inch away from an offense, Miss Blackstone, you can be sure of that. You broke Federal laws and disturbed people. And that directly endangered the safety and life of a family. The Gutierrez or Bolt family, whatever you want to call them, as you figured this out. Do you realize that Ricardo Gutierrez's head, Ricardo the traitor, had a price put on it by Mara Salvatrucha: a two-million-dollar assassination contract? Your little actions could lead to terrible consequences."

"Are you going to arrest me?"

I saw Paul jump out of the corner of my eye when I asked that question. He affectionately put his hand on mine to support me.

Agent Maxim Callaghan seemed to be thinking that over, playing with the point of his pen on his desk.

That repetitive *click-click-click* was irritating. Which probably was what he'd wanted. He finally decided to speak, after what had seemed like eternity and a day to me.

"Everything will depend on what happens with this ongoing incident. If, because of you and your client, something happens to Ricardo Gutierrez or his family, it may be a serious problem for you. Adieu Blackstone Investigations! And for your first investigation, if I believe the very recent date you founded your company, that would be quite the fiasco! It also would be the first failure — the very first one since it was created! — of the WITSEC program."

"The what?"

"The WITSEC."

CHAPTER 79
In their costumes

ZUCCOLI, August 2024

WAS she still really listening to what Ricardo was telling her? Did she still recognize that man she'd loved her whole life... until it drove her crazy? Was Ricardo really as bad a person as he claimed? The head of the gang in his state who had betrayed his criminal organization, given the names of his peers and his bosses to save his own life?

"I never knew if you realized how nervous I was that day at Six Flags," continued the converted snitch to Suzanne. "My life, my family's life, all that was on the table for those precise hours and without knowing it, you were a privileged witness."

"My life was on the table too," she replied bitterly. "You broke my heart, you ruined my life, as if you were playing poker, as if it was just a game for you!"

Ricardo sighed wearily.

"Because you think you're completely innocent, Suzanne? You don't have the feeling that you also poisoned my life? You don't believe that a part of my wanting to flee Nola was because of you? I was fleeing Mara, of course, but also escaping from your insanity! Your threats, the hold you had! Like I told you earlier, that day in Six Flags, I doubled the stakes. Here's what happened. It was both complex and very simple. Paradoxical, right?"

He sat down next to Suzanne and sighed while stretching. Across from them, the two masked men didn't budge. He continued.

"Complex, because there were so many protagonists involved. But simple, because everything went just as planned without a hitch. As soon as we arrived in the park, we were being surveilled by a huge group of federal agents. They'd been tailing me ever since I accepted their deal. Wherever we went in the park, on the rides, in the shops or in the restrooms, there was an agent less than fifteen feet away from Lisa and me. Also from you, but you totally ignored that fact. I knew them though, I recognized them. I knew that under their sweatshirts or in their belts, they had hidden weapons. I could read the concentration in their eyes. I also had fun though when in attractions like SpongeBob SquarePants or Looney Tunes, I could see them wincing so they wouldn't show others their exasperation or how nervous they were. I tried to guess what flavor of ice cream they'd choose after us, if they'd buy a waffle or some cotton candy, so they'd blend in with the others easier. At the same time though I was shaking inside, because I knew that members of the Mara were lurking around us, they wanted me to pay for my betrayal. I didn't trust a soul. I examined faces around us, trying to notice them amongst the thousands of tourists we saw. I also regularly glanced nervously at the cameras dissimulated here and there in the park, knowing that behind them in the huts, there was an FBI agent and a policeman. The Fed's surveillance plan was so well prepared that some of them — probably the ones who'd drawn the shortest straws — had won the grand prize of walking through the park dressed up as the park's mascots. I can still visualize those Daffy Ducks, Bugs Bunnies, Scooby-Doos, and Mr. Six too!" Ricardo remembered, smiling.

The two men behind him also chuckled at that memory.

He continued.

"The only sticking point, one that I learned later, was that the FBI had learned that Mara had also had the same idea to get close to us without being noticed. They were also wearing those ridiculous costumes. That way, no one could have guessed they were there. I understood then later why I'd seen Bugs Bunny attacking SpongeBob SquarePants. A Fed had just apprehended a member of the Mara! Tourists in the park must have thought it was a part of the show."

"I remember that too," Suzanne agreed. "I thought it was funny."

Now Ricardo burst out laughing.

"Funny! If you had known... Let me tell you, that completely stressed me out. I panicked. I could feel that my life and Lisa's life were on the line, a taught line, one in the FBI's hands. I was at the mercy of Mara and had to count on the professional conduct of the Feds. My fate was in their hands. I no longer had any free will, all I could do was to follow the instructions they'd given me earlier. And that's what happened in the afternoon, after you left us for a couple of minutes to go to the restrooms. It was the moment we'd chosen, the restrooms we'd decided on, to start that process rolling. I'd walked over there with you on purpose, knowing what was next. As soon as you walked into the ladies', Lisa and I were whisked off by federal agents disguised as mascots to the service door at the end of the hall. An operation that only took a couple of seconds and that no one noticed."

"Including myself, who would come out just a few minutes later and would never ever see you again! You betrayed me just as much as you betrayed Mara, Ricardo. You made fun of me! You abandoned me just like you abandon a dog when you're going on vacation!"

"I didn't have the choice... Either I disappeared at that precise moment, or I ended up being killed, or I'd spend the rest of my life behind bars, and you know what happens there, the violence in prisons and how prisoners get revenge, stuff like that happens all the time. I'm gonna teach you something, Suzanne. Did you know that Mara says there are three reasons to die? The first one, if you join a rival gang. Second, if you killed, even by accident, a homeboy. And the third one, if you're a snitch, an informer, and you gave the cops info about your *pandilla*, your *mara*, your gang. And the fourth one..."

"You said three," Suzanne cut him off.

"But the fourth one includes all the others: if you're an asshole! I'm sure you can understand why I decided to go with the federal agents who took Lisa and me out of the park. Remember that Maria was supposed to be on a business trip? She was actually already being protected by the FBI as soon as she'd left New Orleans. She was waiting for us where the Feds would be taking Lisa and me. In Virginia."

"In Virginia? But..."

"Yeah, we had to make a few stops before reaching Australia. In Virginia, it was to..."

"She doesn't have to know all the details," said one of the masked men dryly.

Ricardo nodded, understanding.

"Of course... I'll continue. So anyway, behind the park, where the warehouses, garages and workshops are located, there was an unmarked van waiting for us. We rushed into it while other agents made sure there weren't any MS-13 members hanging around that could have seen us. Then the vehicle started up and left the park using the employees and suppliers' access, just a dirt path, a service road that led you directly to I-510 once you'd gone through a gate. Less than two minutes later, we were heading for our new life. As of then, Ricardo Gutierrez no longer existed, Pierce Bolt was born."

Right when Ricardo — Pierce Bolt ! — finished his tale, they heard two sounds at the same time.

Firstly, the characteristic sound of a siren approaching.

Then one of the two guardians' phones rang.

CHAPTER 80
Reset to zero

New Orleans, August 2024

I LEARNED MORE about the Gutierrez case in those minutes than I had during my entire investigation. Thanks to what Federal Agent Maxim Callaghan was telling me, many of my unanswered questions would be finding a logical explanation. There where I'd only seen incoherencies, improbable events, coincidences, in reality were logic, organization, methods and effectiveness by the American government.

"The Witness Security Program, that we shorten to WITSEC, also known as the United States Federal Witness Security Program, sums up in these few words our actions, meaning that we protect threatened witnesses before, during and especially after a trial against a structured criminal organization, as was the case for Mara Salvatrucha. Ricardo Gutierrez, an active member of that gang, was risking many years in prison. But in exchange for his statements allowing us to arrest many of the key players in the American network, especially El Cristo as its leader, the American government assured him impunity as well as a total protection for him and his family."

I sneered, bitterly.

"That's how our tax dollars are used to protect snitches in organized crime."

"Yup, and that's also how we're able to efficiently combat crime. Like my grandma always used to say, 'You can't make an omelet without breaking eggs.' Of course, it could seem unfair that honest citizens pay to protect criminals, but it's to serve a greater cause... A cause that you were about to pull the plug on, Miss Blackstone, with all your nosing around. Just imagine that your discoveries and revelations — and here I'm talking about your Facebook page, amongst others, — were known by the press and general public. Had we not intervened in time, here as well as in Australia, that could have broken the total infallibility of the program since it was created back in 1970! You might say that there's an exception to every rule, Miss Blackstone, but you're not going to be that exception! Gerald Shur, the attorney general assigned to organized crime and racketeering section in the American Justice Department, founded that program and none of the nearly nineteen thousand witnesses and members of their families have never been killed or wounded. That's a hundred percent success rate!" said Agent Callaghan proudly.

I could tell by the sound of his voice, the way he was spitting out words and figures, the veneration he had for the program and its founder, as well as for the FBI unit he belonged to.

"My goal wasn't to wipe out a program I didn't even know existed," I tried to justify myself humbly.

"Of course, you didn't do that on purpose, but because of you and Suzanne Diggs, we're on the brink of entering into the blue zone."

"The blue zone?"

"Yes, the most critical stage of WITSEC: there are three of them. The red zone, when the witness is protected by bodyguards before and during the trial. The green zone that starts when the witness begins living under a new identity and is placed under house arrest, in a place only known to the federal agent, who's a US Marshall, in charge of their case. And finally the blue zone, when the subject has disappeared (dead or alive) or when their identity has been uncovered... Which is about to happen!"

I understood his logic, but still tried to defend myself.

"My job originally consisted just in bringing justice to Suzanne Diggs, someone I sincerely thought was Ricardo's wife and Lisa's mother, two people who had disappeared without a trace. Now I'm starting to understand why they didn't leave any traces!"

Callaghan proudly raised his chin.

"Never leaving any traces, that's the basics of our program. No traces that would allow others to find the protected witness. That's why as soon as they begin with us, the person as well as their family members who want to join the program are all attributed a new identity, something created by the American government. Official ID documents, a new personality with a background, a history, an imagined past, something that was written and edited and produced from A to Z by experts, trying to match their profile as new citizens. And the witnesses have to learn and embody their new identities. And their former identity is completely deleted."

"So that's why I couldn't find any search results about Ricardo or Lisa Gutierrez. Neither on the web nor on the dark web. Same thing for that police file where Suzanne told them about her missing husband and daughter."

"That's true. All of that was destroyed. We had to start afresh with Ricardo Gutierrez's present, his past no longer existed. Our IT experts deleted any traces on internet, extranet, and intranet of those two, and this down to the most well-hidden layers of the web! A complete R to Z."

"An R to Z?"

"A reset to zero. You delete everything and start over. Very discreetly of course."

Paul, sitting next to me, didn't believe his ears either about the breadth of that program.

"New identities, new places to live. The witnesses have to uproot themselves, abandon their lifestyles.

Was the 'Mover's Gang', that nocturnal operation in Chestnut Street part of the WITSEC package?"

"That gang does really exist as one of the Mara's criminal activities, but for Gutierrez, it was the FBI who came in and moved the family out. As soon as a family exits their former lives by exfiltration, they are formally forbidden from setting foot again into a property that those the witness 'sold' know about. Everything is controlled. Without delay, with effectiveness, without leaving any traces. Witnesses are under surveillance 24/7."

"For how long?" I asked, astonished.

"All their lives, if needed."

"So Ricardo, alias Pierce Bolt, is still under surveillance?"

"Even more so ever since you and Suzanne told the Mara gang leaders where he lived."

Agent Callaghan picked up his cell phone, clicked on one of the contacts, and as soon as he picked up, began to speak loudly and intelligibly.

"Blue zone. Let me repeat myself, blue zone activated."

CHAPTER 81
A clean life

New Orleans, July 2004
  Chestnut Street, Garden District

AGENT JOHN COLLINS, the FBI and US Marshals representative, scooted up on the beige sofa in Gutierrez's living room. He was holding a handful of sheets of paper.

Behind him the two other federal agents remained standing, their arms crossed, looking down at the little family. The rest of the team had discreetly gone outside.

On the couch across from Collins, Ricardo and Maria were sitting on both sides of their little daughter, Lisa. The little girl, who undoubtedly didn't understand a thing, kept staring at the two Feds both wearing black clothing and who must have intimidated her.

As Ricardo had agreed to collaborate with the Agency, during his interview, the program was now up and running. The last hours of their former lives were dwindling away like sand in an hourglass. Once the last grains had fallen, they'd irremediably slip into their new existence, the tailor-made one that had been designed for them. Agent Collins began to explain some of the details.

"In the name of the American Department of Justice and as a US Marshal, I must verbally explain the practical conditions and procedures of the witness protection program. I'm going to list the obligations and rights you have. What's expected of you, and what we expect in return. After this, I'm going to ask you to show your agreement by signing this paper, Mr. Gutierrez. Is this clear?"

"It is," Ricardo simply answered.

"You must be aware that you will spend the rest of your life in the program. With three exceptions. The first one, you have the possibility of voluntarily leaving it at any time, but in that case, this would be something that's irreversible. The second, in the hypothesis of a breach of one of the program's rules. Meaning you must always comply with the laws in your new country of residence and avoid any situations that could negatively impact the relations you have with the police. It is strictly prohibited to speak about your new status with anyone outside of the team who protects you. You shall not make any contact with any known criminal nor any former 'associates.' And you will not be able to set foot in your hot zone, which is Louisiana and El Salvador. Lastly, you will not be able to contact any members of your family outside of those included in the program. In a nutshell: the three of you. I'll get back to that later."

Collins paused, leafing through his notes. Ricardo looked at him.

"And the third exception?"

"Your death," said Collins gravely, scratching his throat, uncomfortable.

Ricardo and Maria Gutierrez (they were still referred to using that name) agreed anxiously to each point Collins was explaining to them. Lisa, too young to know what was going on, was simply playing with her teddy bear, tenderly rocking it.

"Each of you will be protected 24/7. There will always be an agent posted near you, each time you go to work, to school or have an outing. When your daughter is eighteen, she will have the choice of leaving the program or remaining in it. Should she leave, it would be considered as if she had 'divorced' her parents and in that case, her visits would be limited and supervised. Outside of this continuous surveillance, the American government will give you funds for your basic expenses for the first six months, any medical expenses, they will assist you in finding jobs and pay for any professional courses required in your new profiles. Speaking of which, we soon will give you your new identities, ones we have created, as well as all the relevant legal documents. And in a few days you'll be meeting with experts who will brief you on your *new past*. A biography you'll have to understand, learn, assimilate, remember, and know by heart so you won't make any mistakes if someone asks you questions. As of tonight, our services will begin working with you and they'll drive you to a safehouse that we monitor in Virginia. It can house three families of protected witnesses at the same time, though they will not be able to see each other nor communicate with each other. This temporary accommodation will last as long as it takes to organize your permanent exfiltration into your new lifestyle. Maria, we'll take you there tonight. For you Ricardo — and for Lisa — that will take place immediately after the operation we planned at Six Flags on August 6th."

Maria was beginning to fear the breadth of sacrifices they'd have to make. But she was far from understanding everything.

"As of today," Collins continued, "you may no longer communicate with your family, friends or colleagues. Your phones will be taken from you, we'll give you others, but they will always be tapped. Your email addresses will also be deleted. We'll supply you with others which will be codified. Each email that you send will go through a secure WITSEC server. Your messages will be read by FBI agents in charge of your file. Once a year, you will be allowed to visit with other members of your family, but the visit shall take place in a neutral and safe venue and will be under surveillance by our FBI liaison agents."

"If everything you say is true," Maria deplored, "our lives no longer belong to us."

Collins nodded his head several times, slowly, looking Ricardo's wife straight in the eyes.

"I understand that this can seem overwhelming and burdensome, Ma'am. I totally do. Your reaction is legitimate, and one I often have. But just think for a moment what your life would be like without the protection of the program... Prison, death. I'm sure I don't have to remind you that MS-13 put out a two-million-dollar award to capture your husband, dead or alive. You wouldn't like your daughter to have a father who's dead... in the best of circumstances. Here we're giving you a new life, of course, we're forcing it upon you, but it'll be one where you'll have a type of freedom. A new profile, a clean life."

"We don't have the choice, darling," Ricardo said, putting his hand on her forearm. "We have to do it."

"Tired," Lisa said, her arms rolled around her little stuffed monkey.

"Let's obey the voice of reason," Collins said, taking advantage of the lull.

"Where do I sign?" Ricardo asked.

The federal agent handed him a pen and sheets of paper, with the heading *US Department of Justice Form 5-K. Cooperating Witness Agreement.*

"Put your initials on each page, and date and sign the last one. Welcome to the program, Mr. and Mrs. Gutierrez."

CHAPTER 82
Lightning strikes

ZUCCOLI, *August 2024*

UP TILL THEN, the Rodriguez family had been peacefully living in the calm little Tindill Court cul-de-sac in Zuccoli.

When Ben, the father, got back from work that evening, he was intrigued by all that unusual agitation in his street. More cars than usual, plus they weren't correctly parked. They were in front of the Bolt's, their neighbors, as well as in front of that gay couple, Seymour and Wayne, those guys who lived across from the Bolt's. He closed the front door, picked up his two kids, Luna and Theo, kissed them and then turned to Cindy, his wife.

"Lotsa people here tonight. Someone must have organized a barbecue, and we weren't even invited... Not cool."

Then he took a can of beer out of his American fridge and completely forgot about that story, until, still holding his can in his hand, his calves immersed in the cool water of their pool, he heard the characteristic sounds of a police siren, tires screeching, and car doors being slammed.

∾

In the empty room where Suzanne and Ricardo were, a phone began to ring. One of the two masked men took it out of a pocket, looked at the name of the contact while frowning and picked up. He listened carefully and then shouted at Ricardo.

"Mr. Bolt! Blue zone triggered. You know what to do..."

∾

A few moments later, another car slowly drove into the cul-de-sac.

"Here's to you, *hijo de puta*!" scathed the passenger, holding his Walther PPQ semi-automatic.

He opened the car door and quickly slipped the weapon behind his back, in his back pocket. He had also dissimilated a serrated knife in one of his boots. Plus a few other little toys that he'd stuffed into the pockets of his cargo pants. Ready to go!

"You stay here," he ordered the driver, "and don't

turn the car off. Make sure you're ready to go immediately if there's a problem."

He walked down the sidewalk in the cul-de-sac that ended in a circular turning zone, looked at the mailboxes, passed the one with the name Rodriguez on it, and then another one with the names of two men, and walked up the Bolt family's sidewalk.

∼

"But who are you then?" asked Suzanne Diggs, astonished, pushing herself up and looking at the two men dressed in black. "You're not from the mafia?"

The person who'd just warned Pierce Bolt, formerly known as Ricardo Gutierrez, that they were going into the blue zone, ripped his hood off and nodded to his partner to do the same thing.

"Agent Seymour Fitzpatrick, US Marshal," he said in an official tone.

"Agent Wayne Jackson, US Marshal," the other one imitated. "We don't have time to explain. We have to evacuate."

"Wayne, exfiltrate him. I'll take care of her."

∼

The doorbell rang at the Bolt's. Maggie was sitting on a sunbed next to the pool doing a crossword puzzle. She wasn't expecting anyone since Johanna and her boyfriend had left the day before and decided not to open the door. It was boiling outside, and it was probably just one of those darn salesmen anyway. He'd get tired of waiting and would go to the neighbors' or keep on walking.

But when it kept on ringing she gave in and slowly got herself up.

"Coming," she said tiredly walking down the air-conditioned hall.

She opened the door and just had the time to begin her question.

"Yes, what can..."

A man pushed her, shoving himself into the house.

That maneuver took just a few seconds, during which that unknown person put his hand on Maggie's (alias former Maria Rivera's) mouth, slammed her up against the wall, and kicked the door shut.

"I'm here to pay a little call on Ricardo, my beautiful Maria. ¿ *Donde está tu hombre* ?*"

"Who are you?" Maggie tried to ask, her lips squashed by El Cocodrilo's smelly palm.

All he heard was something like *wouiewouuu.*

"I'm an old friend of El Rico. El Cristo sent me here to say hi to him. Remember him, El Cristo? He would have come himself to greet you, except that, how can I explain it, he's been a little locked up for the past twenty years. In the shadows."

Maggie's eyes opened so wide they nearly popped out of their orbits. She immediately understood that their past had resuscitated and was exploding in her face. She tried to free herself from his grip.

"Quit moving around, dammit! Take me to your shitfaced husband!"

She shook her head to refuse, her eyes still wide open.

"What do you mean, no? Maybe you want me to heat up your neurons a little?" threatened El Cocodrilo pointing his 9mm to her forehead.

She tried to bite the hand holding her mouth shut. El Cocodrilo pressed it down harder, approaching his lips to one of her ears.

"I'm gonna take my hand away and you're gonna tell me nicely and without screaming where that asshole of a husband of yours is, okay?"

She nodded.

"He left an hour ago," she whispered. "I don't know where."

"Liar!"

"I swear to God I don't know! Please don't hurt me!"

"Okay. So what do you want to do while we're waiting for him? I know, let's have a little fun."

At those words he lowered the weapon and let its barrel wander around below Maria's summer dress, caressing her with it. The contact of the cold metal made her rear back with rage.

"Stop that!"

Tears rolled down her eyes as the intruder dragged her to her bedroom.

AT THE SAME TIME, the Palmerston Country patrol car drove into the cul-de-sac, its flashing lights and siren off. The vehicle stopped in front of the Bolt's property and two men wearing uniforms rushed out, their weapons out in front of them, towards the front door.

The first one to arrive pounded on the wooden door.

"Police, open up!"

∼

IN THE CAR parked at the angle of Tindill Court, its motor idling, El Cocodrilo's partner was trying his best not to panic.

He phoned him, fingers trembling.

"The cops are here!" he shouted when El Cocodrilo picked up. "Right in front of the house! Get the hell outta there!"

∼

US MARSHAL SEYMOUR Fitzpatrick came out first from the house he'd been sharing for months now with Marshal Wayne Jackson, ever since it had been their turn to keep the Bolt couple under constant surveillance. Since the repented family had moved to Zuccoli, there'd been duo after duo of agents in that house across from the Bolt's. A mission that was usually a piece of cake in that peaceful little town. The main drawback for the American marshals was how far they were from home. A whole year without being able to return was long, though it was relatively well paid. So they made the best of things and spent hours playing cards or binge-watching series on TV while of course keeping an eye on their protected witnesses. Each time they'd leave the house, one of them would follow them.

For the last couple of days, things had been spiced up a bit with the arrival of Suzanne Diggs who they had to catch, hide, and detain in a laundry room, a windowless room that they used as a makeshift jail, waiting to know how things would go down.

And they had gone down! Crashed you could even say! Today the situation was getting complicated. As the blue zone had been activated, they had to get Quantico's processes and directives rolling.

Agent Fitzpatrick was leading Pierce Bolt, who'd put on a hood, in front of him.

Behind them, Agent Jackson was doing the same thing with Suzanne Diggs, who had also dissimulated her face.

All four of them were walking to the federal agent's car.

That was when they saw the local police car poorly parked on the sidewalk, then two uniformed men at the Bolt's front door right when it opened onto Maggie.

Maggie's frightened look appalled Pierce Bolt.

"One wrong word and you're dead," warned El Cocodrilo.

Maggie could feel the cold metal of the 9mm barrel of the gun poking her in the back.

"Yes? Can I help you," she said with a scratchy voice to the policemen.

The cops tried to look inside the house, behind Maggie, through the little opening in the door.

"We'd like to come in, please."

"What's wrong?"

Behind the lady, the Australian policeman saw the bottoms of a pair of cargo pants and a ranger's boot.

"Move it!" he shouted, rushing in.

"No!" yelled Ricardo when he saw the cops forcing their way into his house.

"Don't do anything stupid, Bolt," said Marshal Fitzpatrick, holding him back. "We're leaving now."

But Pierce didn't agree and fought like a tiger to shake the federal agent.

"There's something going on there, dammit my wife might get hurt!"

He shook the marshal's hold off him and rushed towards his house like a bat out of hell. Fitzpatrick, after a minute of hesitation, pulled out his weapon and followed him.

At Rodriguez's house, they were wondering what was going on outside. Cindy, Ben and the kids were all peering out of the window overlooking Tindill Court and weren't disappointed by what was going on. People were running right and left, some had masked faces and a hood, cars were parked any old way and panicked people were screaming.

"That ain't no barbecue," Cindy concluded.

At the Bolt's, El Cocodrilo was toppled over by Maggie's weight, who herself was unbalanced by the door that the suspicious policeman had shoved open. He lost his balance and crashed heavily to the floor, with Maggie on top of him squirming and punching him so he'd let go of her.

The cop rushed into the hall, his teammate on his heels, both in combat mode, their arms aimed at the gang member's head.

Behind them, the silhouette of Pierce/Ricardo could be seen in the half-opened door, immediately followed by Marshal Fitzpatrick, a good head taller than him.

The man Isabel Raya Paladar had sent, El Cristo's henchman, regained control of the situation.

"Don't fuck with me or I'll blow her stupid head off!"

His 9mm Walther PPQ was touching Maggie's forehead and they knew he had nothing to lose.

Ricardo was biting his lip, furious that his wife was at the mercy of El Cristo's crony, that gang leader that his testimonial had sent to prison an eternity ago. He understood right then that revenge knew how to wait, a meal best eaten cold. He'd been in the WITSEC program, protected by them for twenty years now, without a hitch. And all it had taken was that crazy Suzanne, assisted by some unknown detective, to topple their new lives that they'd worked so hard to have. He didn't want that story to end like that, not here, not now.

"I'm the one you want, *cabrón*. Let my wife go. Shoot me if you want but let her go right now. She's innocent!"

"Tell them cops to quit aiming at me!"

Right then, the man sitting on the floor, his back against the hallway wall, pulled Maggie in front of him, forming a human shield. She was terrified, and kept on looking at her husband, having much more hope in him than those others, those Australian cops and American Feds together.

"That's not going to happen," Agent Fitzpatrick slowly but firmly said to him. "You're the one who's going to put your gun down nicely and let the lady go. You understand?"

At the angle of the cul-de-sac, in his car still idling, El Cocodrilo's partner-in-crime was struggling with his conscience. Should he run in and try to help his colleague, or would he be better off leaving and leaving right now, fleeing the neighborhood? After all, his role only consisted of escorting him from the airport to Zuccoli, then waiting for him in the car, before rushing off once El Rico had been assassinated. But it would seem that nothing was going as planned. He sighed loudly, his fingers tensed up on the steering wheel. Then he looked down at the number 13 tattooed on the back on his hands. Because of that, he didn't have the right to abandon his blood brother, a *pandillero de la Mara Salvatrucha* just like he was.

"Shit!"

He punched the steering wheel but didn't stop the car, running out of it with his own Walther in front of him.

~

In the house where the FBI agents lived, Marshal Jackson had just closed the laundry room door where they'd detained Suzanne. He had to help his colleague and couldn't risk having the lady who was responsible for the leak flee.

When he reached Tindill Court, he saw a man running to the Bolt's house, a pistol aiming at Marshal Fitzpatrick's back. He raised his own 9mm Glock towards him.

As luck would have it, in the heart of Tindill Court a "Mexican standoff"* which they could more accurately have called an "El Salvadorian standoff," was now taking place. At the Bolt's, the situation was like a single file of characters who were both threatening and being threatened.

The chain looked like this: El Cocodrilo who was aiming his gun at Maggie/Maria; the first Australian police officer who was aiming at El Cocodrilo; behind him, the second officer doing the same thing; next to him Pierce/Ricardo just as immobile as a statue staring at his wife; behind him, Agent Fitzpatrick, who was also aiming at El Cocodrilo, but who's aim was hampered by the police officers, and who was being aimed at by Mara's second crony, the driver; and lastly Agent Jackson who was aiming at him and had just shouted out a summation.

"Hands up and no one moves!"

---

* .
A Mexican standoff is a situation in which at least three individuals or groups of individuals are confronting each other, in regard to a confrontation where no strategy exists that allows any party to achieve victory. Anyone initiating aggression might trigger their own demise. The winning strategy consists in waiting until another person reacts, thus blocking any action.

By extension, this expression has come to designate any situation where the stakeholders benefit from maintaining a standstill, including when it is adverse to them rather than attempting a movement that could aggravate things.

No one was moving anyway...
But suddenly things picked up speed.

~

To really understand the details of what happened, I would have had to write and read in slowmo.

There was a succession of detonations, though to be fair, I must add that that succession seemed like only one salvo, the bullets were shot at infinitesimally small intervals, only separated by minute reaction times of the various protagonists in that Mexican standoff.

The trigger element was a silent message exchanged eye to eye between Ricardo and Maria, leading her to quickly push herself away from the man who was aiming at her. Just like a lizard, she slid down on the tiled floor, and El Cocodrilo's body was up for grabs.

In a fraction of a second, Ricardo pushed the first Australian cop in front of him with his shoulder, surprising him and grabbed his weapon, pointing it at the gang member.

He aimed for his head and pulled the trigger.

The second cop also shot at El Cocodrilo, and his bullet barely missed Ricardo's shoulder.

In the same murderous impetus, El Cocodrilo's henchman pulled the trigger on the person he'd been aiming at, Agent Fitzpatrick, and shot him in the shoulder bone.

Marshal Jackson immediately and by reflex fired off a salvo to the *pandillero* and hit him twice in the neck.

Then complete silence for a couple of seconds before a maelstrom of groans, tears and death rattles were heard.

~

In the laundry room, a cell for her, Suzanne Diggs heard the series of gunshots, smothered by the windowless wall.

She just had enough time to think that if both of her kidnappers were killed, she'd end up dying of hunger and thirst there.

~

At Rodriguez's little Luna was all excited, jumping up and down.

"Mommy, can we go see the fireworks?"

Epilogue

NEW YORK CITY, September 2024

PAUL and I were only allowed to leave the FBI New Orleans facilities after we had signed a sworn statement that stipulated that neither of us would say anything we knew about the Gutierrez case. A formal prohibition to mention anything at all on that subject without being immediately arrested and thrown into jail for obstructing justice.

My investigation had undermined the secret that had been well kept up until now, about the witness protection program involving Ricardo, Maria and Lisa. That partially was my fault, but it was above all because of Suzanne Diggs that the protected family had to enter the blue zone.

Because of that, the FBI had to exfiltrate them once

again in order to protect them from the revenge of Mara Salvatrucha's henchmen, who were now undoubtedly more determined than ever since two of their *pandilleros* had been killed when they had nearly carried out the sanction that El Cristo had ordered from his super-maximum-security prison in Pelican Bay.

Ricardo, Maria and Lisa Gutierrez, after having become Pierce, Maggie and Johanna Bolt now perhaps would become Paul, Barbara and Megan Johnson, or Carlos, Pamela and Vivian Ramirez, or who knows! Would Ashley also change her name, after all, she was born Ashley Bolt? New identities would be created. New official documents would be generated. Would they be living in New Zealand, Peru or Zimbabwe? The FBI would be the only ones to know.

And Suzanne would certainly be the last person to be told. When she returned from Australia, my client was arrested for having uncovered the program. She was tried and found irresponsible for her acts by a psychiatric expert who was assisted by Dr. Petrossian and sentenced to an undetermined stay in a psychiatric hospital, a place where whatever she said would be deemed to be pure delusions.

She'd been alone for twenty years. Alone with her dreams, her hopes, her delusions.

She'd remain alone until the end of her days, only accompanied by her ghosts.

. . .

As for me, following that decision, I had to say adieu to what she owed me in our contract. Something that certainly wouldn't help arrange Blackstone Investigations' finances!

I had to make do with the sum she'd given me at the beginning. By doing that, I was able to avoid the worst-case scenario — being tried, being prohibited from working as a private detective, and going to jail.

Would I say that Blackstone Investigations' first investigation was a failure?

Undoubtedly, though Suzanne, Paul and I had unveiled the truth!

But I couldn't tell anyone.

Yet, my Dear Readers, you may retort that I've just told you all the details of my investigation, all the truth. And I gave you names, places, I told you what precisely took place. But was everything true?

My Dear Readers, never forget that you now know confidential and top-secret information. That WITSEC, the program that protects witnesses, demands total secrecy!

So, keep your eyes peeled, but keep your mouth closed!

. . .

OR YOU MAY BE PROSECUTED…

THE END

Acknowledgments

As usual, I'd like to thank my proofreader, my designer and my little team of beta-readers, you know who you are. And of course I can't forget Jacquie Bridonneau, my favorite French to English translator, who made it possible for you to read this book in English. Your comments, likes and helpful hints have helped me write this fifteenth novel. Sometimes I had moments of euphoria, doubt, and uncertainty, but if I can believe the comments I've had, this novel is one of my best ones. My Dear Readers, what's your opinion?

Whatever it is, I'd also like to thank you all as your numerous messages supporting me, by email or on social media have helped me understand how much you appreciate Karen Blackstone as a recurrent character.

When I first began, I'd imagined Karen in a trilogy that would allow us with the theme outside of her investigations, to comprehend the secret past of the heroin. But once it was unveiled in *The Lost Son*, you urged me, threatened me, forced me :-) not to abandon the Blackstone team. And I must admit that I'd also started to love Karen.

So I gave in, and here is *Alone*, the fourth volume of the opus.

And you know what? I've already been thinking of the fifth volume's plot… Its main characters, the final twist and even the title. I'm sure that you know this, I'll be as quiet as the grave up until the very last moment.

But get ready: Karen will be back! And she won't be… alone!

A tetralogy that will turn into a series?

Bibliography of books translated into English

THE KAREN BLACKSTONE SERIES
Into Thin Air (2022) *(Winner of the Cuxac d'Aude Favorite Novel, 2023 / Finalist in the Loiret Crime Award, 2023)*
I Want Mommy (2023) *(N°1 in Amazon Storyteller France sales 2023)*
The Lost Son (2023)
Alone (2024)
Volume 5 to be published in 2025

THE BASTERO SERIES
French Riviera (2017) *(Winner of the Indie Ilestbiencelivre Award 2017)*
Perfect crime (2020)
Bloody Bonds (2022)

OTHER NOVELS

True Blood Never Lies (2022)
Thirty Seconds Before Dying (2021)
Eight more Minutes of Sunshine (2020)

Who am I?

Nino S. Theveny is one of France's leading indie authors. He's married and has two children. In 2019 he was laid off from a multinational company and decided to make the most of his newly found liberty, turning to writing, his passion, which is now his day job.

With 15 books published to date, Nino S. Theveny, Sébastien Theveny's American pen name, has over 200,000 readers. Translated into English, Spanish, Italian, and German, his thrillers are appreciated throughout the entire world.

With his fourteen-year-old son, he has also co-authored a thriller for young adults which was published in March, 2024.

Printed in Dunstable, United Kingdom